Measure Twice,
Love Once

MEASURE TWICE, LOVE ONCE

Flynn's Crossing Romantic Suspense Series Book 8

Yvonne Kohano

K
E

Nanokas Press

A Division of Kochanowski Enterprises

MEASURE TWICE, LOVE ONCE
FLYNN'S CROSSING ROMANTIC SUSPENSE SERIES
BOOK 8

Nanokas Press/KE Press books may be ordered through booksellers or by contacting:

Kochanowski Enterprises/Nanokas Press
PO Box 1274
Clackamas, OR 97015-9594
www.yvonnekohano.com
yvonne@yvonnekohano.com

Measure Twice, Love Once is a work of fiction. People, places, events, and situations are the product of the author's imagination. Any resemblance to actual persons, living or dead, or historical events, is purely coincidental.

This book contains an excerpt from the forthcoming book *Love's Fiery Prescription* (working title) by Yvonne Kohano. This excerpt may not reflect the final content of the forthcoming edition.

Any people depicted in stock imagery provided by Thinkstock are models, and such images are being used for illustrative purposes only.

Certain stock imagery ©Thinkstock
Cover design: John Kochanowski

ISBN: 978-1-940738-80-2 (e)
         978-1-940738-81-9 (sc)

Nanokas Press First Edition: 04-21-2015

Also by Yvonne Kohano

*FLYNN'S CROSSING ROMANTIC SUSPENSE
SERIES*

*Pictures of Redemption, Book 1
(Serena & Dane)*

*Flashes of Fire, Book 2
(DK & Vince)*

*Naked Intolerances, Book 3
(Gabby & Rick)*

*Tastes and Consequences, Book 4
(Mac & Roxy)*

*Blooms on the Bones, Book 5
(Tess & Powers)*

*Wine Into Water, Book 6
(Marguerite & Deke)*

*Love and the Christmas Tree Nymph,
A Flynn's Crossing Seasonal Novella*

*Love's Touch of Justice, Book 7
(Jake & Marlee)*

*This Proposal Between Us,
A Flynn's Crossing Seasonal Novella*

*Measure Twice, Love Once, Book 8
(Geno and Agnes)*

And more to come!
Learn about upcoming releases at
<u>www.YvonneKohano.com</u>.

Measure Twice, Love Once

Prologue

A promise was a promise.

His gut rotated faster than the speed of his circular saw, and he reached for the roll of antacids in his jacket pocket on autopilot. They barely made a dent in his nausea. This job splintered his nerves to toothpicks, and still, he couldn't stay away.

Staring up at the shop's sign, he debated his approach. There had to be a way to get close to her, close enough to fulfill his mission without raising alarm. He could hide behind a laid-back front, but only for so long. Engagement was necessary. He popped two extra tablets in his mouth, grimacing at the chalky texture and fake fruit flavor.

A shadow moved behind the blinds of the front window. He'd been standing still long enough to be conspicuous. White slats bent and parted. Big eyes he knew to be as deep and complex a brown as well-stained mahogany glanced out, and he spun around before she could see his face. Pretending to examine the vacant building across the street, he caught her momentary reflection in its unlit window before she turned away.

She always had the most expressive eyes, teasing and laughing one minute, turbulent and snapping the next. Had those changed over the years? Life hadn't exactly been easy for her, and yet from what he'd heard, she handled what it had thrown her well. Too bad this was one curve she might never recover from.

He glanced up the sidewalk, tensing as he noted he was no longer alone. Two women waved, and he raised a hand in return. There was no way to avoid them, not without seeming rude. That wasn't part of his character, at least the congenial one familiar to these people. It would cause talk.

He fell back into an examination of the three stories of old brick across the street. The mirror offered by darkened glass shifted as the blind in her shop rose quickly and without pause, and the northern California sun, still low in March at this early hour, lit the interior with a stage set quality. She stood framed in the window as if posing for him.

The buzz of his cell phone, a hard rock melody, gave him an excuse to turn back toward her shop. Acting like any other guy distracted by his call and not looking at what was in front of him provided an excuse to pace closer. With the blinds open, she was clearly visible, fussing with something on the front desk. He didn't bother to check his caller id, distracted by her big smile as she lifted her phone.

"Yes?"

"Hey man. How's life in Flynn's Crossing?"

And of course, the one man he didn't want to talk to would call at this moment. The thick accent and rough cadence reminded him of his childhood, empty except for one person. He was committed to this course of action, but that didn't make it hurt any less.

"Hello. Life is good. How's Boston?"

"The same. Things don't change much around here." The voice paused, as if searching for more idle words to fill the time required for social niceties before he discussed the things he considered important. Time expired and so did his patience.

"You know why I'm calling, right?"

He sighed in response. "I have nothing to report, other than her business is doing well. She seems to have settled in for the long haul. This place agrees with her, and everyone appears to be thriving."

"Have you talked to her yet?"

The question added a fresh wave of acid to his stomach. He paced away from the shop and approaching company, wishing he'd let this call go to voicemail. It reinforced what he already knew. He didn't have much time left.

"No, I haven't. I'm still looking for a fitting opportunity. It's not like I can waltz in without her asking questions." He shoved his free hand deep into his jacket pocket and fingered its contents, closing around cold metal and toying with the clip.

On the other end of the phone, frustration crackled over the connection. "What do you mean? She has a business. You need what she's selling. It's easy."

He grimaced, watching the subject of their discussion hang up her call and turn toward the building's interior. "That would be challenging. I don't need her services." He killed the desire to open the buttons of his jacket at the heated thought of her hands on him.

"Are you stalling? How hard can this be? If you don't need what she's selling, she probably needs you. Troll for business, man. Use your connections. Didn't you say you have friends in common? Or just walk up to her on the street and say hello. She might be surprised, but I doubt she'd call the cops, right?"

Maybe not the cops, but she might call him a stalker, which was correct up to a point. Or give him the cold shoulder. That would hurt his feelings.

"I'll figure something out. You have to give me more time." He paced closer to the shop once more, trying not to be caught staring into the window.

The man on the other end coughed, his aggravation clear as his voice roughened.

"I'm not the one setting the clock. Time's running out, man. You of all people should realize that."

One of the approaching women raised a finger to him as if she wanted to interrupt his call. He nodded in agreement, knowing that any other response would make him appear less than sociable.

"Another month. It's not that long."

The man on the other end swore and began to argue, but he wasn't interested in listening. He had his excuse when the woman swung in his direction as the other approached the shop's front door.

As he hung up on the caller in midsentence, his attention froze on the short package of round curves and abundance framed by the window. His subject greeted her customer with an animated face and big hand gestures punctuating her words. She was as pretty as he remembered, as vibrant and energetic as she'd been growing up. When she left, it was like the sun had set permanently, leaving never ending night in their neighborhood.

"Hi. Do you have a minute? I have an idea for the kitchen I'd like to discuss with you."

He nodded as the woman drew even with him. His mind whirled and his stomach churned. She talked, but his brain couldn't process her words. He tried and failed to keep from glancing into the shop. Memories and sensations heaved through him, making composure impossible.

Over nine years. She had every reason to hate him, while his feelings for her had grown more intricate, more complicated, and more compelling. The sensible thing to do would be to stay away. Despite the consequences, he wasn't going to get another chance with her.

But he had made a promise, and he always kept his promises.

Chapter 1 – A Week Later

The whine of the table saw filled his ears despite his earplugs, and his nose behind the mask twitched from rising sawdust. This pine was like that, dusty, gritty, and messy to work with. But stained right, its sinuous grain shouted its warmth, inviting everyone to caress it with sensuous attention.

A change in the shrill sound accompanied the end of the cut, and the split timbers separated. Geno Altimari eased the smaller piece to the side, adding it to the pile for other uses. No one should ever consider blue pine as scrap. It was too precious and too unusual. Running a gloved hand over the wider board, he marveled at the faint tint of color that gave the wood its name. This would look mighty fine as the counter in his client's kitchen.

"Roxy's going to flip when she sees this. I wasn't completely sure when you told me about it, but now that I see how it's come together, I'm sold. It was worth the expense of transporting the remnants of that old barn down from Oregon."

Mac took off his safety goggles and accepted the board from Geno's hands. If his touch was gently reverent, it was only fitting. Lumber like this weren't available at the big box home remodeling store.

Mac continued, "I really like the idea of having two islands instead of one big one. She gets the prep area she wants, plus this beautiful service space. I'm glad we never let her see the final plan. It's getting harder and harder to fend her off, though. She can't wait to see the final kitchen. She trusts your judgment, but you know how she is. She's used to being in charge and making every final decision. I almost have to hide her car keys to keep her away."

Geno nodded at the words but didn't comment. The men of the wolf pack loved to talk about their women.

"Luckily, she's so busy at the restaurant with this year's crop of interns that she doesn't bug me about keeping her away, at least not more than four or five times a day." Mac chuckled as he returned to the table saw.

Geno smiled along with him. When Mac bought the Prescott Ranch, this main house had been a wreck of a place, dilapidated by years of neglect and scoured by the elements through a damaged roof and courtesy of any creature that happened to take up residence. He'd spared no expense in saving the place, though, and Geno appreciated that. History like this and craftsmanship on a scale uncommon today should be preserved. All it took was money. Luckily, the movie star's pockets were deep.

Selecting another rough board from the stack, Geno positioned it and double- checked the width setting on the saw. It hadn't moved, but precision was important, doubly so when the wood was this unique. It never hurt to spend the extra seconds it took to make sure his cut would be accurate. The tape measure dropped back into the tool belt with a snap of metal on plastic.

"You are one detail oriented dude, Geno. I enjoy seeing a master of his craft in the thick of things. Thanks for letting me help. I know you could probably do all this faster without me underfoot, but I like to be immersed in a project. Someday when I'm watching Roxy cook an incredible meal in this kitchen, I will take pride in the fact that I helped put it together, however minor that role might be."

Mac replaced his goggles and earplugs and put his gloved hands on the end of the board to hold it steady as he'd been taught. It was another trait Geno appreciated about the man. You tell him something once, or show him the way things needed to be done, and he wouldn't forget. Must be all those lines in scripts he had to memorize over the years.

Starting the saw eliminated the need for Geno to reply. He preferred the silence. The wolf pack had come to accept this about him.

The cut boards separated, and Mac hefted up the finished piece and carried it to the island. It was the last board. Soon, it would shine with a light varnish, bringing out faint blue tones and rich, intricate grains.

"This place will look amazing when the appliances are delivered. I can't wait to see Roxy's face when she takes this in. When do you think it will all be done?"

Geno smiled as he swept dust off the saw, wielding the broom and pan with the same patience he'd come to use on everything. Mac knew the schedule in as much detail as he did, involved as he was in every phase of the remodeling and renovation to the degree his schedule allowed it. He didn't need to work on three or four film projects a year, acting or directing or both, but he did it because he loved the movie business. Dedication to craft was a characteristic they shared.

"We're right on schedule," Geno said. "Everything will be ready in time for you to surprise Roxy on her birthday."

Mac's big grin said it all. He was happy, in large part because he could make Roxy happy. Their love affair fifteen years ago ended badly. Rebuilding trust and rekindling their romance hadn't been easy, but they made it work.

Kind of like restarting a long-interrupted friendship. At one point, Geno and Agnes had been best friends, buddies from day one in first grade. Grammar school, middle school, high school, and after. Until he screwed it up. He was better off not thinking about how much the separation hurt. He didn't want to screw things up again.

"Roxy said she and Tess saw you on Main Street the other day. That's not your usual stomping ground. Are you doing work for someone down there?"

Mac's simple question made his insides flip. It might be easier if he was doing a project nearby. He could keep an eye on things. He could keep an eye on her. He'd promised, but even that justification didn't make the step he needed to take a simple measure.

"I happened to be walking down the street. You know, errands. It was nice to see Roxy." Geno figured that was all the answer he needed to provide. It sounded innocent.

"Yeah, we don't all get together often enough anymore. I'm thinking of having a surprise birthday party for Roxy with the big kitchen reveal. You know, get everyone here, and then bring her over like I'm going to show her this room, just the two of us. We can park the cars in back where she can't see them, and I can blindfold her to bring her in. I know she'd love to have you and the rest of the gang here. What do you think?"

Geno always found himself surprised by the acceptance of this circle of friends. Living as a loner seemed easier, with fewer questions posed and fewer explanations required. Friendships were as surprising as the addition of a goofball dog to his otherwise solitary life. The big hound mix rambled up on a job site one day, so far out in the woods that even the locals didn't know their neighbors. No one claimed the dog, probably because he paid no attention and had a mind all his own. But he evidently decided Geno was the human for him, and he jumped in the back of the pick-up as if it had been his place of honor for years. Undernourished and a little crazy, Geno named him Lucky because he figured the dog was lucky to have found a home with someone who understood what it was like to be alone in the world.

The dog, sunning himself on the unfinished front porch, chose this moment to bark like crazy. The noise of a big engine and tires crunching gravel announced a visitor, as if Lucky's frantic greeting wasn't enough. When the motor stopped and a door creaked open, Geno didn't need to look outside to know Lucky was on the receiving end of as much loving as the dog was willing to take. It had become something of a routine. When footfalls sounded on the temporary wood steps and trod across the porch, Geno pulled off his gloves.

Powers strode into the room, glancing around as if cataloging the progress Geno had made in the last three days. His roaming eyes stopped on the blue pine counter pieces and he grinned.

"Man, the boards look amazing. I can't believe those are the same ones we unloaded weeks ago. I didn't think you could plane them down enough to remove those years of grit and paint."

Powers shook hands with Mac, then Geno. Still nodding in wonder over the boards, he ran a slow hand over the surface of the top one. Technically, Powers was the general contractor on this project. In reality, the two men had struck up a business partnership that suited them both, and Geno filled the de facto project manager role. Powers had enough projects around the region to keep him busy as boss of Ashland Construction, but Geno knew the man loved nothing more than pulling on gloves and getting into the work himself.

Which is exactly what he did, pulling well-worn leather from his back pocket and slapping the gloves against his thigh before frowning at the stack of completed wood. When he glanced at Mac and Geno, both with their gloves off, he shoved his back into his pocket with more than a little disappointment on his face.

"Are you done already? Damn. I hoped to get here earlier and handle the woodwork with you. I don't get to see much blue pine these days."

"Relax, Powers." Geno smiled at the obvious regret in his friend's expression. "There's plenty more. I still have to do the build-in cabinets and open shelves Mac wants in the library. And I'm saving the mantelpieces for you. You'll have plenty of opportunities to caress it as much as you want."

Mac added, "I thought you were a little nuts when you suggested we find reclaimed lumber to replace the rotted wood. And going hundreds of miles away for it? Ridiculous. But I have to admit, it was worth every minute of negotiating and every penny it cost. This will make the house shine. If it doesn't, I'll eat my Oscars."

Geno joined in the resulting laughter. How much his life had changed. In his first year in northern California, he'd moved around a lot, living in his trailer and often parked on a job site where he worked. A trip to Flynn's Crossing for a restaurant project had him staying longer than the work required. There was something about the rural setting and history of its buildings that made him linger here. The locals were laid back, at least the ones who weren't as intense as a pneumatic punch. That suited him fine. His reputation as a fine craftsman grew, and he had as much work as he was willing to take on.

And this. Here, he had friends.

The fact that Agnes lived in the area too, well, that was a nice coincidence. He'd heard through the old neighborhood grapevine where she settled down. It wasn't as if he'd followed her, of course. He assured himself of this when the thought of her came up, which didn't happen all that frequently.

Okay, it happened every day at least three times, or maybe it was more like five.

"What do you think of that, Geno?"

He realized he'd taken a mental break from the conversation, which was embarrassing, since he now had no clue what Powers had asked him.

Mac and Powers watched him, each shifting on their feet as if getting comfortable for a long pause. Geno stalled, a trait he'd learned in childhood. He could stay quiet for a long time. But when Powers didn't add anything to give him an idea about what he needed, Geno realized this time, he'd need to rewind.

"I'm not sure, Powers. Why don't you run through it for me again so I can consider it?"

Powers pulled his eyebrows together close enough to create a single dark line and shot him a curious look. He sighed and said, "I know it's a lot to ask of you. But I can't take on the project unless you manage it. I'm full up, and Tess will send me to the spirit world herself if I work more nights or weekends. You'll make your usual rate for the carpentry, and I'll add on to that for the project management aspect. It's a great block of structures, and the merchants are excited to get started. After I did the infill project on Main Street, I get requests from owners of the other buildings on a regular basis. Most of the projects are small and I have no problem fitting them in, but this will be bigger. We'll have to work around the stores, keeping them open for business while we do the renovation. It's right up your alley, Geno. Restoring those old buildings to their former glory while modernizing their functionality is something you're great at. What do you say?"

Did Powers say Main Street? How hard would it be to be working there every day, within touching distance of Agnes? If he ran into her casually, what would he say?

Hey Agnes, it's been a long time. Good to see you again. Maybe we could get together for coffee some time and catch up.

And she'd buy that about as quickly as she'd thrown coffee in his face all those years ago.

Chapter 2

Space limited her at every turn. She couldn't add another station. Every service position was busy. There was always risk in growth, but her business volume supported it. She'd run the numbers, and she knew she could pull it off.

The man on the phone added a cajoling tone to his words. "Bliss, I know you want to lease that space now, but I have to wait until I hear back from the contractor on the remodel. I have no idea how long it will take, or even if your plans can be incorporated into the final layout. It's been so abused over the years that it needs a master's touch. Wouldn't you want it to look great for your spa?"

Yeah, Agnes Amendola did. She continued to scowl at the offending wall blocking her from her expansion as she pressed the phone to her ear. She appreciated that her landlord wanted to return the building to its former glory. But that didn't make the waiting any easier. Everywhere she turned, it seemed, she had to be patient. It wasn't her best trait.

Demanding wouldn't make things happen any faster, and she said she understood before wishing the man a nice evening. Walking through her shop, she clicked off lights and music before darkening the open sign. The street's glow slid through the slats of the blinds, and she stood still for a second, in the same place she had that morning a few days ago. She thought she saw a ghost that day, but when she looked back, it was just a man in a ball cap facing away from her and talking on his phone. If he was tall and slender and reminded her of someone specific, she pushed away the memory. Wherever he was today, he didn't deserve the energy it took to remember him. But she'd been thinking about him more and more recently.

She couldn't be that lonely, could she?

Stalling as she straightened hair products on the shelves gave her time to think. Her daughter needed to be picked up from the sitter. Dinner would follow homework. It amazed her how much a nine-year-old needed to do each night. Even a child as bright as hers needed coaching.

It was more than motherly pride. Her daughter had a gifted mind, a ravenous curiosity about the world, and a determination to accomplish things that almost rivaled her own. She'd chosen the girl's name by herself, despite the urging of her family to name the child after her mother. She couldn't do that. This child was blessed, no matter what her mother said.

"My name means wisdom, if you recall. Sophia is a fine Italian name. Your child will need wisdom to make her way in the world, with her challenges. It is a curse against you, you know. God ruled on your sins and the fates on your indiscretions, and your child is marked as a result. Agnes, it is your penance in this lifetime. What God decides for you in the next world is up to him." Her mother had crossed herself three times with this pronouncement, spat on the hospital room floor, and left the maternity ward without a word of warmth for her only daughter and her new granddaughter.

It was the last time Agnes spoke with her mother, if she could call those post-partum tears and pleadings a discussion. Yes, they lived under the same roof for all of seven months longer, until Agnes couldn't take the silence and the snubs. Most Italian grandmothers would smother their heirs with attention, so much so that parents needed to call a time out, for the grandparents, that is. But not in her case. When she moved out with her baby into a one room flat, she worked as many hours as she could and relied on her savings to fill the gaps.

Leonora's father was no help. Over the years, she'd come to terms with the knowledge that he had to grow up. Someday, he'd be ready to settle down. In that someday, she and Leonora would be ready for the joyous reunion. Her intense feelings for him were never far from her mind, even if years had passed. Maybe that's why ghosts with reminders appeared outside her window.

Glancing at the clock, she noted how much time had passed while she lived in the past. She was running very late. If she didn't pick up Leonora as promised, her sitter would need to delay dinner for her own kids. It wasn't always a fair arrangement, but it was the best she could afford now. Leonora, her little light in the darkness, needed a place to go after school. Bringing her to the shop hadn't been a good alternative. People talked. Some women stared. Others tried to be overly understanding. None of those options made for a blissful spa experience.

Bliss Day Spa, her crowning business achievement to date. Three years of renting space from others taught her she wanted to run her own place. When a salon in a rural foothills town outside Sacramento came up for sale, she made an offer before she could talk herself out of it. One business loan later, she'd updated the equipment and surroundings, staffed the place, and had as much work as she wanted. Leonora entered first grade, and life settled into a frantic but happy pace.

Bliss wondered if her mother would recognize the woman her daughter had become. Working hard and building a stable life for her child had changed her, and with the change, she'd changed her name too. She associated Agnes with fear and dependency. Bliss was a woman who provided for her own, at least until Leonora's father re-entered the picture.

She punched in the security code at the back door, closed and locked it behind her, and checked the length of the alley before setting off at a brisk pace for the city parking garage. It wasn't that the town was unsafe. In fact, many merchants felt okay without a security system, and some might be lax about locking their doors. But she could never shake off the lessons learned from her big city roots.

It helped, growing up, to have brothers. Like, big older brothers. She never grew past five foot three, even if her curves and endowments belonged on a woman much taller. The brother next older in the pecking order had two years and a good foot on her, and he was the runt of the litter. God knows where they got it. Probably the hormones in meats, and it hadn't helped her height when she decided to be a vegetarian for a handful of years when she was nine.

Nine years old, almost ten, the same age as Leonora was now. When Bliss was nine, she was convinced she knew everything and had the world under her control. It seemed her daughter followed in her footsteps a little too closely. If her mother could see her granddaughter now, she'd laugh that evil cackle of hers and point her finger saying, see Agnes? You reap what you sow. It had been a favorite saying of hers when Bliss was growing up. Not that Sophia ever used it on her sons. No, that was a special message for her daughter alone.

Bliss put on her headset and shifted her car into gear. She hit speed dial for the sitter, relieved when the woman picked up herself.

"Hi, it's Bliss. I'm so sorry, but I was delayed and I'm just leaving. I'll be there in ten minutes."

She listened to the woman's rapid-fire words, unable to process the gist of what she was hearing as she drove down Main Street faster than she should. When the message made it through her tired brain, she lifted her foot off the accelerator in shock.

"What do you mean? You've been her sitter for two years, and I thought it was working out. I didn't know the hours had become a problem for you."

A car honked behind her, and Agnes put her foot down again, making the tires screech on the pavement loud enough to draw frowning looks from people on the sidewalk. She smiled apologetically and tried to speed think through the implications of the other woman's words.

"A week? Can you give me two weeks? You know how hard it is to find someone to sit on a regular basis, particularly with the hours I keep. And spring break is coming up."

When she pressed the button to end the call, she hadn't won her concession. One week. Her phone rang on the seat next to her, but she ignored the call. If she could figure out a way to convince her sitter to change her mind in the minutes remaining before she arrived at the house, she could set this worry aside and move on to one of her many others.

Foremost on her worry list were her daughter's continuing needs. Being special came at a price, emotionally, physically, and financially. It didn't help that her little girl already figured out what most kids didn't have a clue about at this age. The world was rough, and it sucked to be different. It was even worse when that difference meant you couldn't try everything other kids did, or what you wanted to do. Yes, there were solutions, but they were costly and so out of reach that Bliss didn't even bother to dream about how to snag them.

She pulled into the driveway of the single story frame house, hesitating behind the wheel and turning the car off. She pulled her coat around her shoulders more tightly to ward off the loss of heat. Usually, this was one of her favorite parts of the day, reuniting with her little light. Her daughter always ignited a sense of wonder in her, even when she was crabby or unhappy. She raised this little person by herself, and she would continue to do so to the best of her ability. If that meant she put her own life and dreams on hold, someday, it would be worth it.

"The last owner didn't pick up. I left a message." Powers flipped the sheet of paper over, checking the back. He glanced up and asked, "Are you okay? You haven't said much."

Geno blinked at his own copy of the list. When Powers gave him the paper, his eyes nailed on the one name he didn't want to see there. While he knew it was a probability, seeing it in ink still hit him hard.

He said, "No, no problem. I'm thinking through the logistics of keeping the businesses open while we do the work. Not only that, but some of the original features of these buildings have been destroyed over the years, or have deteriorated past the point of saving. There isn't much in the budget to replicate those missing pieces, at least, not in restoration-quality materials."

Yeah, that was what was really on his mind. He ran his fingers over the computer keyboard in a meaningless search. He would treat this like any other challenging job. At least until the shit hit the fan. He'd have to meditate on what to do when that happened, because it would.

Powers said, "Make replicas in other materials, as long as the resulting effect stays true to the period. You have the computer capability to design what we need. Didn't you say you wanted to try 3D printing to reconstruct missing pieces? We can figure it out as we go. The owner understands we won't know how bad things are until we take the space apart. It's in the contract. He's already conceded to taking down the styling a notch if we can't make it fit into the budget."

Geno nodded in response, wishing he hadn't been so quick to say yes to this project. Usually he gave himself a day to ponder a new job, but not this time. He'd agreed to be the project manager in record time, knowing it would put him near Agnes. Later, he wanted to kick himself.

He ran his finger back over the list, running down the other names if only to distract himself from the one he didn't want to stare at. He knew some of these people in person, was familiar with the reputations of others, and had a fair idea that for the most part, they would prove to be easy to work with. All except for one.

"So we're set. Tuesday evening, five-thirty, after the shops are closed for the day but not cutting into evenings. I'll have the office send out a group email and confirm the meeting to everyone. I'd like you to take the lead in the discussion." Powers continued to flip through the roll of plans spread out on the drafting table.

"I'm not sure that's the best approach." Geno took a deep breath, knowing that he would never escape the inevitable, but he could delay it, at least for a short time. Maybe it would be long enough to figure out what he would say.

Powers looked up and frowned at him. "Why?"

Geno waved his hand, willing his fingers to relax on the page with its fatal list of names. "They don't know me. You, on the other hand, they already know and trust from the work you've done on your new building, and because of Tess. They might be happier finding out about the plans for the project from you, particularly any issues related to business access while work is underway. After the landlord introduces the project, you can talk about what they can expect."

The frown on his friend's face cleared up and he nodded, agreeing. "You're right. It might be nice to have Tess there too, for the PR factor if nothing else. They all love her. I think I may scare some of them." He chuckled.

Geno didn't join in. He doubted one person would be laughing, smiling, or doing anything other than screaming if his name came up.

There was no if. When his name came up. There was no escaping it. It was destiny, and his karma was coming back to haunt him.

Powers typed a couple of notes into his tablet, nodding as he did so. "We'll have the owner do a rah-rah on the project, introduce me, and I'll talk about specifics and take the initial questions. Then I'll introduce you as the project manager and you can answer more of their questions. That will make them comfortable with you. You'll be point person after that. It will be easy."

Geno knew it would not. He wanted to find the spiritual insight and growth offered by the challenge, but damned if he could.

Chapter 3

"Why do you have to go?"

The plaintive whine made Bliss wish she could find another solution, and quickly. But those fates were laughing at her again, and she must have pissed off her guardian angel to boot.

"It's a business meeting, not a party. I need to go because it's important to the future of the spa. We need to expand, and this will be the path to doing that. You know how important keeping the business growing is to our future, right?"

Her daughter frowned instead of agreed. "Then why can't I go with you? I plan to take it over from you someday."

Bliss felt her heart sink with dismay as it always did when Leonora talked like this. Her daughter's future belonged in the world of big brains and intellects. She should have a better life, a life of fewer struggles and less hardship. Besides, Leonora would never be able to do this work.

Glancing at the little girl, Agnes realized they were about a minute away from a major meltdown. The afterschool upheaval of the past week and subsequent disruptions to her regular schedule made Leonora crabby. Just because she was bright didn't mean she wouldn't act out like every other kid her age.

Losing the sitter was a huge problem. Yesterday hadn't been bad, since Bliss didn't usually work in the shop on Monday and she could pick up Leonora herself. If it was a little challenging to do the ordering and accounting while her daughter asked questions about her homework, some of which Bliss had no clue how to answer, so be it.

She leaned forward and looked her daughter in the eye. "Can you help me out here, sweetie? I miss being with you too, but I need a compromise. How about if you go with Marlee for an hour like we planned, and then next Sunday, we'll do something special for the whole day?"

On cue, the massage therapist stepped out of the shadow of the back hallway and said, "Come on, Leonora. If you want to take over the spa someday, you'll need to understand massages. I'll show you the basics, and you can decide how much you want to learn from there. What do you say?"

Bliss shot Marlee a thankful look. They weren't close, but then Marlee didn't seem to be close friends with anyone. She paid her station rent on time and kept her drama to a minimum, unlike some of the other workers. But they did each other favors, and sometimes, that was all two women on their own could hope for. Friendship, if it came to that, would be much further down the road.

Leonora eyed Marlee carefully, as if sizing up her sincerity. Evidently satisfied with what she saw, she nodded and turned to the treatment rooms. "I'll be waiting," she said as she disappeared down the hallway.

"I can't thank you enough," Bliss said, though she watched her daughter's retreating back and wondered how Marlee was going to handle the inherent difficulties of showing massage to someone who clearly didn't have the physical resources to perform one. "I hate to cut into your personal time."

"Don't stress about it, Bliss. And if you're worried about what I can teach her, don't be. I'll pull out the charts and show her the muscle groups. She'll either become entranced with the human body, or she'll nod off and take a nap."

Marlee's gentle grin of understanding brought an answering smile to Bliss's lips. If tears threatened too, so be it. She couldn't arrange every detail of her life perfectly, but she could roll with its ups and downs with the best of them.

"I should be back in an hour at most. Maybe earlier, since I don't have any questions for the contractor other than how soon they can start next door. God, listen to me. I haven't even signed a lease on the space, and already I'm considering it mine." She glanced at the common wall, aware that on the other side even now, people waited for the meeting to begin.

From the back, Leonora yelled, "Marlee, when are we getting started? It isn't a good idea to keep a client waiting, you know."

To Leonora, Marlee said, "Coming," and to Bliss, "Go." And she pushed her toward the door.

"If you have any problems, text me. I'll come right back, no matter what."

"Bliss, go. Leonora and I will be fine for this little while. It's not a problem."

From the back, her daughter's impatience made her voice screech a little, "Marlee!"

Bliss fled out the front door, hoping the walls were thicker between the suites than she thought. Otherwise, she would be explaining to the people gathered next door why something sounded like a wounded animal howling in her spa.

Ten minutes later, she wondered why she'd rushed. Idle chitchat with other storekeepers passed the time. She and Tess discussed the merchants' association plan to hang flower baskets from the lampposts for the summer. At fifteen minutes, Bliss tried to keep her feet still, but her toes tapped in impatience. Finally, the owner of their building rapped a pen on the side of his water bottle to get their attention. As people took their seats, Bliss took the opportunity of sudden quiet to listen sharply for any complaints or screaming. All was blessedly quiet.

"Thank you all for coming tonight," the owner began.

And he was still droning on five minutes later about the virtues of the period beauty of their building, even as he also noted the restoration couldn't be historically accurate. Bliss watched Tess, sitting to the side of the podium table, nudge the big man sitting next to the owner. She frowned and twitched her head to the side. The big man frowned and shook his a little.

Bliss knew the big man, Powers Ashland, was Tess's boyfriend. Did that word still work once you got out of high school? Lack of a formal title for what they had together didn't seem to impede their ability to communicate without words, though. Bliss noted the thin line of Powers' lips and the answering pursing from Tess. Then the woman raised her hand.

"Yes, Tess? Did you have a question? Or maybe you'd like to move your flower shop into the other vacant space in the building?" The owner laughed at his attempt at humor, and people responded with a polite titter.

"Howard, I think it's commendable that you're willing to undertake this restoration project. I'm sure once it's completed, it will be an excellent example of how the character and style of these old buildings can be maintained, even while they're outfitted with modern conveniences. Perhaps it's time to let Powers speak so the store owners can learn more about the specific plans for the renovation."

Around her, Bliss heard people sigh in relief that someone was willing to yank Howard off his soapbox. If a couple of people applauded quietly, they went unnoticed by the landlord as he shuffled into a seat and allowed Powers to have the floor.

Twenty minutes after that, Bliss was enthralled, even enchanted, by the picture Powers painted of what the building could look like once it was restored. Imagine how stylish and chic her day spa would look, outfitted with replicas of the original molding and window framing. Modern additions, like electrical systems that didn't short out or blow a fuse when styling wands and blow driers were plugged in, would be a huge benefit. And the pedicure stations situated in private alcoves behind the original archways would make the place cozy as well as classy.

Bliss was in heaven. She ignored the legal pad in her lap, the one where she'd started a list of features she wanted to incorporate into the new space. She didn't need it. Her mind had already drawn the picture.

"And we plan to begin our work with this suite, the one we're seated in today. As you can see, it needs a lot of help."

People shifted in their seats, taking in the peeling paint and missing wood framing around doorways and windows. Where the doors themselves had disappeared was a mystery from long ago. Windows to the street now housed mismatched panels of glass.

But she could see it all as it would be, the space perfect for the next stage in her expanding business.

"I understand from Howard that he already has a tenant interested in this unit. Is that correct, Howard?"

The owner stood and searched around the room, stopping and smiling when he found Bliss in the crowd. She waved, happier than she had been in a long time. It looked like she was finally going to have a little good luck.

"Bliss Amendola, ladies and gentlemen. She is ready to expand her day spa next door, and she approached me a while back about leasing this suite. Of course, I couldn't give it to her in this condition, so you might say her interest spurred me into getting the ball rolling. Thank you, Bliss."

Around her, people shared their congratulations and thanks, and Bliss let herself bask in that glow. Her family doubted she could make anything of her life without their support. In fact, they expected her to fail. All she could think was, well Mama, look at me now.

Powers continued, "Bliss will be working closely with our project manager, a man I believe some of you already know. In this first stage, we'll be trying out different renovation techniques to see what makes the most sense for this space. Once it comes time to merge the new space with her existing spa, we'll experiment to find the best methods to keep her up and running, even as we tear the walls down around her."

Everyone laughed, and Bliss beamed at them. She'd expected this. Maybe she'd run a remodeling special, something to make sure her customers were compensated for their inconvenience during the work. In fact, that might even bring in new customers.

The broad smile on her face made her cheeks hurt, and she beamed as Powers said something more, introducing the man who would be the project manager, the man she'd be working with so closely. She couldn't wait to meet him, and she turned with everyone else as a reedy, balding man pushed his way off the back wall and started down the side.

Bliss blinked, unable to process what her eyes saw. As the man passed her, he caught her gaze as if trying to pin her in place, not that she could have moved. She was seeing a ghost. And it was one ghost she'd willingly bury herself if she could dig fast enough.

>>>>>

Powers said, "Geno Altimari, ladies and gentlemen. Some of you know him as a master carpenter. What you might not know is that he's also a whiz recreating period-authentic replications of wood, framing and other unique characteristics of these old buildings. He's also an experienced project manager, and he'll be your day-to-day resource during the renovations."

Geno heard more words, but they sounded like babble to him. His fingers bit around the metal in his jacket pocket to steady himself. She was staring at him like he was her worst dream come true. He hadn't intended to be. Hell, he never wanted to be anything other than her friend.

And she still had the most passionate eyes. Those eyes currently snapped and burned on his. He could almost hear the wheels grinding in her brain, trying to figure out whether to give him the finger or go with her baser instincts and chuck a folding chair.

He broke off the shared gaze, walking forward until he stood next to Powers. Agnes had sunk back down into her seat when he glanced at the crowd again. He wasn't overly fond of speaking to crowds. Standing in the back of the room suited him just fine. But this was now his show, and damned if he wanted to fail in front of her.

People asked him questions, he answered, and evidently, he didn't sound like an idiot. People laughed at a couple of his comments, but he was clueless about what he'd said. People glanced between Agnes and him at one point, nodding approvingly. She looked anything but pleased. In fact, an old country grandmother might say she was giving him the evil eye.

Cold, her look was so cold. He shivered, even though the room's temperature didn't match the mid-

March chill outside. She tipped up her chin and turned her face away as if dismissing him.

"So, thank you all for coming this evening. If you have any questions, Geno is your primary point of contact. I will, of course, be available because, as you all know, I live just up the street." Everyone laughed at Powers' closing comment. Everyone, Geno noted, except Agnes.

People rose and came forward to shake his hand and introduce themselves. He waited through the greetings, somewhat relieved with the delay. He doubted she'd stick around. In fact, he wondered if she'd back out of the whole deal, now that she knew precisely what, or rather, who was in on it.

As the room cleared, though, he saw she hadn't left. She sat in her seat, her face as empty of expression as a carved mask.

"Let me introduce you to Bliss formally." Howard closed his fingers around Geno's upper arm, and short of jerking away, he wasn't sure how to avoid the inescapable. Their steps echoed ominously as they crossed the room.

"Bliss, let me formally introduce to you the man you'll be working with on this renovation, Geno Altimari. Geno, this is Bliss Amendola, owner of Bliss Day Spa next door and one of my best tenants."

Agnes remained seated, and Geno didn't extend his hand.

Missing the fact that something wasn't right, Howard said, "Geez, Altimari and Amendola. It sounds like an Italian pop duo. You two belong together."

And Geno's memory flashed back twenty-five years.

"Children, I will read your names in alphabetical order. When you hear your name, please sit down in the seat I point to. Genovese Altimari. Genovese, where are you?"

Geno pushed away from the back wall, staring at his shoes so he didn't have to meet anyone's eyes. Miss Francis was a wide woman, and in her brown dress with its faint print, she looked like a weird bear. He walked up the aisle towards her, shaking a little bit. There was a dust stain on the knee of his dark blue uniform pants, and he hoped she wouldn't notice.

"Genovese? Welcome to the first grade at Our Lady of Perpetual Sorrow School. You'll sit here this year."

She pointed at the first desk in the first row, pulled in so tight against the one next to it that the arms of the chairs touched. Geno sat where she pointed, still afraid to look up in case the teacher was staring at him. He wondered if she knew he was a new kid. But then, they were all new kids, except the rest of them grew up in this neighborhood since they were born. He was only here because of his dad.

"Agnese Amendola? Agnese? How do you pronounce your first name, dear? Oh how cute, Altimari and Amendola. You two belong together."

"I prefer Agnes, or you can call me Aggie, like my brothers do. Mama makes them stop it, but I don't really mind. But I guess maybe you'd better call me Agnese, so Mama doesn't yell at you too."

Geno smiled at the explanation and the tut-tut of Miss Francis. He knew what it was like to have a weird name. When they were living in Texas while his dad was overseas fighting in someplace called the Persian Gulf, his mother insisted on using his full name in public. On base, the other kids laughed at him, and in the grocery store, they pointed and made fun of him. He *never felt like he belonged. It seemed like Agnes had come to terms with her name, though.*

"Hi, I'm Agnes. I guess it's okay that you're a boy, though I really hoped to make girlfriends in school this year. I have five older brothers. What do you like to be called? Do you have any sisters or brothers? Where do you live with your mom and dad?"

He stared at his hands, folded neatly on the desk like his mother had taught him. Then he stole a glance to his right, and his mouth dropped open.

Agnes had long brown hair, with curls held back in a big pink bow. She was smaller than he was, but she didn't seem uneasy about her size. She watched him with open curiosity and sparkling eyes.

"Class, I want you to introduce yourselves to your seatmates. You'll be sitting next to them for the whole school year, and I expect everyone here will be friends with everyone else. Now you can talk."

Around them, the buzz of conversations rose.

"So, what's your real name? That's the name you pick for yourself. My real name is Rose Violet. I don't like Agnes, or Agnese. My parents speak Italian at home when they don't want us to know what they're talking about, but I know what they're saying anyway. They say I'm a hand full. I hate it when they pronounce my name Agnese. But you can call me Agnes, or Rose Violet."

He returned to staring at his hands, wishing he could sprout wings and fly through the open classroom window. Outside, the air was warm and humid. It was much nicer than the hot and dusty Texas base they left. But they had to leave the base. His daddy died, and he was a hero according to his mom. But he was still dead. Now all he had left was his mom, and she was too busy working most of the time.

"All right, children, let's quiet down now. I hope you had some nice first discussions with your new friends. Today we're going to spend our time on…"

"So, what's your name?" Agnes gave him an elbow to the ribs to emphasize her whispered question. *"Come on, you have to share yours. I showed you mine."*

"Geno," he mumbled, tightening his fingers.

"Geno?" Agnes rolled the name around. *"Geno. I like it."*

"Geno?"

He shook off the intervening years as Agnes said his name in a tone of disgusted disbelief. She was still in her seat, though he could see the coiled energy ready to spring up any moment. She rarely sat still for long, at least when she was younger. He doubted this had changed about her.

"God, I can't believe it. Two thousand nine hundred miles away, and it is you. I don't think I can do this."

She gathered her purse and a big pad of paper, while around them, the remaining people talked and laughed as if a chasm hadn't wrenched open in the crust of the planet. Or maybe it was his heart, tearing open again as it had the day she threw her drink at him.

Agnes jumped up, knocking over her chair in the process. It cascaded into another, which fell at the feet of Powers and the building owner. They looked up, and Powers cocked a questioning eyebrow at Geno.

Geno shrugged, reaching out to catch the paper falling out of Agnes's arms as she whirled for the door.

"Agnes, wait. It's great to see you. How are you?"

She stopped, her back to him. Then she raised herself to her full height, pushed her shoulders back, and spun around to face him.

She stuck a finger under his nose to emphasize her words. "I am not Agnes, not anymore. I am Bliss. You can call me Bliss. But I'd prefer you don't call me at all."

"What if I call you Rose Violet?" He smiled at her, wishing he'd thought through better words of greeting.

She didn't even hesitate in delivering her response. "What if I call you a traitor and an idiot?" The spark in her eyes cracked as sharply as her words.

"Is there a problem here?"

Powers loomed behind Agnes, dwarfing her even more than Geno did. Not that it appeared to matter to her. In fact, she probably didn't even notice their differences in height. She'd always been like that, unafraid of things that were bigger or scarier. Even when things were the hardest for her, she didn't back down.

"No problem, Powers. I was discussing the first steps in the project with Ag-, ah, Bliss. She's eager to begin, and she can't believe we aren't going to start tonight."

She shot him a look, the one that could melt stones when they were growing up. She turned to Powers and stepped forward, so much into his personal space that Geno noticed Powers step back in surprise. Agnes stepped forward again, lifting her hands to begin gesturing. She always talked with her hands when she became agitated, and you had to be ready to duck and dodge as a result.

"Mr. Ashland, I – "

"Please, call me Powers."

"Fine, Powers. I would prefer to work directly with you, not some lackey." She threw a hand over her shoulder at Geno as if discarding him.

"Ma'am, I think you'll have an excellent working relationship with Geno. The man knows his renovations. He'll be completely honest with you about what can and can't be done."

"Ha!" Agnes threw both hands in the air this time, and glanced over her shoulder to give him a dirty look. He was scared spitless of whatever was on her mind based on her expression alone.

"Hi Bliss. Is there a problem?"

Tess joined the ever-growing circle. Geno wished he'd had the nerve to visit Agnes before this, to make his apologies and beg her forgiveness for his unthinking words years ago. He'd allied himself with the wrong team, and it cost him, big time.

"Hi Tess. I was explaining to Powers that I prefer to work with him directly on this project. Surely you have some influence on this?"

Tess frowned, but instead of looking at Powers, she glanced between Geno and the spitfire standing with her back to him. An assessing expression came over her face.

"Oh, I'm sorry, Bliss. I know everyone wants a piece of Powers, but he is, after all, only one man. I know you'll enjoy working with Geno. All our friends do, and the results he's created have been outstanding."

Agnes blinked. "There's no way we can change this?" Her pleading question held a note of panic, and hung in the air for sixty long seconds when no one responded.

"Ag-, Bliss, why don't you and I spend some time with the plans? I'll show you what we have in mind," Geno said.

She gave no response for another full minute, then turned to him and got into his face, her eyes snapping and narrowed. Fingers poked in his chest hard enough to bruise him, as she said, "No, Geno, why don't I show you my plans for my spa instead."

Chapter 4

She could not believe it. Somewhere in the back of her mind, she had the vague memory of one of her brothers telling her that Geno Altimari had married a nice Italian virgin from the old neighborhood. They divorced after three years, if she remembered correctly, much to the shocked disapproval of the regular attendees of Our Lady of Perpetual Sorrow Catholic Church. Her own mother even had a Mass said for their souls, since everyone in the church knew they were now doomed to burn in eternal hell.

At the time her brother shared the story, she'd said Geno undoubtedly deserved to burn. Inside, though, she'd felt a pang of regret, of too many words said that neither one of them could take back. And since, according to her mother, she was going to hell too, so at least she'd be there with someone she knew.

"Mommy? What's wrong?"

Leonora stood with her head tilted, a worried frown on her face. Agnes knew she charged into the spa like a blow drier set on high. Once she'd realized there was no way she was going to change their minds about working with Geno, not if she wanted this renovation, she couldn't stand there any longer. No one commented when she blasted out the door.

"Nothing, sweetheart, nothing at all. Listen, I need to talk with Marlee for a couple of minutes, and then we'll go home. How do you feel about pizza for dinner tonight?"

"Are we having a treat for something? We never have pizza on a school night, unless it's for a treat."

Over Leonora's head, Agnes saw Marlee give her a frown. She must look as frazzled as she felt. Geno Altimari in Flynn's Crossing. Damn.

Her little girl began gathering her things and putting them in the backpack. Marlee leaned in to whisper, "Is everything okay? You don't look like you're happy. Was there a problem at the meeting?"

She couldn't share it, not until she got her emotions under control. And not until she came up with a plan to get what she wanted, without the help of Geno.

"No, everything went fine. They're going to work on our new space first, using it as a test, I guess. They aren't sure what they'll find under the old wood, how much can be reused and how much needs to be replaced. Stuff like that. I just, ah, didn't expect things would be so complicated."

Marlee nodded sympathetically. "I guess major restoration projects always have some element of surprise in them."

A six-foot-three surprise.

"Mommy, I want vegetables on my pizza. I'm cutting down on meat." Leonora didn't even turn her head as she delivered her pronouncement.

She didn't need to think about like mother, like daughter. Not now.

To Marlee, she said, "Thanks again for helping me out. I promise not to ask you to do this – at least not too often." Agnes gave a weak laugh. She needed to solve that sitter issue, now more than ever.

"No problem, Bliss. Leonora and I had a great first lesson in massage therapy. She's a natural."

Agnes heard the rest of what was unsaid. She's a natural, even if she'll never be able to practice it.

"Yes, Mommy, I learned about how muscles and stuff attach to the spine. And how they work. Marlee showed me. I'm going to learn more next time. Can I come back after school tomorrow?"

"We'll think about it, okay? You know Marlee has clients, so she wouldn't be able to work with you all the time. And I have to work too, so you'd have to sit in the office and do your homework. Will you be able to do that?"

Her daughter's mutinous face told her this would be another battle. Leonora pushed her own limitations while she pushed every one of Agnes's guilty buttons. She wouldn't want to sit in the office; she'd want to be at the front desk. She wouldn't be doing her homework; she'd be talking with the clients about whatever popped into her head, some of which would be inappropriate. And the clients wouldn't be getting their blissful relaxing environment for their treatments.

"Thanks again, Marlee. See you tomorrow."

The other woman called out goodnight as she left through the back door. How long could she impose on the other woman's kindness? Not long. And she shouldn't take advantage of the goodwill of her clients for many days, either.

"Come on, let's go home and order that pizza. I bet they can have it to us in no time, and meanwhile, we'll work on your homework."

A reminder about the upcoming pizza went a long way toward improving Leonora's mood, and she grabbed her backpack and jacket while Agnes did her final walk-thru of the day. She glanced at the wall that would one day be gone, opening up the suite next door to hers. If only opening up her heart to an old friend who'd betrayed her was as easy as knocking down a brick wall.

>>>>>

"What just happened here?"

Powers stacked the last of the folding chairs on the cart while Geno collapsed the table legs. The air still held electricity from his encounter with Agnes. Bliss, she called herself Bliss now. He'd have to get used to that. He didn't want to think about how she could have earned that nickname. A lot of years had passed since he knew every intimate detail about her life.

"Nothing I can't handle, Powers. I think Bliss might be the kind of client who wants to be involved in every decision and overseeing every activity."

In fact, he was sure she would be in his face and second-guessing everything he did. She was nosy when they were growing up, and he doubted that would have changed about her. Unless she wanted absolutely nothing to do with him, which could also be a troublesome possibility.

Furniture corralled, Powers stood with hands on hips turning in a slow circle. Geno glanced around as well to take in the interior of the space, not that he hadn't examined it in detail already. The brick, stone and masonry had been built after the fire in 1900 wiped out wooden structures on Main Street. Natural decay brought on by its age, coupled with less than original modifications made for various tenants over the years, hid most of its character.

The part that intrigued Geno most was the woodwork. Here and there, segments of old wainscoting and ceiling moldings, carvings along the stairs to the upper level, and ornate railings surrounding the level above gave a hint of the building's opulent past. It had always been a store or eating establishment of some sort, but once upon a time, an elegant balcony wide enough to accommodate tables and chairs encircled the upper level, now hidden behind a false drop-down ceiling. Opening that up, exposing brick covered haphazardly with drywall, and replacing the wood detailing would go a long way to restoring its former glory.

The question would then be how to transform it into the day spa extension that Agnes – no, Bliss – wanted. Damn, he'd have to work hard on that name thing.

"This was once an amazing space, back when craftsmanship meant something," Powers said. "And we'll restore it to that glory again, eh?"

Geno nodded, but he wasn't thinking about the building now. He couldn't help but wonder if there was any way to restore his relationship with Agnes to its former wonder.

Chapter 5

"Are you sure I can't talk you into a manicure for those tired fingers of yours?"

In the mirror, Roxy shook her head at Bliss. "No, it's a waste of time. I'm in the kitchen all the time and bare nails are a must. Maybe when Mac and I take our next vacation, whenever we can both get away. The remodel, or maybe I should call it a gut and rebuild, is taking what limited free time he has. If it was for anything other than that ranch, I'd be jealous."

Agnes understood those kinds of priorities. She hoped she'd soon be elbow deep in the final design touches she wanted on the space next door. As long as she could avoid Geno in the process.

Bliss asked, "How is that remodeling coming along?"

Roxy sighed deeply, frowning at her reflection.

"Mac hasn't let me near the place for weeks now. The kitchen is close to completion, but he won't let me see it. If anything needs to be changed, I need to tell them now, don't you think? But Mac's sworn Powers and Geno to secrecy, and none of them will give me so much as a hint about how it's working out."

Her client's mood could be measured in the delivery of each frustrated word. Bliss held in her own exclamation when Roxy spoke. Geno again. Now that she knew he was near, he was turning up everywhere. Besides, even if she still hated him, she was curious.

She snipped at the ends of Roxy's long blonde hair and attempted to inject a casual note into her voice. "Geno? What's he like?"

"His work is amazing. He was able to find a few pieces of the original woodwork throughout the house, and he's carving us new decorative moldings to match. He's building our cabinets and shelves from scratch, to replicate as much of the original design as possible. I can't wait to see it. Now if they'd just hurry up and finish it."

Bliss didn't want to hear how great Geno was. Through a sleepless night, she'd convinced herself she didn't want to know what happened in his life. The fact that he'd become a success grated on her nerves. Did he deserve to have a great life after what he did to her?

Roxy continued, "He worked on details in the restaurant for me when he first moved to the area. He lived in a trailer behind the building, and he worked around our schedule. I'd come down from my apartment in the middle of the night, and there he'd be, installing some fancy new wood. It was interesting to watch him work. And he's such a nice person. So laid-back and easy-going."

He was not a nice person. And she should know. Well, maybe he was nice, except for that one time when she needed him the most.

"Wait. I'm thinking Tess told me Powers hired Geno as the project manager on this building's remodel. You'll get a chance to see how he is in person. He's a wonderful man. And I hear he's single." Roxy cocked an eyebrow as she added the final sentence in a sly tone.

The last thing she needed was people trying to set her up with someone she deplored. She liked that word, deplored. It summed things up quite nicely.

"Thanks, Roxy, but I don't have the desire to get fixed up. I have my daughter to take care of, and I have this place to run. Between those two things alone, I'm so busy I can barely think. Plus the expansion next door. I had hoped to work with Powers directly on it, but

I guess he's sloughed it off on this Geno guy. I'm not looking forward to that part."

"Oh, well, you'll see. You'll be working closely together, so you'll learn more about him. He's kind of quiet, at least until he gets to know you. Then he's only a little less reserved."

Roxy smirked at their reflections in the mirror. Bliss tried to smile back, but her mind stuck on Roxy's assessment of Geno. Yes, he'd always been quiet, but then when they were kids, she didn't know how to be.

"Are you shy?"

She wasn't sure what made her think he was, this silent new kid she sat next to. It had been a whole week, and he had yet to say a full sentence. Maybe he didn't know how to talk. How did anyone live if they didn't know how to talk?

She knew who he was, because he and his mother moved into the tiny house three doors down from hers. She'd heard her parents discussing it, in Italian of course. Gossiping was a sin according to her mother. Why wasn't what they were doing gossiping?

"You just moved in, didn't you? You came from another state. Why did you move here? Where does your dad work? Why does your mom work too? My mama says that women should stay home and take care of their children. What do you think?"

He slid his eyes to hers, and she caught a quick glimpse of hurt before he dropped his gaze back to his hands. He said nothing in response.

"Do you know how to talk?" Because she just had to know. She'd never met a mute person before.

He shot her another glance, angrier this time, but still said nothing.

"Agnes, Geno, are you talking?"

They were supposed to be working on their penmanship in silence. Miss Francis stopped in front of them, staring down through her thick glasses. Agnes thought she often looked mean, and her brothers said sometimes, she would smack a desk with a ruler to make sure a student knew she meant business.

That wooden ruler landed on Agnes's desk with a clap loud enough to make everyone in the room jump. The pencil she'd been holding flew out of her hands, landing at the feet of the teacher. Now she'd gone and done it. She'd probably end up in the principal's office. Her brothers said getting punished was scary.

"I'm sorry, Miss Francis. It's my fault. I asked Agnes how she makes her letters so neat. Mine aren't like that."

She forgot about being scared, because the person speaking was the boy sitting next to her. He rose out of his seat and bent down to retrieve the pencil, handing it back to Agnes solemnly. Then he went back at his desk, hunched his head down, and started tracing letters once more.

Miss Francis made a sound like the dog before it threw up, then rounded Geno's desk and showed him how to hold his pencil differently. She watched him and corrected him until another student called her name. Once she walked away, Agnes leaned over and whispered, "Thank you."

Geno shrugged in response, though he looked at her for more than two seconds this time.

"You're very brave," she said. The boy lifted his shoulders again, and then sat a little straighter in his chair.

Agnes saw the hesitation in his eyes. She knew none of the other children approached him and no one seemed to want to be his friend. But he was her personal hero now.

"Mama packed lasagna for my lunch. It's a big piece, and she makes really good lasagna. Want to share it with me?"

She thought he might be trying to smile. Then he said, "Okay."

And just like that, they were best friends.

"Oh Bliss? Where are you?" Roxy's singsong voice brought her back to the present, to the scissors clutched in her hand and the vintage rock music playing low in the background. Around her, the acidic smell of nail polish remover and metallic sting of hair color solution clashed with the scented candles she burned to make things spa-like.

"Sorry, stuck in old memories. What were you saying?"

Roxy smiled, her head tilted to one side as if assessing Agnes and wondering what was really going on.

"I was mentioning what a great guy Geno is, that he's single, and that once you get to know him, he's very friendly. He's very supportive and he likes to solve problems. And you drifted off."

Yes, she knew. He was always very supportive of her, protective even. But the one time she really needed him to step up, he wasn't the same knight in shining armor. And it wasn't as if he'd had a good reason.

Agnes flipped Roxy's hair, making sure the cut was even and full the way her client liked it. She reached for product, not that the mane needed volume, but it was habit. And it meant she didn't need to look in Roxy's too-observant eyes and give anything away.

"I'm sure he's a very nice guy, but I don't do nice. In fact, did I ever tell you the story about my first boyfriend? Man, my mama was out of her mind with that one. You see, he came to the house in a black leather jacket, and – "

She rambled on in the story, not really paying attention to the words. She'd recited this fiction so many times over the years, she almost believed it was true herself. Roxy didn't need to know she almost missed her junior prom because no one asked her. She'd been crushed. Until Geno asked, and they went together, much to their mothers' joint happiness. Nothing happened, because they were best friends, but he made the night special for her.

Then Geno went his way, and she went hers. He went to community college for computer technology for two years, then quit because he decided he wanted to be a carpenter. His mother was outraged, but she couldn't force him at his age. And at that point, he'd grown tall and lanky, and would still stare unspeaking if he didn't like the topic of conversation. It could be freaky if you didn't know it was because he was shy. Agnes remembered talking almost nonstop more than once, only to grind to a halt when Geno uttered a single sentence.

He'd said a lot that day when she asked her favor of him. His shocked face had morphed into resolution as he shook his head in denial. The part she recalled most vividly was the red checked tablecloth and dripping candle stuck in the wine bottle both getting drenched when she threw her coffee at him. All because he'd said the one word she'd never expected after all of the years when he'd protected her.

No.

Chapter 6

He loved the buzz of a saw, any kind of saw. The sound always reminded him he'd picked this trade by choice. His mother hadn't been pleased, thinking he'd be much better off in computers. But two years of school convinced him sitting behind a desk all day wasn't how he wanted to spend his life. Computer work was now a hobby, not a chore.

He released the trigger on the circular saw, setting it down in its rack besides his other tools. Keeping things orderly meant he could find what he needed quickly and easily. It was harder on a job site, particularly when he had to share space with other trades. He loved the workshop he'd set up at home. The stereo system added the perfect touch of energy.

"So, Lucky, what do you think of this piece? Pretty, isn't it?"

The dog lifted his big head, his ears cocked up and his nose sniffing hard. When the action didn't produce a scent he cared about, he dropped back into his leisurely recline and returned to snoring almost immediately.

Geno didn't expect much more of him. Lucky had two speeds – turbo and snoring. He reserved the turbo version for chasing cats and squirrels and diving for food. Snoring was for the other twenty-three hours in a day. He often spent hours on a job site lying in the sun, baking his belly or a side. It was only when Geno's lunch box came out that he got excited, and then he was like velcro.

The furniture pieces for Roxy and Mac's living room were coming along well. This special table would be part of the entryway. While Mac kept the project's finish work a secret from Roxy, even he didn't know about this unique item.

It was one of a kind, using the blue pine installed in the rest of the house. It fit the entry alcove perfectly, and Geno had spent long happy hours creating scrolls and fretwork mimicking original designs he'd been able to salvage from the house. His movements flowed with the rising crescendo in Puccini's lovers' duet between Mimi and Rodolfo as he ran fine sandpaper back and forth. It was a labor of love to create something this different.

Lucky lifted his head and let out a woof, listening hard. He wasn't much of a guard dog, but he made a good doorbell. By now, Geno could hear the sound of an engine too, and he brushed off his hands and glanced around to make sure everything with a power button was turned off. He pocketed the mp3 player and left the coolness of the space, Lucky bounding ahead.

The large garage was built away down the driveway from the house and out of sight of it. It was one of the things that attracted him to the place. That, and the big patio under the span of an old fig tree. Massive branches formed a canopy covering that space, and in the summer, it stayed cool even on the hottest days. With spring around the corner, buds had begun to swell on the tree. It looked like it would be an early start to the season this year. Already, he could feel a pronounced temperature difference on his balding head between the direct sun and the limited shade of the big tree.

"Hey man, how are you? I hope you don't mind us dropping in unannounced, but I wanted to leave you the plans and specs for the building downtown, and he needed something to do."

Powers stood up and brushed Lucky's fur off his palm before extending it to Geno. He tightened his grip on an expanding folder and a roll of blueprints. Jake came around from the passenger side and through the gate, scratching the dog's head before extending his hand as well.

Geno asked, "How's the back feeling? Any better?"

Jake shrugged in response, a noncommittal gesture that communicated little. As if to deflect attention, he turned towards the house and followed its lines from roof to foundation.

"Boy, you have done an amazing job with this place. I've driven by here many times over the years, starting when I was a teenager. It was always a mess as a before shot. The after is nothing short of incredible."

Geno paused and took in his surroundings. When he bought this small piece of land, the structures had been run down, the yard overgrown, and the fruit trees all but inaccessible with wild blackberry canes woven into thickets covering the hillside. He'd cleared the land, happy to see the trees still producing fruit. He put in a small vegetable garden where the only lawn used to be. The garage had been full of a variety of old stuff, from truck parts to farm tools. Cleaning it out had been a major undertaking. Every bit of work had been worth it.

Together, the men turned toward the patio flanking the house. Jake whistled when he saw the fig tree. "That must have been planted when this place was first built. How old is the house?"

"It was built for one of the children of the original settlers when he got married. The main house is up the road about a mile. This land was only settled about a hundred years ago, and this house was built about seventy-five years ago." He loved the history of the place almost as much as he loved the building itself.

The house had been a labor of love from his first day there. It wasn't big, but it suited him. He rarely had company, so he'd remodeled it to suit himself. It was spare, neat and comfortable. When he pushed open the back door and led the men down the narrow hallway between the two bedrooms to the main living area, he felt quiet pride in saving the structure.

Powers glanced around, nodding approvingly. He'd been there before, but Geno had added the woodwork and paneling since then.

Jake took longer to assess the room, his gaze sweeping the walls and settling on the big windows looking out to the trees and the doors to the wrap-around balcony. He said, "This view must be amazing when the snow's falling. Or when it rains."

Geno nodded, staring outside as well. In some ways, it was like living in a tree house. He'd always wanted one of those when he was a kid, but that was impossible in the confines of the city.

Heading for the fridge, he said, "Are you done for today? Want a beer?"

Powers nodded to his questions, running his hand over the raised wood grain Geno had coaxed out of salvages from another old building. He had enough in the garage to make every piece of furniture for a small house. He considered it his personal stash. Jake moved closer to the balcony doors, staring out at the view from the open expanse.

"You do amazing work. I am constantly amazed by what you can make out of what other people would consider scraps," Powers said.

Geno opened the beers and headed for the stairs with the bottles in his hands.

"Come on, let's go down to the office."

He ducked at the entrance to the staircase. It was low, even lower than a person of standard height would find comfortable. He'd had the choice to raise its ceiling, but he didn't want to spoil the original hovel-like feel of the place. It was one of its many charms.

If the upstairs was a tree house, this lower level was his cave. Reached by these narrow interior stairs or by walking around the patio and down a short set of stone steps, it served as his office set into the hillside. Sets of windowed doors stretched the length of one long wall, opening out to a patio covered by the balcony above. He'd gone for wood and concrete for finishes here, making each piece himself to fit the specific needs of the space's constraints and how he used them. His drafting table faced the garden. His computer sat on a built-in desk. Corkboards lined the interior walls. Other people used a social media program to share their photos. He used old-fashioned paper and tacks.

Geno gestured to the long worktable against the inside wall of the office, handing Powers his bottle when he'd set everything down. Jake accepted his, and the three of them clinked glass and took sips. When they dropped their bottles, Jake eyed him closely.

"You're looking a little tense, Geno. Pained, even."

Powers frowned as he examined him more closely. "You are mister laid-back, so I have a hard time thinking of you as stressed out over anything. Is something wrong? I thought we were doing well on Mac's project, on time and on budget. Or is it something else?"

Geno hesitated, wondering how much he should reveal. These men had become his friends, but he'd never explained his past. It wasn't something guys did. In this case, though, it might come back to haunt him. If Agnes decided to make things difficult, it would come back to bite Powers too. But he didn't know where to start.

Powers unrolled the blueprints, and Geno set his bottle on a side table and leaned in to examine the plans. Setting weights on two corners, he started flipping through the sheets, pausing occasionally to look more closely at a figure or calculation.

"You know that if something's wrong, we'll help you out. That's what the wolf pack does. We stand up for each other. Hell, you've been driving Jake around, and you barely knew him at the start of it. You jump in and help people. Don't turn down returned favors."

Geno nodded absently as he flipped more pages without seeing the text and lines in front of him. All he could think of was how Agnes was still as amazing and energetic as she'd been when they were growing up. No matter what life threw at her, and a significant load of crap had come her way, she lifted her chin and kept moving. She'd need to do that again, soon. Some actions caused hurtful consequences.

It was the summer they were waiting to turn twelve, bored with free days of no activity after only two weeks. Her brothers wanted nothing to do with them, the youngest all too eager to be in high school in the fall and the older ones working part time jobs and chasing girls.

Agnes said, "Hey, let's go downtown and hang out in the Commons. There's probably a concert or something we can listen to."

"You need money to get there, and you need money for the concerts. I don't have money. Do you?"

She'd shaken her head, her expression drooping with disappointment. He hated to see her sad like this. Usually, she was bubbly and happy, but recently, she'd been moody and unpredictable. He'd heard their mothers whispering together about it. They said Agnes was at the age when girls got the curse and boy troubles started, whatever that meant.

"Let's get our bikes and ride someplace. Where, do you think? A park?" He hoped she'd brighten up at his suggestion.

"Yeah, let's get our bikes and ride as far as we can, until we run out of road and we're in the country. Let's do that."

Riding that far wasn't exactly what he had in mind, particularly with the midday sun beating down on them, but she was smiling and laughing once more, extending a hand to him in that easy way she had. Her brothers teased that they acted like boyfriend and girlfriend. That suited Geno. He didn't want to lose Agnes to anyone.

They got on their bikes and pedaled hard. Flying across the city proper, far from the tang of the bay and familiar cooking odors of their neighborhood, things changed. The houses looked different here, nicer, with big yards and plenty of trees surrounding lawns so green, it hurt his eyes to look at them. It even smelled cool and green.

Despite his feeble protests, they rode long and far. She asked, *"Where do you think we are?"* She leaned her arms on the handlebars of her old bike, a blue hand-me-down boy's model from her brothers. She didn't seem particularly worried about their location, her face carrying a dreamy look as she gazed around at the houses.

Geno was worried enough for both of them. He had no idea where they were. More importantly, he wasn't sure how to get back home again. They'd taken so many twists and turns on their ride. He had his emergency money tucked in his pocket, but he knew a cab cost way more than what he carried.

Agnes didn't care that they were lost. She started making up stories about the people who lived in the big houses. A prince and his court. A world-famous musician who was a recluse, with the love of his life *tragically gone. A man who made a lot of money, who attended amazing parties with his beautiful wife, and who adored his lovely young daughter, showering her with presents galore. Even back then, the stories circled around an accomplished man. She had stars in her eyes, and she told him often that she expected to find a dashing man to marry someday.*

"I think we should go back," he'd said.

She didn't want to. She argued with him, saying the sun wouldn't set yet for hours, and they weren't far from home. She kept arguing while she peddled, taking random streets and stopping to admire more houses and make up more stories. They did this for so long that he wondered if they were even still in Massachusetts.

"I'm thirsty," she said. He dug in his pocket and pulled out two damp folded dollars. Without asking, she grabbed the money and dropped her bike in front of a gas station mini mart. Moments later, she came out with two big cups of crushed ice, handing him the cherry one, his favorite.

He thanked her and held out his hand for the change.

"I spent it all."

"All of it?" He didn't have much more.

"Actually, there wasn't quite enough, but the lady let me take the drinks anyway. She was nice. She said it's a hot day and I looked really thirsty." She sucked some of the drink up through the straw, her lips and tongue already turning purple from the mix of flavorings she always added to hers. She said it tasted like a fruit salad.

They stood on the sidewalk, sipping their drinks and watching nice cars go by. Agnes said people were rich and their kids must have swimming pools in their backyards. The sun started sinking in the sky, and Geno wondered how they were going to get home.

Agnes sucked down the last of the drink with a messy bubble and hollowed out cheeks. She took his empty cup and threw both of them in the trashcan by the store's door. Her straight brown hair had begun to come out of its elastic band as they rode, and she refastened it in a sloppy knot before picking up her bike.

"I'm getting hungry, so let's go home. It can't be far." She started pedaling in the opposite direction they'd come from.

"Wait. I think we need to go the other way." He pointed, but she wasn't looking.

"Ha. I don't think so. I think we need to go this way. It's a shortcut." She pedaled away faster, and Geno bent over his front tire and pumped his legs harder to catch up to her.

"Do you know where you're going?" The street didn't look familiar, and he thought they needed to have the sun at their backs, not in their faces.

"I don't need to know exactly where. I have an excellent sense of direction. Come on, I'll race you."

And she took off.

He pedaled fast, but she was quicker. Years of chasing her brothers taught her that. She laughed as she stayed ahead of him, a rich sound that did funny things to his insides. She often made him feel funny and he didn't understand it.

Then she hit something with her front tire, and the bike went one way while she went the other. She yelped when she hit the ground, and by the time he rode up to her, her lower lip trembled and tears filled her eyes.

"I fell." She held up a bleeding elbow for him to see. He dropped his bike next to her and sank down.

"Are you going to be okay?" He thought the scrapes looked bad, and blood was leaking out fast enough from one knee to drip on the ground below.

She seemed to think about this for a while, and then wiped an arm across her face, streaking escaping tears.

"I don't know. My butt hurts too."

"Agnes, you can't say butt. Your mother will kill you."

She sniffed, the tears shut off as quickly as they'd come. *"It's not a swear word, silly, at least, not a real one. Ass is a bad one, but not butt."*

"Agnes," he said again, but she must have missed his exasperation, because she examined her knees, huffed loudly, and stood up. The rise was slow, but she looked determined and only a little pale.

The sun now kissed the tops of the tallest trees. It was late, and they would probably miss supper. His mother was going to kill him, if she didn't spank his bottom raw first.

"Oh damn," she said.

"Agnes Amendola, that is so much a swear word. I'm surprised you haven't been hit by lightning." His mother would soap out his mouth for even thinking the word. And they would be in so much trouble for taking this adventure.

"My bike. Look at the front tire." She had it up on its wheels, but it didn't stand straight. Looking down, he saw the front wheel was now bent too crooked to ride, and the tire was flat.

Strangely enough, Agnes seemed more perplexed than upset. She frowned in that weird way she had, her face pulled more to one side than the other and her eyebrows knit together. One hand held up the *bike. The other was propped on her hip in a picture of attitude.*

Finally, when it seemed the world might have stopped because neither one of them talked for so long, he asked, "How are we going to get home?"

She looked up at him, a bright smile covering her face, her injuries long forgotten. "We'll figure something out. We can call my brother. He'll know what to do."

She didn't even wince when she started walking back in the direction of the gas station. Because it only seemed fair, he picked up his bike and walked it alongside hers as they wobbled down the street.

Shaking him out of his reverie, Jake asked, "What's the problem?" His cop-mode face was serious and he had a hand resting in the place he usually carried his gun.

If he could have said and kept Agnes out of it, he would have. He turned to Powers, waiting a beat while he tried to figure out how to explain it, but only the blunt truth came to mind.

"I have a past, a past that includes Bliss Amendola."

The response wasn't what he expected. Powers said, "Really? Because according to Tess, she hasn't been dating anyone."

He let that hang in the air between them, glancing between the two other men. Both had their eyes fixed on him.

"We didn't date, exactly."

Jake frowned, shaking his head as if he was confused by that clarifier. "If you didn't date, what did you do? It's not like Bliss has a reputation for much more than hard work and great mothering. She has a daughter, you know."

Geno nodded. Oh hell yeah, he knew she had a daughter.

None of the men said anything for a while, until Powers' patience ran out and he said, "Tell us what's going on. You're worrying me. How do you two know each other?"

Geno only paused for a moment. There was no point in hiding things. "We grew up together. We were best friends, in fact. Then we had a fight about something important, and we haven't spoken in years. Until the meeting the other night, that is. Powers, you have to know she's not pleased I'm going to be the project manager. She doesn't want to work with me." She didn't even want to speak with him.

Powers shook his head. "Our contract isn't with her, it's with the building owner. We aren't working on any suite she currently occupies. She hasn't signed a lease on the new space. You are only working directly with her as the potential tenant, and as it impacts her present business. I don't think it will be a problem, Geno."

He didn't know how to explain it. They had been best friends for years, and he'd disappointed her when she probably needed him most. The reasons, the problem, weren't something he felt free to explain.

Jake's hand no longer rested on a pseudo-gun, though he still frowned. "So you have a history with her."

Geno nodded. Powers looked like he was going to burst a vein, waiting for an answer. Geno provided the only one he thought he could.

"It won't be a problem for me. But Bliss's opinion is a completely different story."

Chapter 7

In the week since the meeting about the building's restoration, Bliss had talked with everyone she could think of about the project manager situation. She refused to work with Geno. The man was a traitor, and she had a long memory about that.

"Mommy, can I put color in someone's hair? I promise I'll do exactly like you tell me. I want to try it. Please?"

Leonora sat at the front desk, as Bliss worried she would do. She lasted in the back office only long enough to finish her homework, and then she glided out into the main area and talked up the customers. She'd probably burst into the massage room too, if Marlee hadn't locked her door.

"How about this? Why don't we take some color home, and you can practice on me? You'll get better and better at it that way." God only knows what her hair would look like after this, but Bliss was ready to make that sacrifice.

Any sacrifice was worth it, when it came to her daughter. Her young life had been difficult enough.

Leonora's frown deepened.

The street door opened and shut, though no steps rang out other than the first two bringing someone inside. Bliss was worried Leonora would start a tantrum at any moment. The girl was often moody, and she tested every boundary in front of her.

But instead, she suddenly smiled, looking past Bliss at their visitor. Before Bliss could turn around to welcome the person, Leonora said, "Good afternoon. May I help you?"

The person said nothing, forcing Bliss to turn around to see who it was. Her heart skipped around in an irregular beat when she saw the man standing just inside the door.

Geno. After a week of cajoling, pleading, and trying anger as a means of convincing, she'd given up. Long and short of it, Powers Ashland wasn't going to budge on Geno as the project manager, and the building owner thought that was fine.

He didn't stare at her daughter as she expected him to, though. He looked her in the eye, his expression guarded but friendly. She remembered that look from years ago. He often waited to see what direction things seemed to be taking before he acted. She'd admired that about him, because she often spoke first and suffered for it later.

He nodded in her direction. "Hello Bliss. How are you?"

She'd spent long hours over the past week thinking about him. She remembered his quirky ways of expressing himself, and the happy chuckle he gave when something pleased him. He'd always been the one person she could tell anything to. She didn't realize how important that was until she didn't have him around anymore.

But now, how was she? She was damned mad. She wanted nothing to do with him, even as her heart lurched to see him.

Pulling herself up to her full height, she still had to lean her head back to look him in the eye. He took a step forward, and she forced herself to stand her ground when she wanted desperately to step back.

"Geno, I'm fine. Thanks for asking." She didn't return the question.

"Mommy?" The single word held too much curiosity. Bliss groaned inwardly, not wanting to make a bigger deal out of this and raise a whole lot of nine-year-old questions. As Geno broke their joined gaze and glanced over to where Leonora was hidden behind the height of the front desk, Bliss stepped up and grabbed his arm.

"Mr. Altimari and I are going outside to talk business, so sit still while I'm gone, okay? Don't answer the phone. Or make an appointment for anyone. Or play with the computer." Though she knew her words meant nothing and her little light would do whatever she wanted.

Geno held the door open for her, following her out on to Main Street and closing it behind them. A sudden gust of early spring wind rustled down the street, raising goose bumps on her bare arms and the distance between her boots and her skirt. She should feel the cold, but she was too revved up with Geno so near for it to matter.

"What did you need to see me about?" She rubbed her hands up and down her arms and kept her face turned away from him. He'd always been too good at reading her emotions.

When he didn't reply, she was forced to turn to him. She didn't want to see what he was feeling. Everyone had judged and condemned her, and he'd done nothing to save her.

But she was surprised to find him staring at her with a bland but friendly expression. It was the kind of look two acquaintances shared. Its neutrality gave her time to examine his features, seeing the changes brought by age and life. He looked relaxed, but watchful. Lines radiated from the corners of his eyes. If there were matches at the corners of his mouth, she couldn't see them in the shadow of his thick beard. Her fingers suddenly itched to stroke it, to see if it was as soft as it looked.

She stopped short of shaking her head, but not by much. She wasn't here to drink him up like a slurpee on a summer day. They had business to do. She shifted, and her eyes tracked down his body. Too much was hidden by denim and corduroy, but she remembered the view at the building meeting. His body had aged well with hard work over the years. His fingers, always long and thick, bore calluses and scars. Now, his hand came out of his pocket with a red tape measure, and he extended the metal and retracted it in an absent-minded gesture. When it rolled back in a particularly loud snap, she blinked and realized she'd been staring.

She should feel pissed off with him. He deserved it. And he certainly shouldn't treat her like he barely knew her. They'd shared years, damn it, and would have shared more if he hadn't screwed it up.

Geno said, "I wanted to tell you I'll be starting the work on the suite next door this week. I'll try to keep the noisy activities to late night, after your regular business hours, or on Sunday or Monday. I don't want to disturb you. When I'm around during the day, please feel free to come over and discuss any ideas or concerns you have."

He nodded once and turned away, strolling down the street without waiting for her response or saying goodbye. His rolling gait was longer than it had been the last time he'd walked away from her. His jacket rode high enough to expose his behind, and she couldn't help but notice he had her favorite kind of butt, narrow and almost flat where most men's were rounded. She stared at it until he turned the corner past the bakery and was out of sight.

Bliss sighed, realizing she'd stopped rubbing her arms or feeling the breeze in the short minutes it took for his words and disappearance. If her heart beat a little faster and she felt lit up inside, she wanted to believe it was because she had her mad on. She was so angry with him for back then, and for intruding on her dream now. But she knew she'd have to call herself a liar on both counts.

The spa door opened and one of her customers came out, laughing as she did so.

"I swear, Bliss, that daughter of yours is a trip. I can't believe the stuff that comes out of her mouth. It's a shame, the way she is, really a shame." The woman walked on, shaking her head.

Bliss wondered what Leonora said this time. She had no filter between her thoughts and her mouth. It was a trait Bliss herself had been accused of, years ago. She never understood what a pain it was until she was on the business end of it with her kid.

She grabbed the still-closing door and went inside, taking in the sight of another customer standing at the counter and writing a check while Leonora looked at something on the computer.

"That will be fifty dollars. You can make the check out to Bliss Day Spa. Would you like to make another appointment?"

The woman looked shocked, her pen poised above her checkbook. Bliss hurried forward, putting a hand on her arm and rubbing soothingly before rounding the desk and shooting a hard look at Leonora.

"I'm sorry. My daughter got the total wrong. It's twenty-five. I'm happy to make another appointment for you. In six weeks?" She hip-checked her daughter to the side and poised her own fingers over the keyboard.

The young woman seemed to recover, finishing the check and tearing it out with more speed that necessary. She snapped the cover closed and shoved it into her purse as she shook her head. "I'll call you, Bliss, when I think I'm ready. Tell me, will your daughter be working here long?"

As Bliss assured her this was a temporary thing, the customer waved and walked out faster than she usually did. When the door closed behind her and the coast was clear, Bliss flipped around in her chair and stared hard at her daughter.

"What did you say to her?"

Leonora looked down, her sudden fascination with the vinyl flooring suspicious. As she tried to move away, Bliss put a restraining hand on her arm and asked more firmly, "What did you say?"

The modern art on the wall behind the desk now had the child's full attention. She bit her lower lip, something she did when she was trying to figure out how to lie her way out of a situation. Then she shrugged her shoulders as if it didn't matter, and nodded her head back and forth as if listening to a favorite tune.

"Nothing," she said.

"Leonora Amendola, look me in the eye and tell me what you said." She leaned in to let her daughter know she was serious.

Her kid kept up the head-bopping thing, and Bliss remembered as she herself was growing up, her mother said more than once that someday, she'd have a child who'd misbehave exactly as she was doing, and that would be her penance. Of course, her mother believed anything bad that happened to anyone was penance for their bad behavior.

Bliss shook her daughter's arm, not hard or a lot, but to get her attention. Leonora slipped a sly gaze back to her, and she kind of smiled, except it wasn't a funny or kind look. Bliss never wanted to believe she was evil or spiteful, but she was afraid she was doing something very wrong for her child to be turning out this way. Sins of the parents, ways of the children, her mother used to say. At times like this, she almost believed it.

Leonora finally stopped bobbing her head and said, "If you must know, I told her she should put some colored streaks in her hair, like purple or green or pink, and wear more make-up. That's the only way she was going to get a man, I told her. She's so plain, and she's so tall. Men aren't crazy about tall women, I said. She didn't say anything back to me. I know it's because she knows I'm right."

Bliss wanted to weep, right after she called the woman to apologize.

"None of that was nice, and you know it, young lady. And why did you tell her the haircut cost so much? You know it doesn't."

Leonora smirked at her and huffed in apparent disgust. "For the advice, Mommy. People pay good money for that kind of lifestyle advice. I know they do. I see it on TV all the time."

Bliss shook her head, wondering where she'd gone wrong.

"You need to go back to the office, young lady. You can't stay up here."

"But Mommy, I hate the office. Nothing's happening back there." The whine in her voice was shrill enough to send any cats in the neighborhood scurrying for higher ground.

"You're happening back there. You have homework."

"I finished it."

God, the child was a whiz. Her teacher's instructions for today's assignments stated they should take three hours. They took Leonora only one.

"You have your tablet, and your music, and you can write me something, a story."

Leonora frowned at that, tilting her head to the side. The expression pulled her face to one side in a charming uneven way. It was familiar, uncomfortably so.

"Like what kind of story?"

Bliss sighed. Once upon a time, she believed in princes and knights and happy daddies who cherished little girls, and rich men who took care of big ones. She never shared those dreams with her daughter.

"Write me a story about a famous lady who runs a big company all by herself, and what a wonderful world she lives in."

Her daughter sputtered out a derisive noise, a cross between a cough and a hiccup. "That's a fairy tale."

"And why would that be?"

Leonora lifted her chin and sent a worldly but sympathetic glance Bliss's way. "Because everyone knows that if you run a big company, you're a man, and you have to take care of your family." She paused long enough to move from behind the desk to the hallway, taking her time as she approached the door to the back area. "But I guess I could work on that. What kind of business should she run?"

Bliss felt a sudden surge, the twin sensations of gratefulness and sadness she should be used to by now as she watched her daughter disappear. "I don't know, sweetheart. It can be any kind of company you want. Surprise me."

"Okay Mommy," the distant voice replied, as a door shut in the back.

She avoided banging her head against the wall, but barely. She'd always wanted a big family of her own, kids she would shower with affection and never ever judge the way she'd been judged. She wanted her children to feel special, not because of what they looked like or where they were in the birth order, but because of the wonderful human beings they'd become. And she wanted a caring husband to stand beside her, sharing the remarkable life they'd created together.

None of her dreams had been fulfilled. She only hoped Leonora would be able to live out hers. And even as she thought it, she knew that there was a very good chance this would never be true.

Chapter 8

"I appreciate what you're doing, man, I really do."

Geno didn't reply, holding the cell phone to his ear as he stared at the wall that would one day be a doorway. Tearing down the physical wall was easy compared to the emotional one he struggled with. He pulled the tape measure out to a foot-long length and let it snap back into its roll, the movement doing little to calm his agitation.

"Are you still there?"

Snapping the tape again, he realized it wasn't working. It always worked, but it wasn't now. He shifted the phone to cradle between his shoulder and ear, reaching for the hammer and cat's claw to remove more molding. "Yes, Luke, I'm here. You can rest easy. I have an eye on Agnes and Leonora."

A humming sound came through the receiver, followed by a low curse. "I hate this," the disembodied voice burst out. "I fucking hate this."

"Geez, man, language." Geno should be used to the swearing by now, but even after all these years, he wasn't. Luke Amendola started cursing when they were kids. He claimed he was entitled because he was two years older. When Geno got to be the same age and tried it, his mother washed his mouth out with soap, and the taste stuck with him still. He saved the curse words for times that counted, when nothing else fit.

"Sorry, forgot what a good altar boy you are."

Geno pushed the claw behind a piece of wood that already looked like it might disintegrate under any gentle pressure. He barely tapped the hammer against the claw, and the piece loosened enough to hang on a single nail. Changing position, he tapped again, and the piece came off in his hand. The rot on the back of it was a mix of angry colors, as dark as a tough bruise.

"I'm not an altar boy any longer," he said, putting the wood in a stack he intended to take home to work on. If he could carve duplicates, he would, but they would take a time, and the budget didn't allow intricate work.

"Graduated to distributing Holy Communion now? Planning to enter the priesthood?" Luke chuckled on the other end.

"Not exactly. I'm more of a Buddhist now."

This surprised a sharp bark of laughter out of his old friend. "A Buddhist, really? Don't you have to go meditate on a mountain top or something to be a monk?"

It was Geno's turn to laugh. "No, I didn't become a monk, though at times, my life feels like that. I've just changed my thinking, my acceptance of the world and my sense of karma. I'd be happy to tell you more about it, if you're interested in ditching the whole Catholic thing."

Luke's guffaws of humor rang through the connection so clearly, Geno felt them in his chest. When the hilarity died down, both men said nothing for a space of time. They didn't need to. Geno missed Luke, but a few years back, he thought he was better off not being close with any member of Agnes's family. It hurt too much.

"Seriously though, man, this is about Mary Margaret, isn't it?"

Geno let the name and accompanying self-reproach wash over him. He'd never made her happy, not the way she should have been anyway. He regretted not being man enough back then to stand up to the pressure, because he'd known it wouldn't work before they even started. He'd given it his best shot despite his misgivings, but there were some things that couldn't be forced.

"This isn't about my ex-wife. She deserved better than me. Always did."

Luke snorted, adding a few more curse words that had Geno wincing. "No, that's not true and you know it. You're a great guy, a terrific friend, and much nicer than the idiot she married next. He's so lazy, I'm surprised anything gets done in his warehouse. But she seems content, since she gets to bitch to anyone who will listen in the old neighborhood about how hard her life is. Some women like that kind of stuff."

But not Agnes. She'd never been one to accept the way things had to be. No, she'd moved on, moved up, and moved out. By the time Geno figured out what he wanted, what he needed to make things right between them, she was gone.

"So, it's been a long dry spell for you?"

Moving to the plans on the board set over sawhorses, Geno rummaged through the pages until he found the elevation he wanted. Confirming which sections of wall would eventually be removed, he grabbed the hammer again and went to work on fake wood paneling that should never have been installed in this old beauty in the first place.

"What do you mean, dry spell?"

"You know, getting some. Bonking anyone. Sex."

That was a theme Luke repeated too often in their calls. In the early years after his divorce, Geno had been self-conscious and felt clumsy, unwilling to put himself out there for more ridicule. As time passed, though, he'd dated a bit. He'd learned more. His technique improved, or at least, he hadn't had any complaints from women sharing his bed.

Recently, though, he found he wasn't interested in any of them. The one woman for him wanted nothing to do with him, and in many ways, he couldn't blame her. Karma.

"I'm fine in the sex department, thanks. Listen, did you have a purpose in calling, or did you just want to annoy me?"

Silence greeted him on the other end of the phone. It lasted long enough that he finally asked, "Luke, are you there?"

"Yeah, I'm here. You know why I'm calling. Your promise. Things are heating up."

Geno stopped mid-swing with the hammer, finally letting it fall down to his side. He wasn't sure he could trust himself to speak. He still felt anger with the way that family treated one of their own. Except for Luke, none of them seemed to care what happened to her. And now, Luke expected Geno to fix things.

Of course, he hadn't been close to her for years either. Agnes had deserved better from him. But at least he was trying to make it up to her.

Was that what he was trying to do? Make up for past mistakes? Or was there something more? He hadn't examined his motives for a while, intent on reconnecting and paving the way for more civil communications. With time, he'd hoped she would forgive him and allow them to become friends again. He swung the hammer harder, taking his guilt and frustration out on the wall.

"I remember the promise, Luke. These things take time. I'll let you know when I have something new to report." Though he doubted it would turn out well.

Geno heard Luke's unsteady breathing on the other end of the phone, as if he felt the agitation.

Finally, he said, "Watch out for my sister, will you? And my niece? I worry about them."

As they disconnected, Geno let the weight of intervening years and remorse wash over him. Luke had every right to worry. Agnes had become even more vivacious with time. Her daughter would probably become the spitting image in both looks and personality.

The paneling in front of him was old, ugly and splitting apart in layers. Those layers were significant, similar to how his relationship with Agnes had peeled apart at the end. She offered him the glue to put it back together, but he turned her down. In a sudden fit of fury, he picked up the heavier sledgehammer and slammed it hard into the ugly wood.

It splintered, coming off in big shards of laminate and old glue. It felt good to give in to his frustration and disappointment. His life would have been so different today if he had said yes when she'd asked. He banged into the wall again, and more wood flew apart. Soon, he couldn't stop the cadence of whacking hard, his anger building rather than letting go.

One swing for each time he'd disappointed her. That took down a good four feet.

More swings for each time he'd turned her down. Another panel fell.

And a final hard whack for the stupidity that kept him away for so long. Being prideful was not a commendable trait. He didn't want her to turn him down this time. Turnabout would only be fair, though.

The front door burst open with enough force to give it a bounce against its hinges. When it settled back into a more leisurely swing, a hand reached out in a fist to stop it. And Bliss blew into the room like a summer tornado.

"What the hell do you think you're doing?"

Geno looked at her, his anger and frustration vanishing as he drank in her perfectly styled hair, clothes that looked as coordinated as a fashion ad, and dark eyes sparking at him like metal on stone. He let his arms drop to his sides, nearly letting go of the sledge completely as he contemplated her stance, hands on hips, feet wide, and fury in every line of her body.

He knew that look. He'd seen it before many times, though only one time when that full force had been aimed at him. Back then, there had been a touch of pained disappointment in her eyes. But not today.

"I said, what the hell do you think you're doing?" Each of her words held a crisp note of allegation.

"I'm taking down the wall."

She paced up to him, the heels of her boots echoing on the bare floor. As hard as she stomped them, he wondered if the old wood would stand up to the strain.

"You are only supposed to be doing this kind of work," her hands waved wildly at the disintegrated wall, "when the spa is closed. Remember?"

She wagged a finger under his nose, and he fought the temptation to grab it and use it to pull her to him. This close, he could smell the sexy scent she wore, some mix of spices as evocative as she was. It was different from what she used at twenty. But then, so much of who they were now was different.

Instead of grabbing her in his arms like he wanted, he took a step back and carefully set the sledgehammer on the floor. When he straightened, it was to find Bliss still staring at him, but the anger in her eyes had been replaced by confusion. She glanced away quickly as if sorry she was caught.

He said, "I'm sorry. It's Sunday, so I thought you were closed. At least, the list of businesses and their hours noted you were closed today, as is the butcher on the other side of this space. Has that changed?"

He watched her shoulders sag a little, exposing the line of her neck where she'd pulled her brown hair up into some sort of clip on the back of her head. She'd always had the prettiest hair, the color of a clear walnut stain, deep and rich with natural highlights like fine grain. At least she hadn't changed that.

Facing the torn apart wall, she said, "No, officially it hasn't. I'm sorry. A long time client called and begged for an appointment. She's traveling to see her sick mother back east and needed to get in today. As long as I was coming in, I decided to start early and get some paperwork done. But it's not going well."

He made a noise he hoped she took for sympathy. "I'll stop pounding. Again, I'm sorry, I didn't know you were there, and if I did – "

Well, he wasn't sure exactly what he'd do if he'd known she was alone next door, on a day when no one expected her to be there. But he was alone with her now, and he could begin the process of making amends. He had a lot of things to make up for.

"Agnes, I wanted to talk with you."

She turned her head, looking over her shoulder at him even as she kept her body turned away. The position would be considered deliberately provocative on some women, but he didn't think that was the case here. She didn't want to face him, any more than she wanted to talk to him.

She opened her mouth, and despite his reservations, he leaned toward her, waiting to see if she'd deny him this. As she inhaled, the door burst open again, and a small voice said, "Mommy, your lady's here. And she's in a hurry."

He watched Agnes shut her mouth with a snap and spin away, turning now toward the door and the small figure framed in it by the light from the street.

"Mommy? Are you coming? I can help you, right?"

He followed Agnes's eyes to the girl, and his heart skipped a beat. The last time he'd seen her, she was an infant, a bundle of yellow blanket and a bright pink hat, sleeping soundly or cooing happily in her stroller despite the fury of the adults standing over her. When he ventured into the spa, she was hidden behind the desk. Today, he couldn't see much detail due to the sun reflected behind her, but her hair was long and her figure skinny.

"Mommy?" The voice held more concern than demand this time.

"Right there, sweetheart. I need to say goodbye to Mr. Altimari, and I'll be right there. Okay? Tell her I'll be just a minute."

The figure disappeared, leaving the door hanging wide. Cars and trucks passing on the street broke the silence of the room, and occasional pedestrians stopped talking as they glanced in the open doorway. The intruding noise made it feel more intimate, much more than Geno thought he was ready to handle.

Agnes's voice was quieter when she said, "It's my turn to say I'm sorry. My daughter has been raised with manners, believe it or not. But she tends to overstep boundaries every chance she gets. I guess it's compensation."

"You had to bring her to work with you?"

She nodded in response to his question. When she walked to the door slowly, he wondered if she'd draw more lines he wasn't supposed to cross. But she shut the door quietly, and turned back to lean on it and face him.

"I don't usually bring her with me, but no one was available to babysit today. On top of that, my weekday sitter quit two weeks ago, and I haven't been able to find someone new. At least, not someone I can afford. So Leonora has been coming to work with me for two weeks, and it's been the longest two weeks of my career. Do you know what it's like to have a nine-year-old constantly asking questions, wanting to do things she can't?"

The closing of the door brought shadows to the corners of the room, but Geno could see her face clearly. She closed her eyes, and anguish was obvious in her expression. He wanted to go to her, take her in his arms, and tell her it would all be better. Years ago, he did that. He'd had the right. But not anymore. That kicked his possible ulcer into high gear.

Agnes opened her eyes, composing her features into a professional calm that he would bet his new table saw she wasn't feeling. Pushing off the door, she turned and reached for the handle, pausing with her hand there but her face turned away.

"Do you ever wonder how things could have been different, Geno?"

Her question hung in the air as she opened the door and disappeared outside, closing it with such a soft click that it took him a moment to register the sound. What would she have said if he told her that yes, he wondered how things could have been, all the time, if he hadn't been such an ass.

Her client chattered, moaned about her life, and recited her frantic to-do list. Bliss nodded and made noncommittal noises as she applied color to the woman's hair, as she painted her nails while the color processed, as she washed out the color solution, and now, as she cut the newly bronzed hair. Red didn't suit this woman's flesh tone, but Bliss couldn't talk her out of it.

Besides, she had other things on her mind.

Blowing the hair dry and into a casual shape, she was saved from commenting on the client's negative descriptions of her family and how she alone worried about their poor, dear mother. Pulling off the drape and giving the hair a final fluff, Bliss stepped back, relieved she'd soon be in silence.

Leonora hadn't taken well to being told to stay in the back and play her video games. Today, though, Bliss wanted to move quickly, not only because her client wanted it, but because she wanted to get out of there and hide as far away from Geno as she could. Her apartment would work fine for that, but she'd have to tame the wild Leonora first.

What did Geno think of her, and of her daughter? She hadn't seen any emotion on his face, but then, he'd always been good about hiding those.

"I swear, Bliss, you are a miracle worker. I feel much better now, like I can deal with whatever life throws at me. And talking with you always helps. You have the best way with people."

There hadn't been any talking, only listening. She'd gotten very good at that skill, one she hadn't necessarily been great at when she was growing up. The fact that Geno was the one she most often gabbed at incessantly back then was an irony not lost on her now.

"Okay, Leonora, you can come out now." She waited to hear the sound of the office door opening, but only silence met her ears. She swept the floor and put away her tools, washed out the sink, and generally straightened up. Her daughter was going to punish her for being, as she always put it, locked away in the dungeon.

What did Geno think? It was hard to forgive him for turning her down all those years ago. The situation was awful on so many levels, and added to the reality, her mother had spared no opportunity to remind everyone that the reason this all turned out the way it did was because her daughter didn't listen to her good advice. Back then, Agnes had taken it, until she couldn't anymore. Then she left. When she landed in Flynn's Crossing as Bliss, she didn't intend to look back.

But having Geno next door forced her to do just that. Okay, she'd admit that she thought of him from time to time, usually when she was feeling lonely and carrying more despair than hope. He'd always been so good at seeing the bright side of the most dismal circumstances.

From what she heard, he had developed quite a following for his professional skills and expertise. To hear Roxy tell it, he had singlehandedly transformed the old ranch she and her boyfriend bought into a masterpiece. Roxy had worked with him before, too, on her restaurant. She said he performed miracles.

She's always thought that about him. No matter what kind of jam they got in, he found a way to get them out of it. And yes, she'd admit it. She was often the reason they were in that jam. That didn't make Geno's heroic actions any less majestic. Until the one time she'd begged him to help her, and he turned her down.

She should feel rage at that. For years, she did. She hadn't been able to forgive him, and so she never answered the phone when he called and threw away the letters he sent unopened. When he emailed her, she blocked him.

Time passed, though, and she found herself wishing she could talk to her old friend again. They'd been best buddies. So much had changed, yet so much had stayed the same. He was still silent unless he had something meaningful to say. Still watchful and assessing until he figured out how to act. Still compassionate and easy with others. She saw that in his eyes when he looked at Leonora.

But other things had changed about him. He held himself with more confidence. His spare frame was muscular and powerful. She watched the way he handled that sledgehammer. It couldn't have been light, but he held it with ease as if it weighed no more than her styling comb. The hair on his head might be disappearing, but he'd grown a thick gorgeous beard instead. And his green eyes, so expressive and intent on hers the whole time she was yelling at him, sparkled with knowledge and wisdom.

She could eat him up.

Chapter 9

When Powers appeared at the end of the day on Monday, Geno was wiping his hands on a wet rag and taking inventory of his progress. He'd accomplished a lot, helped along by spurts of anger over the way he'd mishandled the conversation with Agnes. Actually, he wasn't sure who he'd been talking with, Agnes or her new alter ego, Bliss. He'd have to ask her about the nickname sometime. He turned down the opera blasting from mini-speakers as Madame Butterfly bemoaned her fate.

"Wow, you've done a lot in two days." Powers walked through the empty room, bare to the bricks or studs.

"Yes, but it was perfect timing. The butcher is closed on Sunday and Monday. So is the spa, though I had a run-in with Bliss on Sunday. Thought you should know about it." In case she complained to Powers.

Powers frowned. "Isn't she supposed to be closed on Sunday and Monday too?"

Geno nodded, tossing the rag into his tool bag to take home. "Yeah, but she had a special client on Sunday, so she was here. I interrupted her time for paperwork, and she told me so in no uncertain terms."

Powers shook his head. "I don't get it. She's the force behind getting this space done. If the building owner could have leased it the way it was, he probably would have. But Bliss wants this space for the spa expansion, and she was very excited about it. I hope that hasn't changed."

Geno didn't think it had, but then, he could only base his knowledge on the Agnes he knew years ago.

The woman known as Bliss was a force he didn't completely understand. She had a daughter she took good care of by herself. She ran a business that hummed with activity five long days a week and then some. Did she have a relationship too? He didn't think so, because he'd bet he'd have heard about it already. There was nothing like a few well-placed questions in a small town to provide all sorts of interesting gossip.

Not that he liked to gossip. It tended to come back around and bite you. Karma.

"Geno? Did you hear me?"

He shook his head, wondering why any thought of the woman produced a mental fog he found hard to navigate.

"How did you leave it with Bliss? Do I need to talk with her, calm her down?"

Geno shook his head again. "I don't think so. We worked it out."

At least, it seemed to him they had. She'd popped her head in later in the day to tell him she was leaving and he could make as much noise as he wanted. She hadn't come by yesterday, so if she'd visited her shop, she hadn't been bothered by his continuing hammering and sawing. Tomorrow, he scheduled quiet activities of measurements and verifications of the plans. It was mind-emptying, Zen kind of work, taking him outside of himself. At least, it usually did. If he thought about Agnes being on the other side of this now-thinner wall, he'd have a hard time concentrating on anything.

"I said, did you discuss the plans with her? Does she have any changes? Man, Geno, you are not paying attention."

No, he wasn't. He was thinking about the gentle sway of her hips as she left on Sunday, the sad note voiced in her question. He wanted to undo that bun of her hair and let it fall in a thick curtain around her shoulders so he could bury his face in it.

He focused with a deep breath, letting it out on a hiss loud enough to draw attention from Powers. "You okay, man? Is working with her freaking you out? If it is, tell me now."

"No, it's fine. I'm fine. I've got it. I'll talk to Bliss tomorrow and go over the plans to see if she has any additional changes." Even if it put him in her line of fire.

>>>>>

"Really, Mother." Leonora drew out the second word into more than two long syllables. Bliss didn't need to think long to figure out where that trait came from.

"Really, Leonora." She mimicked her daughter's frustrated tone.

"Come on, please? School's out tomorrow because the teachers have to go learn something, and Dr. Kinkead said we could sleep over. Charlotte said we're going to eat Chinese food, because that's her favorite. Her dad's really nice, and he's single, you should date him."

"You're right, he's very nice." And undoubtedly safe, based on her in-depth check into his background. While he hadn't been in Flynn's Crossing for long, his colleagues at the hospital thought highly of him. Her daughter was special, and because of that, every time she went for a play date or a sleep over, Bliss was extra careful.

"He's a doctor." A sly wink accompanied Leonora's mischievous tone. Even her daughter was trying to fix her up.

"I know that, sweetheart."

"You should date him. For bleep's sake, Mother. He's a doctor."

"What did you just say?"

Leonora didn't look in the least bit downcast. "I said, he's a doctor."

"Right before that, young lady. You know what I'm talking about."

"It's not a swear word, and you say it too. It's just a bleep. Besides, you can swear if you have to. You have a difficult life."

Bliss blinked, unsure where this new line of conversation originated. She made sure she never told her daughter she was a burden or a problem. Just the opposite, in fact.

"Why would you say I have a difficult life?" Bliss busied herself with the salad for dinner, even if she felt less like eating it with each passing minute.

"I didn't say it. One of the old ladies who comes in every week to have her hair washed and curled said it. She said you have a difficult life, what with being single and alone and having to take care of me. She says it every time she sees me, when she comes over to pat my head if I'm behind the counter. And she gets all teary and says how she prays for us every night."

Too shocked to say anything in response, Bliss sliced radishes on top of the greens. She was sure the woman wasn't trying to be mean or thoughtless, but the result was the same. People believed Leonora was her burden, not her gift. She gave thanks every day for her little light, even if others didn't necessarily see her as that.

"Mommy, that's a lot of radishes."

Bliss glanced down at the bowl, realizing she'd sliced almost the whole bunch. Their mound outsized the lettuce leaves and trickled down the edges of the bowl.

Others didn't see their life as normal, but this was the only adult version she knew. Bliss did everything she could to provide Leonora with what she wanted. Maybe she did overcompensate at times.

She pushed the three remaining radishes back into plastic and grabbed the bag of greens, storing all of it in the fridge. She kept her head inside the box to gather her thoughts. If normal meant she needed to let her daughter spread her wings a bit, then so be it. She'd cope. At least, she hoped she coped as well as Leonora seemed to.

When she straightened and took out dressing and the chicken she planned to cook, she said, "I'll call Dr. Kinkead after dinner to make sure he's on board with this. I'm not promising anything, yet."

But her girl screamed anyway. Sleeping over was a big deal, the biggest of deals. If there was anything Leonora loved, it was a chance to do something different. And Bliss knew where she got that too.

Chapter 10

When Geno opened the door to the spa, his nose twitched with smells he wasn't used to. Sharp scents and bitter aromas made him want to sneeze. When the tickle got too bad, he did, and three women in various stages of having things done blessed him in response.

If only it was that easy.

To the unfamiliar woman behind the counter, he said, "Is Bliss here?"

"She's in the back with a client. I'm Marlee. Do you have an appointment?"

"No, I'm the contractor working next door, and I need to discuss the plans with Bliss, to make sure she doesn't have any further changes. I'm Geno, by the way."

He extended his hand across the counter and was surprised when the woman squeezed it tightly. He must have grimaced, because she withdrew hers quickly and said, "I'm sorry. Occupational hazard. I'm a massage therapist."

He smiled at her, assuring her that she didn't do any permanent damage. "Can you ask Bliss to come next door if she has time today? Or she can call me and we can set something else up. She has my number."

He left without saying anything more, and let himself in next door, turning on the bare ceiling lights. Open to the studs as it was, the space looked bigger and colder. Someday, it would be a chic addition to Bliss's spa, but now, it echoed like an empty warehouse.

Dropping his tool bag on the floor by the table, he turned on the desk lamp clamped to the edge and flipped through the plans until he came to the page with finished elevations of each wall. The common wall to be opened was almost completely blank except for the doorway. He'd been looking at its plain square boxy structure and thought it didn't do the space justice. There were curved arches elsewhere in the building, and a curved opening here would dress up the rooms.

Nice molding, wainscoting, and maybe some built in cabinets for products Bliss sold to customers would make for a more finished effect. And if she wanted, he could build her other furniture to match, so that everything had a unified look. He could even use some of that special wood he'd kept to make a custom countertop for her front desk. A light paint color would offset the darker wood grain and floors nicely, maybe with a texturing to make it look like old plaster. He wasn't an expert, but he thought his texturing turned out pretty darned good.

What was he thinking? All he was responsible for was buttoning up the walls and woodwork. Whatever Bliss chose to do to finish the space was up to her. Yup, just make the woodwork and complete the drywall. The rest was her responsibility.

He began the painstaking process of measurements for drywall and moldings, double-checking everything. The materials order took no time, nor did the scheduling of trades and inspections. Electricians would start work by the end of the week, and after that, things would move along quickly.

And soon, he'd be done. He'd been so worried, working mere feet away from her, and yet, Agnes, or Bliss, had done nothing to make his work difficult. Well, nothing other than occupy his thoughts.

When a light knock sounded on the door, he looked at his watch, surprised to find the afternoon had passed so quickly. Usually this part of the process didn't take him long. But if he was honest with himself, he knew it was because he'd spent a significant amount of time musing about the woman next door.

When that same woman poked her head around the doorway and gave him a tentative smile, he couldn't help grinning back. Today, her long hair was pulled back into a clip, with pieces hanging in front of her ears. It made her look years younger than the severe bun. It took him back.

"My mom wants me to get my hair cut short."

He stopped working on the wooden train he was building for the Christmas bazaar. He learned how to do this in a class his mother sent him to on weekends. She said it would give him a hobby. He thought it was so he wasn't underfoot. Mom was trying to date guys again.

"Why does she want you to get your hair cut short?"

Agnes shrugged, pushing that same hair out of the way behind her ears. "She says I get it too tangled and she has to spend too much time brushing it out every night. She said that if I want to have it long, I must take care of it myself. She said I could go to beauty school, to learn how to do hair, so I'd have a job when I get out of high school."

"That sounds like a good idea. I mean, the having-a-job part." He wasn't sure why she looked so sad.

"I know. It's just that I don't like things like that. You know, fussing with my hair and doing make-up and things." She'd pushed at her hair with a harder shove this time, and returned to painting the pieces he'd completed. When red paint somehow landed on her nose, he laughed, and she laughed along with him, a wonderful sound that made his chest fill up and his

heart beat harder. They were thirteen, but they were still best buds, and he knew that would never change.

But things did change. He'd had first-hand experience with how much they could change. Agnes went to beauty classes, and he went to woodworking or computers. Before long, she dressed differently and didn't want to do anything that would mess up her fancy hairdos. Soon, she was trying to catch the eye of first one guy, then another, until she set her sights on the high school quarterback.

Then one day, she finally caught the quarterback's eye, and the rest, as they say, was history. Until she needed him, of course. Then she couldn't run to him fast enough, in tears. And he couldn't do a thing to help her.

"Wow, this place is big, isn't it? It didn't look that large when it was boarded up, but now that you've demolished the old walls and ceiling, it is amazing. Is that original brick?"

Bliss walked to the far wall and rested a hand on the rusty colored stone, and Geno tried to remember why she was here and what he was supposed to be doing. She still wore her clothes with style, and her hair held that same glossy texture it had way back when. If her curves were more generous, they only enhanced her look. She was a woman meant to have curves, the kinds of softness a man could get lost in.

"Geno, what's wrong?"

"Oh, sorry. I was lost in thought for a moment. Yes, that's the original brick. That's one of the reasons I wanted you to come over today. The plans call for covering it up, but it's beautiful. What do you think about leaving it unfinished and building it into the design instead?"

She cocked her head and got that lopsided look she favored when she was thinking hard about something. He thought she looked charming. Back in their childhood, he used to tease her about how funny her face looked, like one side belonged to someone else. But he'd come to love that look. He'd come to love a lot of things about her.

Bliss frowned, spinning in a slow circle as if assessing the overall effect. Then she shook her head.

"I don't know. I'm having a hard time visualizing it. I'd have to make different arrangements for the hair stations. That's what I planned for that wall. I'd need to be able to hang the mirrors. And I planned to hang shelves there too, so I'd need to buy furniture to match everything else."

"I could make you pieces to match," he said, trying to bite his tongue as words poured out. Why had he opened his mouth? Even his subconscious tried to keep him close to Bliss for any amount of additional time it could.

"That would be expensive. Probably more than I can pay, I'm afraid."

He took a step forward, putting a hand out to deny her words. "No, it really wouldn't. And it would give the place a stylish look. I've been thinking about it, and I have some ideas."

What was he doing? If he could have kicked himself without falling over, he would have. But his fingers pulled a pad from his tool bag and grabbed the pencil from behind his ear, sketching fast. When Bliss came to stand next to him and watch, he thought he'd have a heart attack from the jungle beat of blood through his system. Meditative breathing wasn't helping, and he tried to concentrate on the pages in front of him to avoid falling on her like an over-eager kid in high school.

"You're really good at this," she said, and she pointed a perfectly polished nail at something on the page. He wasn't looking at the drawings, but at the crown of her head. In the harsh overhead lights, it looked like she had a halo. Not that she did, he knew. Agnes had never been one for reverence.

She glanced up at him, and he couldn't meet her eyes. This close, he knew he'd give himself away. But when his gaze fastened on her lips instead, he forgot about that too. She still had the lush lips of her childhood, the bottom lip plumper than the top. Now, she dressed them in a lipstick that matched her nails. Back then, unadorned, she'd looked just as ravishing.

He gulped, trying to remember why he'd stayed away from her for so long. Oh yeah. She'd said she would never forgive him. And over the years, in all of the instances when he'd tried to get back in touch with her, she'd lived up to that.

He heard a gasp, realizing he had stared at her lips for so long that minutes had probably passed since he'd moved the pencil on paper. It was Agnes's gasp, though. He glanced up to her eyes quickly, wondering what was wrong, to find her staring at his mouth too.

He pushed up and away from her, watching her shake her head as if trying to clear it. She got a funny look on her face before she shook her head from side to side more vehemently. Picking up a tape measure he'd left on the table, she rapped it on the table in a quick tattoo. When she started playing with it, pulling out the tape and pushing it back in slowly, he thought he'd lose it completely. Did she even know how sexy she looked right now?

"I don't know if I can see what you're seeing in this place, Geno. I think you'll have to give me drawings for ideas. Do you have time?"

Hell yeah, he had time. He'd drop everything for days if it meant he could stay here, watching her absently stroking the tape like it was a lover. It might make the top of his head blow off, while his jeans grew uncomfortably tight, but he'd do whatever she asked.

But she had obligations. He dimly remembered that it wasn't just the two of them hanging out anymore.

"Do you need to get Leonora from next door? Or from school or something?"

She shook her head, her face sad but resigned. "No, she's having a sleep over with friends. I'm proud of her. A new family moved in mid-year, and she befriended the girl. They've become quite close, and now they're both part of a bigger clique. Remember how we were in high school? Well, they're like that even younger now. She has a posse, or at least, that's what she calls it."

"You let her sleep over?"

He watched the defensive curtain fall in her expression. She straightened her shoulders as she turned away, and he wished he could see her face.

"Yes, I want her to have as normal a life as possible. Her friends are nice. The parent of the girl, an emergency room doctor, assures me it's no big deal. The girls take care of each other. And he's a doctor after all."

He suddenly wanted to slug the doctor, because she seemed to regard him with more than a passing familiarity. Then she laughed, and the sound echoed off the bare walls and ceiling, settling into his chest and making breathing difficult.

"Get this. My daughter is trying to fix me up. The doctor is single. As if I have time to date anyone, and I doubt he does either. But my little light wants a daddy. She's been asking about her father a lot recently, and I just don't know what to say."

His heart did a flip, then settled into an uneven beat. He didn't know what to say either.

She walked the length of the space, her heels echoing with her slow gait. From the back of the room, she said, "You'd think I would have come up with something, after all these years. But every time I thought about it, I pushed it away. Now, she wants to know. What do I tell her, Geno?"

Once upon a time, he didn't know what he wanted to tell her, but now, he did. But she'd never hear him out. This was the first time she hadn't turned away from him, and he wasn't going to waste the opportunity.

"Do you want to get dinner?"

She stopped, looking back at him over her shoulder with sudden confusion. Then she chuckled.

"No, I don't think that's what I can tell her, but thanks for the laugh."

"No, seriously, dinner, you and me. We can work on the plans." If she knew he was grabbing any excuse to stay close to her for a while longer, she didn't show it.

"Okay, let's get dinner. Can we get it delivered?"

"Pizza?" He remembered how much she loved pizza. That couldn't have changed, could it? He could still remember the way she liked it.

"Pizza is for treat nights."

"What?"

"It's a saying Leonora and I have. But I'd say this qualifies. You're going to show me how awesome my new spa is going to look."

He tried to look down at his cell phone to call for delivery, but he couldn't take his eyes off her smile. If anything, she was even more beautiful. And this time, he wasn't going to deny her anything.

>>>>>

"I can't believe you remembered my favorite toppings after all this time." She mopped at her fingers, messy with stickiness from the pineapple and ham.

"It helps that they've always been my favorite too."

She watched him work the paper napkin back and forth between long fingers. His hands had been bigger than hers from day one, even when she briefly grew taller than him in fourth grade. Then he suddenly shot up, and before long, she'd had to lean back to stare up into his face a full foot above her.

He'd aged well. Yes, he lacked hair, but balding on Geno looked classy. His beard was neat and trimmed, but she'd shape it differently. All the better to show off his sensuous mouth.

Bleep. Shit. She didn't need to be thinking about Geno in those terms. They'd been friends, best friends, but there was nothing sexual about it. Not that she hadn't wanted to think about something sexier more than a few times. Okay, maybe more than a few times.

He said something about molding and pointed to the pages in front of them, but she missed his words. She was stuck watching his lips move.

"Have you ever kissed a girl?" She'd asked the question, betting she already knew the answer.

"Kissed a girl? No. Hell no." He stuttered over the statement. They'd been experimenting with swear words, though she was more eager to embrace them. Still, he was trying.

"Have you ever kissed a boy?" He didn't look at her as he asked the question, continuing their slow amble home along the alley after school.

"What if I have?" Not that she had.

His face got red and he scuffed his feet in the gravel and dirt. His feet were already big. His mother said he'd probably be tall, very tall, like his father. Geno had told her this with pride in his voice. She felt sorry for him, not having a dad. Not that hers was all that great.

"Maybe we should practice, you know, so that when we do kiss someone, we know what we're doing."

He stopped and frowned at her. *"Who would we practice with?"*

"Each other. Come on, it's no big deal. I know I'll be great at it. Don't you want to know what it feels like?"

She watched his face grow ruddier, a contrast to the red streaks in his blond hair. He sighed with a resigned shake of his shoulders and glanced up and down the alley.

"Where should we do it?"

Her heart sped up until it felt like a hammer in her chest. Yeah, he was her best friend, but she was going to kiss a boy. A thirteen-year-old boy. Wow. No, damn and hell. Those words felt better.

She grabbed his hand, wondering whose palm was sweaty, his or hers. When she dragged him between two garages, in the narrow path where no one could see them, he didn't fight her. She stopped, her back to a wall, closed her eyes, and puckered up.

And she waited.

And she waited.

Finally, she cracked open her eyes and squinted into Geno's face, his eyes screwed closed, and his lips squeezed tight. God, did she have to do all the work?

She leaned forward and planted a big kiss on his lips. At least, that's what she thought she did. A zap like *sticking her finger in a socket – because she'd done that, since people told her not to – hit her lips and ran through to her fingers and toes until they curled. She couldn't move back, and Geno leaned forward. After what felt like hours, they both broke off. Breathing hard, they leaned back on opposite walls in the narrow passage and stared at each other.*

"Wow," she said, meeting his confused eyes. He looked mad. Then he looked worried.

"Was that okay?"

She shrugged, as nonchalant as she could manage. "I guess."

He frowned again. "Maybe we should practice some more, so we know we can get it right."

"Yeah," she'd agreed, "maybe we should."

And they probably would have, except the garage door slid open on squeaky wheels behind her back, and they bolted out into the alley and down the block until they had run out of breath. When they'd looked at each other, they both burst out laughing. Yeah, fun times.

"You can get a feel for it, and tell me what you think. I want us to get this right."

She shook her head, bewildered by his words. He looked at her with a strange expression, like he wasn't sure if she was paying attention. Which she wasn't, of course.

That first kiss had been, to coin a word her daughter recently started using to death, awesome. She wasn't sure why, exactly. They didn't know what they were doing, but somehow, she'd secretly compared every man's kisses since to that first one. Maybe you never did forget your first kiss.

Of course, she suspected they'd each gotten better at it since then. She'd obviously done more than kiss, since she had Leonora to prove it. And Geno had been married for three years. She didn't expect that he'd been a virgin going into that relationship, either. She bet they'd be better at that whole kissing thing now. The fact that she'd never find out left her feeling empty and lonely.

"*Agnese*?"

His use of her birth name should have set her back up and made her angry, but strangely, it didn't. He was a part of that time in her life. The time since, she'd created for herself.

"Sorry, *Genovese*, sorry." His name in Italian rolled easily off her lips, even after all this time. "I was thinking about what you were saying. Why don't you run through the options for me again so that I'm sure I'm clear? Then I can give you an answer."

His sudden knowing grin disappeared almost as quickly as it lit up. He wiped the latest addition of pizza juice from his lips, took a new napkin to re-wipe his hands, and pointed to the plans.

"I think you'll get style points if you use the brick for focal interest. Leave it exposed here, and here. The rest of it can be covered, since those areas are private rooms. What did you call them, treatment rooms?"

She nodded, trying to capture her errant thoughts. Where his sleeve rose as he gestured, an exposed forearm defined by sinewy muscles left her feeling slightly lightheaded. He was lean, but then, he'd always been lean. She liked lean men. And if anything, his body had toned to perfection.

"What do you do in treatment rooms?" The simple question, accompanied by honest interest in his eyes, made her heart do a little flip. She had all sorts of ideas about what they could do in a treatment room together. But she didn't think that was what he was asking.

"Can I show you?"

>>>>>

He didn't think he'd heard he correctly, not the words, and certainly not the low, seductive tone. Or at least, that's how it sounded to him.

All he could do was nod, and she set aside the remains of their pizza and took his hand, pulling him up. Geno followed Agnes as obediently as Lucky did, waiting for him to lock the suite door before unlocking the one to her shop. Then she took him by the hand and led him through her domain.

Each room had a purpose, each station a specialty. At least, that's what he gathered from her tour. He was too busy watching her eyes, the way they shown with pride at her accomplishments. This was her space, her kingdom.

"Now, sit here. There's something I've been dying to do since I saw you in that beard."

She pushed him into a chair in the front area. Only a handful of lights were on, illuminating the mirror in front of him when she turned him to face it. In the glow, her face looked mischievous. It was the heat in her eyes, though, that made his blood run a little faster than necessary.

When she left the room, Lucky settled on the floor with a series of thumps. Water ran in the back. A heavy sigh from the dog combined with a series of beeps that sounded like a microwave. Geno counted to twenty, slowing his breathing. As soon as he'd finished, his blood raced once more. Relaxation techniques weren't working.

Agnes glided back into the room, a small smile on her lips. She stopped behind him and caught his eye in the mirror. In the semi-darkness, the reflections of their faces looked mysterious. He forgot about counting, about breathing, about the dog, because her eyes bewitched him.

"Do you trust me, *Genovese*?" Her expression dropped into seriousness with the question.

"With my life, *Agnese*." Because it was true.

From behind his back, she pulled a white cloth and wrapped it around his face, blocking his vision. Ah, a hot towel. It smelled of laundry soap and lavender.

"I want to trim your beard. I like what's left of your hair all wild and crazy, but your beard needs some work."

He wanted to laugh. Wild and crazy? That was hardly him.

"I want to keep the beard, Agnes." His voice came out muffled, and he hoped she heard him.

"I understand. I want you to keep it too. I didn't think I liked it to begin with, but it's kind of grown on me. Now sit still while I work."

She leaned over him, and he wished the towel wasn't blocking his vision. He could still catch her scent, unique and spicy, mixed with a hint of pizza toppings. He felt her fingers combing through his hair, giving his scalp a deep massage. When she concentrated on the soft spots behind his ears, he thought his eyes rolled up in his head. Whatever she wanted to do would be fine with him.

He missed the caress of her fingers the moment they left his head. A clatter, running water, a plop of something. The calm settling through him was the first he'd felt since he'd been talked into seeing her again.

The promise. The thought washed over like a cold slap of ice. He was supposed to be watching out for her, not heating up for her.

He put his hands up to his face, only to find his fingers closing over hers on the edge of the towel.

"Hey, not yet. This is my job. You stick to carpentry. I'll do the shaving."

Her husky voice made him stop, but not before his rough fingers stroked over her soft ones. She gave the towel a little tug, and he let go.

His eyes felt misty and unfocused when her face popped into view. She held up a fuzzy brush with white foam on it, and with it, she began to soap his beard.

"Just a little trim around the edges, and a little touch-up on the length. I promise, Geno, this won't hurt a bit."

She smiled at him. He wanted to smile back, but she pursed her lips and scolded him to keep still. He watched her fierce concentration as she shaved a little, trimmed a little, and shaved some more. He wouldn't have been able to move if the place was on fire.

Chapter 11

"What do you know about Noah Kinkead?"

Geno posed the question as casually as he could, thinking that his friends would be likely to know any back-stories or nasty rumors.

Powers shrugged his shoulders, saying, "He's grabbed a beer with us a couple of times. His brother brought him along. Talk about opposites. He seems as steady as his brother is nuts. He's a doctor at the hospital, if I remember correctly."

Mac shook his head, saying he had no idea who they were talking about. But Jake nodded. "He treated me the night of my accident, and I've run into him a couple of times since then around town. Cute girls, his daughters. He told me he moved here to be close to family after a nasty divorce. Seems like a nice guy, and I haven't heard of any problems. Why?"

His cop friend always wanted to know why. Geno wasn't going to enlighten him. He shrugged instead, the universal guy symbol that encompassed a range of emotions and signaled the topic was done.

The acid in his stomach churned and his ulcer sent out a bite of pain in warning. It did no good to worry about what Agnes was doing. If last night had been any indication, she was fine on her own. She knew what she wanted. She was still as much of a risk-taker as she'd been when they were kids. It had gotten her in trouble in a major way, but even then, she'd seemed to relish the negative attention as much as she did the positive. Today, she was proud of her achievements, and her business was only one of them.

There had only been a handful of times he'd seen her confidence and composure crack. The last time he'd seen her in Boston, it had been wrenching to witness. If he could have one wish in the world, it would be that Agnes Bliss Amendola never had to feel that kind of hurt again. It was the best he could do to make it up to her.

"How does Bliss like the new drawings?" Powers leaned to the side to make their conversation more private.

The drawings were completely forgotten. When she focused on his beard, he closed his eyes. If he watched her work, this close and personal, he'd have had a stroke. By the time she massaged his shoulders, he was putty in her chair. She looked as flustered and hot as he felt at the end, and when she shooed him out the door with the dog, he was only too ready to go. It was lucky he didn't see anyone on the street, because his agitation would have been impossible to miss. It took him a good half an hour in the stillness next door to compose himself.

"I haven't been able to show them to her yet. She's been busy, and spring break is coming up for her daughter, so she's putting together activities to keep her busy. I never realized how much goes into keeping a child's schedule on track."

Powers nodded. "I see our friends with kids, and it's not for the faint of heart. That said, Tess and I would like children someday."

Geno drew back in surprise. "You're getting married?" The wolf pack and the girl tribe had relegated this couple to the forever together but never getting married stack.

A sheepish grin filled Powers' face. "Yeah, I know. No one thinks we'll get married, but there's no other woman I want in my life, ever. That kind of commitment deserves a ring and a ceremony, don't you think?"

Geno nodded. He'd had the ring and the ceremony, but not the right woman.

He often wondered where he'd be if his life had been different earlier on. If his father hadn't died in the war, his mother would never have moved back to her family's old neighborhood. Even if none of the relatives were welcoming, she felt better surrounded by roots, as she put it.

Then, if he hadn't had his last name, he probably wouldn't have been friends with Agnes. She changed everything for him. And if Agnes hadn't been the crazy wild child she'd been, she'd never have gotten into trouble and with a child of her own. Up until then, everything had been happenstance. Karma.

After that, though, he'd made his own choices. He hadn't always done a good job of them. From the woman he left in angry and disillusioned tears to a wedding that never should have occurred, he'd made a long list of mistakes. One thing had become crystal clear to him over the years, though.

He still loved *Agnese*. Whether it was love like friends who'd known each other for decades or an adult kind of emotion, he wasn't yet sure. The tug of sexual interest was impossible to deny. One thing he did know for certain, though, was that he wanted to be back in her life in whichever way she'd have him.

"Hey Geno, what about Saturday? Are you in?"

He nodded in response to Mac's question, too distracted by his thoughts to care much about what they were planning. He would rather think about Agnes, about their years together and how much he wished he could change their future.

>>>>>

"I don't know her all that well, Tess."

Bliss busied herself on the computer, even though there was nothing she needed to do. Tess stood on the other side of the counter, consulting her phone.

"She talks about you frequently, Bliss. Really, she does."

The mechanics of working through a sitter were overwhelming to think about. Besides, she didn't belong with these people. While a number of the girl tribe came to Bliss Day Spa for services, and even Jake came in for Marlee's massages, it wasn't like she was part of their tight-knit group.

"Hey, Sarge and Stuart from the bakery can make it – yeah. Maybe you can carpool with them. Since it's a surprise party, we're trying to hide the cars out of sight, but there's limited space. If you ride with them, it would be easier."

She started to protest that she couldn't leave her daughter at home in the middle of the day, but that wouldn't be a real excuse. Noah had already invited Leonora to join his daughters and a couple of their other friends to see the latest princess movie. In her book, the man should be considered for sainthood.

"Leonora's welcome too, you know. She won't be the only child there." Tess waited expectantly, the smile on her face saying that if Bliss said no, she'd only wear her down until she agreed.

"Actually, my daughter has plans for the day."

"Well, we can't leave you home alone, now can we? Say yes, Bliss, please? We feel like you're part of the girl tribe already, and this will make it official."

Bliss opened her mouth to protest, shutting it again just as fast. Maybe it was time she did something fun for herself. She couldn't remember the last time she attended an adult party. She couldn't remember the last time she'd been to a surprise party either, at least, not one that involved anyone out of single digit age. On impulse, she nodded, getting more excited by the minute.

"I'm in. I'll call Sarge and ask for that ride. What can I bring? And thanks, Tess, for including me."

Chapter 12

"I can't wait to see the movie, Mommy. Cindy saw it already and said it's awesome." Leonora fidgeted as Bliss tried to brush out her hair. Her excitement made the room bristle with energy.

Of course, Bliss felt herself doing a little bristling too. She had a grown-up party to go to, and the idea made her nearly as giddy with happiness as Leonora was over the fairy princess.

"Are you sure you don't want to come with us? You can sit next to Dr. Kinkead. You don't have to sit by me. He's really nice, Mommy, he's – "

She searched for the word, a lopsided look of concentration on her face, before brightening. "He's respectable."

Bliss burst out laughing. She wasn't sure who put these ideas in her daughter's head, because it sure wasn't her. The fact that her little girl felt she needed a nice respectable man should make her feel like she missed out on something.

Her cell phone buzzed on the dresser, and she ignored it, plaiting Leonora's hair quickly once her daughter sat still for a moment.

"Aren't you going to get that?"

"I'm busy, sweetheart. If it's important, they'll leave a voicemail."

"But Mommy, it could be Dr. Kinkead asking you personally to the movie today." Leonora made a lunge out of the chair as if to grab the phone before it stopped ringing, only to be held in her seat by her mother's firm grip on her hair.

"If it is him and that's what he wants, he'll leave a message. Besides, I told you, I have plans today. I'm going to a grown-up party." She paused as she wound the elastic band around the end of the braid. "Are you okay with that?"

Leonora shook her head in agreement, even if her expression was a little disappointed. The little matchmaker was trying very hard. Maybe if Bliss introduced her to Geno as a date possibility, Leonora would be fixing them up instead.

She still shivered when she thought about the forced intimacy of trimming his beard. At the time, her hands shook, but gratefully, his eyes stayed closed as she worked. Shaving around his lips had tried her skills, but the result was worth it. Revealing a mouth that had grown sensuous in the past nine years was like getting a surprise gift. She was delighted when he caught her eyes in the mirror and smiled at the outcome.

And then he tried to pay her. In shock, her mouth opened and shut a couple of times like a gasping fish before she told him it was on the house. He nodded once, shedding the cloak as if he was allergic to it and striding out the door before she had a chance to thank him again for the pizza.

He'd called her or stopped by three times since then. She let the calls go to voicemail because she didn't know if she could keep her emotions out of her voice. When he showed up in person, she vanished as fast as possible with the excuse of a client. Their limited conversation was all business, though. If he'd had an inkling of how amazed Bliss was about the attraction buzzing every time she looked at him, he gave no indication of it. Today, disappointingly, the phone had been quiet.

The message beep sounded, and Leonora shook herself free of Bliss's hands and pointed. "Go get that. It could be important."

The imperious tone was so like Agnes's mother from years gone by that she almost dropped her jaw. The finger pointed with firm determination wasn't too off the mark either. Leonora didn't know her grandmother at all, and yet, she mimicked her moves and her tone almost perfectly.

"I don't know who this is. Who is it?" Leonora held up the phone so that Bliss could read the number. If her heart suddenly accelerated, it was simply because she'd gone from sitting to standing too fast.

Geno.

"Well? Who is it?" Her daughter frowned at the phone again.

"That's the man who's helping us make the spa bigger." And while she was eager to hear his ideas for a different layout, tonight was party night, and it would take her some time to get ready. Geno would have to wait.

"Is he nice?" Leonora wiggled her eyebrows and gave Bliss a pert little grin. "Is he single?"

Bliss barked out a laugh. Of course, the first thing her daughter wanted to do was hook her up. That she picked Geno for this exercise would be comical, if she was old enough to understand the implications and had the full story.

"His name is Mr. Altimari. You've seen him next door." The fact that she'd known him longer than Leonora had been alive and then some didn't need to be discussed now, did it?

"Can I talk to him after school this week?" Leonora took special interest in the pattern in the placemat on the table, trialing her hand along the design.

"Yes, I'm sure he'd love to spend time with you." Though Bliss might be worried about that reunion. Knowing her daughter, she'd have two million personal questions for Geno, and he'd probably tell her the truth in answer to every one.

The phone rang again before Leonora could ask any more questions, and she answered it before Bliss could grab the device from her.

"Hello, you've called Bliss Amendola's phone. This is her daughter Leonora. How can I help you?" She looked proud of herself as she stuck her tongue out at Bliss.

"Oh hi, Dr. Kinkead. Yeah, she's right here. Do you want to talk to her?" She looked excited at the prospect. If Noah was planning to ask her out, Bliss hoped he knew better than to do that through an emissary.

"Okay, I'll ask her." She dropped the phone from her ear. "He's asking if I'd like to stay over tonight. Charlotte wants to go out for burgers after the movie, and he'll take me too. Then we can watch more movies at their house. He says he'll make popcorn. Can I stay over, Mommy?"

Bliss held out her hand for the phone. When her daughter got that suggestive grin on her face again, Bliss frowned and shook her head. One minute it was Noah, then Geno, and now, Noah again. Leonora must think she was desperate.

Putting the surrendered phone to her ear, she said, "Hi Noah. Leonora would be delighted to stay over tonight. Are you sure it's not an imposition? I'm happy to bring over more snacks for the girls too."

Noah chuckled on his end. "I'm not sure we need more snacks. The house seems to be bursting with junk food, and I'm not sure how I get talked into buying it. You're welcome to join us, you know. For the movie at the theater. For burgers. I'd say for the sleepover too, but you might get the wrong idea."

She laughed at that, delighted the man took the time to tease her. How long had it been since someone flirted with her?

"Thanks, but believe it or not, I have plans."

It was the perfect surprise, and Roxy burst into tears before grabbing Mac around the neck and pulling him into a big kiss. When she danced over to Powers and Geno and thanked them with only slightly less exuberance, Bliss told herself the pang she felt wasn't envy or jealousy. After all, it wasn't like she wanted an excuse to kiss Geno.

She sipped her wine, running her hand over the smooth granite surface of counters. She had kitchen envy. Growing up, she'd secretly loved beautiful homes. She never told anyone, except Geno, of course. Back then, they told each other everything. Of course, she might have stopped telling him some things when she got interested in boys. He wouldn't understand.

Since having Leonora, she doubted she'd ever get a custom kitchen. There were days when her dream of owning a house seemed so unreachable, it was like a mirage on the horizon. But then, having her day spa had been a dream at one time too.

"I'm going to need Geno to build me cabinets." Tess came up behind Bliss and ran her long fingers over the built in shelves lining one wall of the space.

"I know." Serena repeated the gesture. "It makes me crave a great big piece of barn wood to play with."

Bliss was sure Serena meant real wood and not something sexual.

"I can build you cabinets." Powers stood behind Tess, looking more than a little put out. Next to him, Serena's husband Dane seemed to puff up his chest.

Both women looked at their men with indulgence, shaking their heads. Tess said, "You guys are good, great, even. But Geno is a master."

Bliss joined the other women regarding the carvings he'd done by hand and the joints that showed no nails. And they all sighed.

"Come on, brother. I don't think we're wanted here. Let's go find Geno and beat the crap out of him." Dane swung an arm around Powers' shoulders, leading the still mutinous man away.

Bliss giggled at their antics.

"Yes, I know, we shouldn't tease them. But they don't have time to do this kind of craftsmanship. Woodworking is not a primary job for them. Geno, well, he's been able to perfect his skills. I wonder why he got into this in the first place." Serena looked at Tess and they both shrugged.

Bliss opened her mouth, thinking she'd tell them the story of how much he liked to build things, even as a kid. How the wooden toys he made from scrap lumber were prized possessions in Christmas bazaars. How she'd watch him for hours, amazed when his young hands produced something that looked better than the stuff in the department store window.

But then she'd have to tell them how she knew. She took a sip of wine instead of speaking.

The women turned to her anyway. Tess said, "How is the remodeling coming along, Bliss? I heard that Geno has some new ideas on the design. I know he and Powers poured over the plans for a couple of hours, moving things around. It seemed they were both delighted with the outcome. What do you think?"

"We haven't had a chance to meet about the final plan changes yet. I've been busy, between the shop and taking care of Leonora. Our after-school sitter quit, and I'm having a hard time finding someone to replace her. And this week is school break, so I guess I'll be taking time off. I have my hands full," she finished, then cringed at her unfortunate choice of phrasing.

If she thought they'd be shocked at her bad choice of words, they gave no indication of it. They might not even be aware. Serena even linked an arm through hers and began pulling her back toward the company in the big kitchen.

"If you ever need to talk, just let me know." Serena's whispered words were delivered before they arrived at the counter covered with all sorts of appetizers.

She didn't have a chance to respond before Roxy appeared from the center of the crowd and danced over to them. Yes, she danced, which was so charming that Bliss joined the others in a big grin and a laugh of her own. Someone poured more wine in her glass, though when she turned to thank them, they were gone. And when she circled back, Roxy swung an arm over her shoulders, the other around Tess, and the four women stared at the counter.

"I feel the need to cook something," Roxy said. "Anything, everything. Look at this place. Can you believe it? And the guys pulled it off without spilling a word about it. Yes, I definitely need to cook something immediately."

Bliss felt the giggle rising again, and when the others laughed, she joined in.

"But really, what would you cook? Look at all this." Tess motioned with her free hand to encompass the islands, the side areas, and the long rustic table set at an angle in the dining area. Every surface groaned under the weight of platters and containers overflowing with food. "Mac catered it so that you wouldn't have to worry about anything."

"I know, the bastard. Damn, but he's sneaky. And he catered it out of my own restaurant and store. I'm going to have a talk with the crew when I get back to work tomorrow." She laughed again, taking any sting out of her words.

Bliss felt a new stab of envy. The few people she called sometimes-friends were friends of the moment, drawn together by the place where they worked more than any other reason. Not one knew Leonora's story, or her own. She hadn't let herself grow close to anyone since coming to Flynn's Crossing. These three held each other in high regard and carried their deep friendship like a cloak to protect them.

"I know," Roxy cried out as she released Tess and Bliss and swung her arms wide. "We need a girl tribe night. I'll cook. We can't do it here yet, but I feel like a cooking celebration. We'll send the guys to Mallory's and make it just us."

Bliss began to fade back, since their party wouldn't include her.

"Where are you going, Bliss? You're invited too. You have to come. You're one of us now, you know. How about Thursday night?" Roxy looked at the others and Bliss watched them all nod.

"I can't, I'm sorry. I have Leonora, and no sitter, and – " She fluttered her hands, nearly spilling the wine in her glass. She took a sip to lower the level, wishing she knew who kept filling it.

"Bring your daughter along. She can cook with me." Roxy didn't seem to think there was anything odd about her statement.

"I – she – we – " Bliss tried again, unsure of how to respond.

Roxy frowned at her. "I'm sorry, was I being rude? I don't think of your daughter as a girl with obstacles, you know. I've taught plenty of kids to cook, and you'd be surprised about the problems some of them had. Come on, you'll both have fun. We haven't had a little girl in our gang before. I promise, we'll take good care of her. And of you."

Tess and Serena nodded, adding their encouragement. In this group, no one saw Leonora as strange or disabled or unable to do normal things. Maybe it was time she stopped thinking in those terms too. She took a sip of wine to buy herself time to think. Damn, the glass was full again.

"At least promise me you'll think about it," Roxy said. "Six o'clock at my apartment above the restaurant. It isn't as big or as nice as this, but I make it work."

Bliss murmured her pledge to consider it. If she did it, it would be the first time she and Leonora had a mother-daughter night out that didn't involved a school event or a bundle of kids. She took another sip of wine, thinking it must be making her tipsy to consider the idea.

"Ah, there you are." Sarge and Stuart stopped in front of her, arms linked. "We thought we'd head out, if you don't mind. We get up early, you know? But we checked and Tess and Powers are happy to give you a ride home. If you want to stay that is." They watched her expectantly.

What did she have to go home to? Leonora was at her sleepover. Bliss wasn't scheduled to pick her up until noon tomorrow. She had nowhere she had to be and nothing she absolutely had to do.

"I'll drive her back."

The gentle voice didn't boom, though in her bones, she felt like it did. She and Geno, in the confines of his truck. Being with him in a small space would be as unnerving as sharing pizza, or trimming his beard.

Sarge said, "Oh thanks, Geno. Come in when you're next in town and get some scones on us. Blueberry is on the menu tomorrow, by the way, and cherries the day after."

She suddenly remembered Geno's penchant for all things baked, and the fruitier, the better. Funny how something that made no difference in the overall scheme of the world would suddenly make her feel warm and comfy.

Geno thanked them, assuring them he'd make a special trip if he had to. When the bakers were gone, he didn't fill the air with words or even take her hand. At least a friendly arm around her shoulders would be nice. Everyone else seemed to be doing it today. When she glanced around, she realized her new friends had disappeared as if spirited away by magic.

She sipped her wine, relieved to find that the level finally seemed to be going down. When she spun around to look at Geno, the heel of her boot caught on something, and she suddenly lost her balance and tripped into his hard chest.

He stared down at her in apparent surprise, his hands tight on her arms. His palms seemed to sizzle through the material of her blouse. She peered up at him, wondering why the edges of his face were fuzzy.

"How much have you had to drink?" His question accompanied a frown that pulled his beard down at the corners. He looked funny from this angle.

"Just this one." She tried to raise it to show him, but he kept his hands on her arms and it was difficult to move.

He narrowed his eyes at the glass she clutched between them. "I'm betting that Mac's been refilling your glass. He's like that. He probably also has a fleet of designated drives waiting outside to drive home whomever gets too tipsy. Stick with me, Agnes. I'll take care of you."

She thought that might have been the nicest thing she'd ever heard him say.

Chapter 13

His truck tires whirred with a reassuring hum on the county road. The distance from Roxy and Mac's ranch to town wasn't that far, but on a night when the stars were hidden behind a layer of clouds and fog billowed at the edges of the asphalt, it could seem very long. Beside him, Agnes faced the windshield and said nothing.

When he'd discovered her tipsy at the party, he'd wrapped his arm around her and kept her close to his side. When Powers looked over with eyebrows raised almost to his hairline in surprise, Geno chose to ignore him. No one else was going to be as responsible as he was when it came to keeping Agnes safe.

He'd replaced the glass of wine in her hand with a bottle of water. She had protested only a little, then squinted at him and meekly took a long drink. After two bottles, she'd excused herself to find a restroom, and he guided her down the hall and outside to the porta-potty, holding a flashlight to help her along. He stood guard, hoping she didn't fall asleep inside. It would be hell jimmying the door lock if she did. And then what would he find?

He didn't want to think about what she would look like, partially undressed. He didn't want to wonder how her body had changed since the last time they'd skinny-dipped as teenagers. But he couldn't help himself.

She'd be lush and inviting, he decided. Having a child and maturing into a woman had changed her in many ways. Her breasts were large, the perfect size for his hands. Her height would never be an issue. He was used to women finding him tall. He could scoop up

Agnes without a problem, working with heavy lumber and construction materials as he did all the time. And then he'd –

He needed to stop thinking about Agnes like that. They were friends, nothing more. Maybe that one beer he'd nursed for two hours earlier in the evening was one beer too many. He'd be better off thinking about things that were the same.

The smart mouth and quick temper were still there, but he'd seen glimpses of patience too. It was in her voice when she talked about her daughter. Her excitement when she had an idea was still as passionate. Spunky and quick to act, those were there too. In fact, if anything, the best parts of Agnes Amendola had gotten better with age, and she'd mellowed on the rest.

"Thank you." Her voice was small as she almost whispered the words.

"For what?" He found his response coming out in the same quiet tone.

"For saving me from making an ass of myself."

He shrugged, though he doubted she noticed it. Her gaze stayed on the road ahead of them, so he added words. "You'd have realized the problem soon enough. I don't think it was deliberate, either on your part or on Mac's. It's just the way he is. It's a party, and he wants everyone to be bubbly and smiling."

He glanced over to find her frowning. "I didn't look bubbly and smiling? I'm always bubbly. And I smile most of the time."

He grinned. Agnes had a certain image of herself, and damned if it pissed her off to find she wasn't living up to her standards.

"I thought you looked bubbly. And you were smiling. You were laughing. What were you up to with the girl tribe?"

Because he'd watched her, seeing the gentle way Tess and Serena enveloped her in their companionship. The way Roxy included her as she continued to celebrate the grand design of the kitchen. The urgent discussion that took place afterwards, until she finally gave a hesitant nod. He'd watched everything.

In fact, he'd almost dropped his beer when she walked in with Sarge and Stuart. All dolled up in her party best, she commanded his attention. Other than accepting Roxy's thankful kiss, he positioned himself to watch her for hours. What started as an afternoon get-together had morphed into an early evening event, complete with blaring music. When the men he talked with moved to block his view, he excused himself on the pretense of finding someone and repositioned to keep his eyes on her.

If he was being honest with himself, he would say it was because he couldn't look away.

"They invited me to one of their girl tribe parties."

He waited for her to continue, but she stared at the road again.

"That sounds like fun."

"Don't be silly. I can't go." The stern command in her tone did nothing to hide her disappointment, at least from him. He knew her better.

"Of course you should go. You'll enjoy yourself. Those are pretty amazing women, and they invited you because they know you're amazing too. You should go, Agnes."

He could almost hear the wheels turning, manufacturing excuses.

"You can get a sitter for Leonora."

Agnes flipped a hand in his direction, dismissal, from the look of it. "That's not it. They invited her too."

It was his turn to frown. "What's the problem, then?"

Agnes gave a sigh so strong, it might have sucked the air out of the truck cab. "If I take Leonora, there will be questions. And she can't go. This is a cooking party. You know why she can't go."

He thought there might be a pleading note in her voice, and it cracked his heart. Years of saying no, of disappointment, of being brave and wishing there was a magic wand to change the outcome, had worn her down. She did her best to keep her daughter safe. But who kept Agnes safe?

They pulled up to her apartment in a nice building on the perimeter of Flynn's Crossing downtown area. It was a short drive to the spa. In fact, it would be a nice walk on most days, if Agnes had the time for that. He doubted she did.

He stopped the truck, engaged the brake, and killed the motor. They sat without speaking. Upstairs, window boxes hung in decoration. At this time of year, they were empty, but he imagined in a couple of weeks, someone would plant colorful flowers to grow throughout the summer and into the fall. Someone would tend them and water them. And if he was correct in his assumption that the second story apartment covered the whole small floor's footprint, that someone was Agnes.

"Would you like to come in, for coffee or something?" Her voice sounded small in the quiet of the space.

"Are you sure you want me to?" If his heart sped up and his blood pumped harder than it had in a long time, so be it.

She smiled now, turning to look at him. "Of course I'm sure. You kept me from making an ass out of myself tonight. You're always saving me, Geno. Thank you."

And he remembered another party a long time ago, when she uttered the same words.

"Please come, Geno. I can't get anyone to drive me home, and I don't want to stay here."

He listened to her words, already putting on his jacket and grabbing his keys. His beat-up truck, the one he'd paid for with his first few carpentry checks, stood in the driveway of the small house he still lived in with his mother. He couldn't afford to move out. If Agnes's brothers thought this was funny, so be it. Besides, moving would take him away from Agnes.

He knew the house she was at by the address she gave him. It was in a nice neighborhood, a whole lot nicer than theirs. The kids were rich, driving brand new cars given to them by their parents. They spent their college break at the fancy country club or going to the beach. He should ask what she was doing there, but Agnes had been touchy of late.

She was sitting on the wide front steps when he pulled up. She ran down the sidewalk and heaved open the door before he could come around to open it for her. By the time he was at the passenger side, she'd fastened her seatbelt and tucked her purse into her lap, looking forward and not smiling. Silent. All very un-Agnes-like.

He closed her door gently, rounding the front and climbing in. She didn't look at him, but from this angle, he could see her make-up was smeared and she seemed to be crying.

"Are you all right?" He thought it was a legitimate question.

"Just drive the fucking truck, okay?" The angry words contrasting with her scared expression jolted him into action. He might have left a little rubber he could ill-afford to lose from those old tires as he tore away from the curb.

They drove in silence for a while. He doubted she wanted to be taken home yet. She hadn't tried to fix her face or mop her teary eyes, and in his experience, these were things she usually did before she faced whatever combination of her family would be in her home's sitting room.

There wasn't far to drive in the city, so he went to the bay, parking in one of the lots along the water and killing the engine. They sat and watched the lights reflecting on the water. It was one of their favorite talking spots.

He didn't ask questions, because she'd tell him when she was good and ready. He'd known her for fifteen years now, and most of those years had been damn good ones. It was only in the last couple when she'd started dating that they seemed to find it harder to spend time together. Maybe it was because sometimes, what they wanted to tell each other was no longer appropriate for their friendship. He missed their old easiness.

Finally, she sighed, released her seat belt, and pulled down the visor to look in its little mirror. She gasped, or maybe he imagined it. He watched the tears drop again, faster this time. Then she gave a huge shudder, pulled herself together, and wiped her face. He liked her better this way, not adorned with layers of paste and color to make her into something she wasn't.

"Do you want to get a coffee or something?" Her big brown eyes sparkled in the reflected lights as she turned to him. She pulled her hair back and wrapped it

with a rubber band she'd dug out of her purse. And she watched him. If her eyes looked a little pleading, he wouldn't comment on it.

"Are you sure you want to?" He didn't mean the hour of the night, because she stayed out late all the time now. It was one of the things he didn't understand about her, this wild streak that started in high school. He'd become even more quiet, some even said laid back. In contrast, she'd become even crazier.

She smiled now, though the expression was tentative and looked like it could break into sadness at any moment. "You're always saving me, Geno. Thank you."

He nodded, not sure what to say. Then her smile disappeared, and she added, "I hope I didn't make a big mistake."

And she burst into tears again. He slid across the bench seat and pulled her into his arms, and let her cry all over his jacket. He had to be at work early in the morning and he'd be tired before his long construction day started. But it would be worth it.

How long they sat like that, he hadn't been sure. She didn't tell him what had happened. He was afraid to ask. He was afraid he already knew.

"Geno? Coffee?"

He shook his head, as much to rid himself of the memory as to tell her no. She sighed again, a lonelier sound, and he almost caved.

"Thanks for the ride." She'd said that in his memory too, after she'd finally quieted in his arms. When she lifted her tear-stained face to his and sniffled the words, he'd kissed her on the nose. Unable to stop, he'd kissed her on the lips, and his body raced in unfamiliar ways, crazy ways, the ways it did when he dreamed of her and woke up with an erection harder and heavier than his sledgehammer. He dreamed of that kiss often over the years.

In the present, she pushed open the door, and he leaped out of his side to help her. Like before, she did things for herself. But this time, he wrapped an arm around her and led her to the doorway nestled between two retail stores. Taking the key from unresisting fingers, he inserted it in the lock and turned it, pushing it open before handing the keychain back to her.

She looked up at him. They were standing too close together, but he couldn't bring himself to step away. She didn't seem to be any more inclined to turn inside. He didn't want to avoid the inevitable.

He dropped his face to hers and kissed her nose, then stood straight. She smiled up at him, lifting her arms, and pulled him down again. And as she kissed him full on the lips, blood drained from his brain and pooled behind his belt, making things hot and hard in an instant.

If that kiss when they were thirteen had been remarkable, and the one at twenty turned his insides out, this one topped them both and then some. It was the best pressure, deep, without tongue or teeth in the way, dancing along his skin like a shorted circuit. It went on for a long time, subtle movements and changes driving him more than a little nuts.

At least, that's what he told himself was the reason he couldn't pull away when she did. He tightened his hold, giving her a scant second to breathe, then dove back in, taking control this time. And this time, he let his tongue run across her lips until they parted, and he ran his tongue over her teeth until he heard a moan. When her tongue danced out to join the fun, he wondered why he'd waited so long.

She moved in closer, running her fingers through his beard and over his head. He loved the way she caressed his skin, and he had a fleeting thought about what her hands would feel like on the rest of him. He knew they'd feel amazing. If there was one thing he'd learned, it was what he liked. And he knew he'd like Agnes's hands on his body.

The tightness in his jeans worsened, making him wish for sweat pants or better yet, being naked. Naked with Agnes in his arms. On a bed. In the one room apartment she shared with –

His whirling thoughts stopped. Her daughter. Was the babysitter up there, waiting to be paid? Was Leonora steps away, looking out the window and wondering why her mother didn't come up the stairs? What would he say?

Drawing back was tough, one of the hardest things he ever did. He'd done it before, and it had pained him then, but for other reasons. Now, the hurt was physical and emotional and timeless, all rolled into one.

She blinked up at him, her lips wet and swollen and parted slightly. He couldn't help the urge to trace that wonderfully plumpness with his thumb, even knowing his skin was worn and calloused and wishing he had softness to give her. If he didn't send her inside, he wouldn't be responsible for the consequences. He didn't want to think about what those might be.

Giving her a nudge with his hip pained him, given the confines of his jeans and the arousal waiting there. Unfulfilled, it seemed to be mocking him. Her little breaths of panted air meant she wasn't immune to their kiss either. But he was a gentleman, and he turned her toward the stairs and pushed harder.

"I'll check on you in the morning. Maybe we can go over the new plans." His voice sounded winded. He wanted to continue to say pretty words to her, words like, maybe in the morning, they could crawl into bed and do wonderful things with each other. But he shut up. He gave up his rights where Agnes was concerned a long time ago. But that didn't mean he didn't long for them back.

She gave a perplexed nod, as if she wasn't sure what just happened. He pulled the door, waiting for it to click shut, then waited longer as she continued to stand there, staring at him.

He finally realized someone had to break this stalemate. He took the hands he'd shoved in his pockets to keep from grabbing her back and made a shooing motion to send her up the stairs. Slowly, she stepped back, going up the first two steps backwards. Then she turned on her booted heel and climbed the stairs slower than a snail, her hand trailing along the railing.

He waited until she closed the door at the top of the straight stairs. He stepped back, watching the lights across the second floor. He stood watching them for quite a while, until one by one, they turned off.

Chapter 14

Lucky resettled into his usual spot on the pile of blankets, with a sleepy whine that quickly turned into a raucous snore. Geno had long since given up trying to get him to use a dog bed. If it looked like it was meant for a dog, Lucky wanted no part of it. A stack of human blankets and towels, on the other hand, was deemed perfect.

Geno stared at the bulky shape in the darkened corner, willing his heart to stop racing and his body to unclench and relax. His erection had a mind of its own, pulsing from the remnants of the dream that held him in its strong web. He might have cried out in his sleep, which raised Lucky from the dead long enough to give a low growl. The noise pulled him out of the forbidden fantasyland. His intellect argued that he needed to ignore it, and ignore its implications. His heart wanted to fall back to sleep and enjoy every second of it.

Her hand glided up his chest, pressing and caressing, until he thought he'd burst. These were not the playful hands of a child, or the tentative strokes of a teenager. Agnes was all grown up, and perfect for him in every way.

Her wavy curtain of hair hung free, brushing against his skin with feather-light touches. Her brown eyes held humor, an emotion he longed to change to heat. He thought he could do it. He wasn't the bumbling oaf he'd been when they were in high school. He'd made it a point to learn his way around women, just in case.

Just in case of what? He tried not to think about it, not consciously. Things had worked out the way they were meant to. Agnes realized her dream of capturing the one man she wanted. When it didn't work out as she'd hoped, she'd still been the belle of the ball in Geno's eyes. Others might curse her as stupid, but he knew better. Agnes always got what she wanted, so she must have wanted this.

He rolled toward her, intent on showing her everything he'd learned to please her. His hands shook as he pushed the waves of rich hair over her shoulders, and his fingers tangled there, unwilling to let go. Only her skin could beckon them onward, and he skimmed his fingertips over the creamy perfection of her shoulders, lower, down the valley between her breasts. They were the perfect size, engulfed in his hands as if molded for him alone. He doubted anyone else could please her the way he knew he could.

"Genovese." Her soft voice broke as she caught her plump lower lip between white teeth and leaned towards him, filling his hands further. As he plucked her nipples and listened to the sounds of her breathing accelerate, he knew this moment was something he'd built toward his whole life. Everything he'd been, everything he'd learned, everything he'd done, was for this. Destiny. Things were never meant to be any other way.

When he entered her, the tight glove of her body welcomed him even as it drove his pleasure higher. They were suspended together in mid-air, laying together on a cloud with brilliant sun shining down on them. It made her skin glow in pearly perfection, as her eyes sparkled with dancing excitement. He kissed her then, the sensation so deep, so immense, that he wondered why he'd waited for so long. This was Agnese, his best friend, who understood him better than anyone else ever had. .

"Geno, please," she begged, her entreaty sounding more desperate than before. Yes, he would please her. He pushed a hand between them until he

found her hot center, toying with the nub first slowly, than faster and harder as their bodies smashed together in a primal rhythm. No amount of enlightenment tempered the craving he had for her. He pushed them faster, higher, harder, until – until – .

Lucky gave a particularly loud snore ending in a muffled bark, scratching his nails against the wall as he lay on his back and galloped his legs. Geno felt the dream drift away and grabbed for it, only finding that the harder he tried to tighten his eyes and return to its wonder, the further it receded. It would have played to its logical conclusion, he'd hoped. Or it would have, if his dog hadn't been having a dream of his own, one that probably involved chasing deer in the forest behind the house based on the continuing scuttling of his legs in mock pursuit.

Panting himself, Geno tried to force his mind into a peaceful state, one where erotic dreams of an adult version of his childhood best friend weren't riding him as hard as he rode her. Arousal throbbed through him, and no amount of deep breathing seemed to diminish it. If it went on much longer, he might need to take matters into his own hands. It wouldn't be the first time he'd awoken to thoughts of Agnes in his arms.

He had to admit that even when he was married, there were times he'd turned to his inexperienced bride and pretended she was someone else. Regrets about that still ate at him, though he doubted he knew enough back then to make her happy, no matter what. She didn't want to be happy, considering it her right to be as miserable with her lot in life as possible and his responsibility to be as melancholy as she was. She was never happy, not even when he'd signed them up for a couple's intimacy week at a swanky resort in the Poconos. She'd bitched about that too.

He wasn't sure why he'd married her back then, this Agnes-substitute who was so different in every way. When the divorce came through, he couldn't wait to move out of Boston. Following the trail to California was unconscious, or at least that's what he told himself.

Agnes had only asked one thing of him, and in his stupid pride, he'd been unwilling to give it to her. He wanted to be the one she wanted because of who he was, not because she thought he'd understand and go along with things. She'd seen it as a personal rejection then, of both her and her baby. He didn't blame her, though he'd never made peace with it himself. Maybe she'd forgiven him, since she'd kissed him back last night.

And gods and goddesses, what a kiss. He could live happily for months remembering every taste and texture. But he wanted another one. And he didn't want to wait that long.

A rapid thump sounded against the wall as Lucky's tail expressed his happiness with whatever image he enjoyed in his dream. Geno envied the dog his simple goals. Mindfulness didn't make his own dream life any less real. None of the practices leading to higher wisdom could compete with thoughts of Agnes and her pleasure. He'd never have the chance to show her what he'd learned about life, about himself, and what he thought he came to know about her.

The shards of the dream still pierced his sleep, and he gave up trying to reason his way to a refuge from carnal sensations. He wrapped a hand around himself, pumping fast and imaging it was Agnes's body. And he gave himself up to the inevitable as he heard her wanton cries in his mind, joining her with a guttural groan.

Chapter 15

The sound of the horn in the street wasn't gentle, and Bliss started at the blare of noise. Early Sunday morning wasn't a time she expected a cacophony on this end of Main Street. And she resented the fact that someone had pulled her out of a luscious dream, one where she felt safe and desired and more than a little hot and bothered.

Because Geno Altimari kissed her last night, and she'd gotten very little sleep as a result.

The years had been good to him. Scratch that. If the kiss was any indication, he'd put them to good use. Long gone was the nose-knocking grate of teeth and tissue. Even that first kiss years ago had been fantastic. The one that night her life changed was even better, letting her know how much was missing. If she'd compared other kisses to those over the years and found current boyfriends lacking, it shouldn't have been a surprise.

She knew he hadn't had many girlfriends by the time they'd graduated high school. In contrast, she'd been a little wild and crazy over boys, and she hadn't necessarily been proud of her actions as she got older. The consequences had been steep. The fact that he married a virgin when he was barely more than one himself had given her a pang of envy. In her honest times, she thought how nice it would be to learn together about their bodies and what pleased them. The exploration, the shared surprises, the safety.

As it was, she'd learned the hard way. But that didn't mean she didn't think about Geno more often than was healthy for her rest and rejuvenation, even if it fueled a rich fantasy life.

His hands were gentle but demanding, not letting her turn away and intent on making her cry out in stunned waves of heat. He molded her, caressed her, pulled her closer, until he'd settled her on his erection, hot and throbbing.

"Ride me, Agnese. Take your pleasure. I'll find mine in yours."

She didn't need any more encouragement, and she lifted and dropped over him, first slowly, to savor every impression of his body. He was big, bigger than her first lover, and hard, like steel or granite. And insistent, unwilling to allow her to back down or slow the pace. When she did, he surged up into her, impaling her more deeply than she thought possible.

"Genovese, I'm coming." No matter how many times, it was like the first time. And it was, for her. He pistoned faster, and she fell hard on him, until she wasn't sure where her skin ended and his began. They were fused together as one, as they had been emotionally all these years. Now, they had the physical union to match it.

His clever fingers found her clit and he rubbed her just the right way, the way that ensured she'd be screaming any second now. When he smiled at her, that gentle loving expression she'd seen countless times over the years even before she knew what it was, she couldn't stop the roaring in her blood or the convulsions of pleasure bending her body over his, dropping her lips to his in an endless kiss as he throbbed with life beneath her.

Her rapture in the dream was something she'd never experienced in real life, not with any of the short list of men she'd allowed close enough. The bright lights flashing in front of her eyes faded, as the heat of her body faded to a new chill. The image of Geno's face, carved in ecstasy she created with him in the dream, melted away, replaced by the bright prints on her bedroom walls and the light beginning to stream in around the curtains. Chalk it up to the first morning she woke up alone with time to feel horny. Add in Geno's kisses last night, and she was justifiably screwed.

Rolling to her side, she stared at the empty single bed against the far wall. Leonora had no idea what sex was, and boys were still in the gross and disgusting category. Bliss hoped beyond all hopes that by the time she figured out they could be fun and pleasurable too, she'd have better self-esteem than young Agnes. She'd ruined many things by being too intent on what didn't matter, while ignoring the people who did.

What must Geno think of her after all this time? He'd been nothing but kind and gentle with her. Even if he stubbornly refused to call her Bliss, she knew why he did it. In his eyes, she would always be Agnes, his *Agnese*, and their friendship would be sacrosanct. The façade she cultivated as Bliss was just that, an image meant to build a shield of protection for her and her daughter.

The doorbell rang, shaking her out of the heat of her dream and the sad thoughts about her regrets. Nothing would erase that past, not when a reminder of it lived in her life for the rest of her years. She didn't regret that part of it. Leonora was the best thing she'd ever done, despite the issues.

The bell jangled again, and Bliss crept to the window to peek out through the curtains. Despite the early hour, the spaces on the street were filled with the cars and trucks of customers at brunch along the street. Joggers and bikers on the trail at the edge of town parked here too. The sun was up, the day was probably warm, and it made everyone giddy with false spring excitement.

She glanced down, seeing the shadow of a shoulder. Then the visitor stepped back and looked up, staring into her eyes.

Geno carried a bag from Brew Bank Bakery in one hand and four coffees in a tray in the other. His head was covered by a knit cap, the brimless kind with the edges rolled up like he used to wear during cold weather when they were kids. The red strands in his beard reflected the sun. Behind his sunglasses, she imagined his dark green eyes would be smiling, even if she couldn't tell about that from his mouth.

What a mouth. What sensuous lips. What a kiss. If he hadn't pulled back, she would have dragged him up the stairs last night for more.

He waved the bag by way of greeting, and she waved a hand back from her perch in the window. It looked like he frowned, then he stepped out of view. The bell sounded again, and she started in surprise. Oh yeah, she needed to buzz him in.

If she'd delayed long enough to make sure her hair was pulled back, so be it. She didn't want to look a mess, despite her lack of sleep. She hoped the heat of her dream about him had faded from her cheeks. Just thinking about it, about coming in a way that she imagined he'd evoke from her, made her start to heat up again. That wasn't an option, and she fought to kill the memory so he couldn't read it in her face. When she opened the door at the top of the stairs, he was already almost there.

He stopped at the top, and this time she could see his smile clearly, filling his face and his eyes, the sunglasses now dangling from his thumb on the hand with the bakery bag.

"Good morning, Agnes." He nodded, and if anything, the smile got wider.

"Don't call me Agnes. I'm Bliss now." She wanted to bite her tongue to fight the bite in her tone.

He frowned.

She sighed. What the hell was she doing? She closed the door on him, breathed for a count of three, put a smile on her face, and opened the door again.

"Good morning, Geno. So nice to see you."

He chuckled, shaking his head.

"You used to do that when we were kids, a rewind, you called it. You still do it?"

She chuckled too. "I doubt I've done it in years. Rewinds don't seem to work in my life. But with you, somehow, it fits."

His smile disappeared, his eyes gaining intensity until she felt heady, like her pulse was beating in time with the one she could see hammering in his temple. Behind him, a car honked as it passed, and he blinked a couple of times.

Shoving the bag and tray toward her, he said, "Here, take this. I have the new plans in the truck. Would this be a good time to go over them?"

She found herself blinking too, trying to figure out how to quiet her racing heart and cool the sudden heat that doused her body like a torrent. She hadn't imagined his interest, she was sure of it. Or maybe he looked at every woman this way now. After all, what did she know of his private life today?

Taking her silence for agreement, he jogged down the stairs. She nearly followed him down, just so she could follow him back up. But he wouldn't let her, she was sure. Ladies first. He'd always been a gentleman. She'd miss one of her favorite views.

He must have propped the street door open, because soon he was back inside, a roll of plans in his hands as he loped back up.

"Where did you park?" She hadn't noticed his truck.

"In the lot behind the building across the street. It's closed on Sunday, so the lot is empty."

She watched him do a swift perusal of her apartment. Momentarily wishing she kept the place neat and organized, she saw his eyes freeze on the array of pictures on the top of a bookcase.

Leonora. From her first baby picture to her last school shot, and everything in between. She'd always loved having pictures of her daughter up, even if she was the only one to admire them.

Geno moved slowly across the room as if he was sneaking up on the photos, and he paused in front of each one, assessing and watchful in that quiet way of his.

"She's quite a beauty."

Bliss nodded, afraid to speak because the big lump in her throat might choke her.

"But then I knew she would be, you know. Because she's your little girl."

She bit back words she almost said. No, those words would only hurt him.

He glanced around the room again, expectantly. "Is she here?"

Bliss shook her head, unable to get her mouth to work right. The bag and coffees shook a little in her hands, and she turned away and placed them carefully on the dining table, taking a deep breath to pull herself together.

"She's still at that sleepover with her friend. I have to pick them up at noon." When she turned back, she made sure her face was bland and neutral.

He'd crossed the room without her realizing it and stood in her personal space. At one time in their lives, they didn't have personal space when it came to one another. Now, though, things were different.

"You look good, Agnes."

She cringed. No she didn't. She had dark circles under her eyes and her skin was pale, symptoms of too little sleep. She'd blamed the difficult sleeping on the unfamiliar wine, but in her heart, she knew better. She hadn't been able to get that kiss last night out of her mind.

"I had a hard time sleeping." Now why the hell did she admit that?

He paused, turning his head slightly and looking at her from the sides of his eyes. The gaze of assessment was so familiar, it took all of her willpower not to grab him for a kiss to end it.

"Me too," he said, in a tone lowered and husky.

The honesty ringing in his words, the implication in his hushed reply, floored her. She wanted to ask him why, wanted him to say the words, say that the kiss bothered him as much as it bothered her. And maybe they should do it again, just so they could both make sure it was the reason they were sleepless in Flynn's Crossing.

But he stepped back and broke the spell, clapping his hands as he did so.

"But then, I'll be able to take Lucky and go home, grab a nap, and be like new. You'll be wandering the mall with little girls dragging you from store to store, trying to buy everything in sight. I think I have it better than you."

She felt like her brain was clogged, unable to process in anything other than slow motion. "You nap on Sunday?"

He seemed to stifle a chuckle at her questions. "No, I don't usually nap. Usually, I work on projects around the house. That's my at-home day. I don't make it a practice to work on Sunday. Saturday, sometimes, but not Sunday. A guy needs down time." He unbuttoned his jacket and stood six feet away.

"Ah, that's why you say you're lucky." Her brain was definitely scrambled. The man was dressed in cold weather layers and she was imagining what he looked like underneath.

This time, he did chuckle. "No, I have a dog named Lucky. Or rather, Lucky has a human named Geno. I'm thinking that's a more accurate picture of the world."

He'd always wanted a dog. When they were kids, he'd begged and begged, but his mother never wavered. No dog. Now he had a dog.

She had to pull herself together. The past and the present were scrambling up in her brain.

His gaze was intense, but not in a scary way. His intensity had always been, well, intense. The subject of his scrutiny should, by all rights, burn up under those piercing green eyes.

What did his eyes look like when he was aroused? Was it like this, only more so?

"So, can I stay?" He did the partial head turn, corner of the eyes thing again.

Yes, she thought, you can stay, and let me show you the bedroom.

"You know, to go over the plans?" Now he regarded her even more closely, though his words were softer.

She shook the lust-filled fog from her brain and tried to focus. Reaching for the coffees, the presence of four cups registered. "Is anyone else coming?"

He shook his head, evidently taking her question as agreement he could stay as he took off the hat and stowed it in a jacket pocket. Then he took off the jacket, looking around. "Do you have a closet?"

She sprang into action. "No, no closet. It's a small apartment. Here, I usually do this." She hung the coat up on the back of a dining room chair. It was so long, designed to fit his tall frame, that the lower edges folded on the carpet.

"Damn. Sorry. I'll hang it up in my closet." She made a move to grab it again and his hand on her wrist stopped her.

"No, don't worry. Trust me, that jacket is being treated with civility compared to some of the places I've had to leave it on job sites."

She nodded, looking up at him. He hadn't released her wrist, and she wished he wouldn't, not for a long time. Maybe he'd link fingers with hers, then slide them up her arm, and maybe she'd see how the muscles filling out his shirt felt under her hands.

This was ridiculous. She needed to stop this, and now, before she did something embarrassing. Like climb all over him and revisit that kiss.

She forced herself to turn away, taking the four cups of coffee out of the tray and placing them on the center of the table. Then she took shaky steps to the small kitchen, grabbing plates and paper napkins. Putting them next to the cups, she turned back once more, got a larger plate, and placed the pastries on it like a serving platter. Then she stepped back when she had everything arranged, and had a brief flashback to being a waitress in high school.

"Ah, you didn't have to do all that. I don't want to make things harder for you." His voice had that gruff and edgy tone again, though his expression as he stared at her was kind.

Oh baby, Geno, you already have.

>>>>>

"What do you think? Will this work for you?"

He waited for her approval, desperately hoping she'd love it. He'd spent hours working the design, molding it, prodding it, nudging things into place. It worked on paper. The only important thing, though, was that it worked for Agnes.

She tapped a finger on the page, running it along the dotted lines he'd placed to indicate the space for each workstation. If his mind drifted to how that finger would feel tracing the lines of his body, he let it drift. There was no harm to Agnes if he dreamed of her. She'd never know.

Finally, she nodded, the motion becoming more decisive, until the ponytail of rich hair bobbed at a rapid pace. In the sun's light coming through the windows, he saw the streaks of color she'd placed there. They weren't natural. He wondered why she'd messed with perfection.

"Yes, yes, I think this will be perfect. Better than that. When I drew up my original ideas, I didn't understand how I could separate the stations enough to give the stylists the space they need. And this remodel in the old space, to change the private treatment rooms? Genius."

She smiled up at him, a big grin that made his heart beat unevenly as he shifted uncomfortably in the chair. He made her happy. That's all he ever wanted her to do.

"When can you start on it?"

He focused on her eyes. She'd donned little reading glasses, she said because her eyes were tired today. He thought they were kind of cute on her, and her fake admission about why she needed them even cuter. All of her brothers needed glasses. Maybe she had contacts she used at work.

"Geno? When can you start?"

He did a mental head slap and tried to focus. "Well, this will delay things a little bit. Powers and I need to finalize the documentation, and we have to get the city and the county to approve the changes. I don't think it will take long, maybe a week or two. Then we'll need change orders for the materials. I'll spend this week doing preliminary work to get ahead of things."

He felt zinged with energy, like he could run faster than his drill and pound harder than the pneumatic nail gun. Pleasing Agnes did that for him. It could be the two coffees he'd consumed too.

She'd been so cute about them too. "Four coffees? Why?"

He'd been honest. "Because I wasn't sure what you were in the mood for today. Stuart says you don't have a usual, so I got my usual and brought all of your choices."

Her smile lit up the room more than the sunlight.

"And that must be the reason for the pastries, too." She said that with another smile as she bit into a jelly-filled roll.

"Sarge said these are all your favorites." He took another bite out of his scone, but it could have been anything in his mouth. He really didn't care.

Because he made her smile again. Not the gee-we-used-to-be-friends smile, but the one that rang out with true happiness and joy. It had been too long since he'd seen this one.

She glanced at the clock. "I have to pick up the girls in half an hour, and I still need to shower and get dressed. Thanks for coming by this morning, Geno. It's been nice."

She might have paused a little on that final word, like she wasn't sure which word she wanted to use. In reality, he wasn't clear on half of it, because once she'd said shower, he'd been imagining her naked body with fine spray on it, drops of water caressing her the way he wanted to.

She took his plate and napkin and turned away to the kitchen area. It was just as well. If he stood up fast enough and dragged his coat on with similar speed, she'd miss the decided bulge in his pants. But even that discomfort was welcome.

Agnes Amendola smiled brilliantly at him, and he felt like the luckiest guy in the world.

Chapter 16

Her head pounded. The week was going from bad to worse and she had no idea how to stop the downward spiral.

"Mother, this will be fine. I can work here. Don't worry, I can run the computer."

Somewhere in the past two days, Leonora had decided only babies used the term mommy, and she now elevated Bliss to the moniker of Mother. Add to this Marlee cancelling a string of appointments and not answering her phone, while her clients called with desperate requests to reschedule with anyone available. The drumbeat was strong enough to make Bliss's eyes twitch in tempo. It was Monday, and she was working.

"Leonora, you can't run the computer." Please, God, don't let her touch the appointment system. Who knows what services she'll screw up and who she'll delete. Sending her daughter to the back on the pretense of finding color solution in the storeroom, she locked the system down with her private password.

The door jingled, a sound she usually muted during regular workdays because someone was always up front. It was another thing she needed to consider, how to structure the front desk and waiting area. Geno would want to know, and soon.

If she spared a thought for him now, she'd break down and cry. The fact that he'd taken the time to find out what kind of coffee she liked, what kinds of pastries, was too sweet. She still didn't understand the intense gazes of yesterday. Was it only yesterday? It seemed like a lifetime ago, time filled with mall craziness and arguments with her daughter and the massive headache of a worker suddenly missing.

"I'm sorry, we're closed today." She didn't even look behind her, trying to manage her face so that when she did turn around, the person wouldn't be shocked by the woebegone look she knew must be there.

"That's what I thought. So why are you here today?"

Oh god, Geno. As if he heard her thoughts and showed up. He'd always been a little clairvoyant.

With him, at least, she didn't have to pretend, at least not about how shitty her week was already turning out to be.

"Well, if you must know, Marlee cancelled her appointments for the next two days, and her clients are calling in an uproar. I'm trying to reschedule her appointments, many of which I have to do myself. That means working today. The shipment of supplies due last week is missing, and I need that stuff. And it's Leonora's spring break, and I can't find a sitter, so she's here with me."

He looked so sturdy standing there just inside the door, and so tall that she wondered if he ducked to get inside. No, that was fanciful. She knew he wasn't that tall. But he still looked like a tree you could lean against and tell all your troubles to.

Now wasn't that even more fanciful?

"I can't help you with the first issue, though it seems strange she'd cancel things without telling you. Is she sick?"

Bliss waved her arms around, flapping them at her sides. She was sure she looked ridiculous, but this was Geno. She didn't need to impress him.

"That's just it. I don't know. She has her phone turned off. I'm sure there's a man involved. She started seeing someone, and she's very secretive about it."

"Okay." He drew the word out into two long syllables.

"And don't tell me you can't help me with the missing shipment, because evidently, no one can. Not the company I ordered from, not the delivery service who can't find the boxes, no one."

"Okay." He said it the same way this time, rocking back on his heels and rubbing his beard. The movement drew her attention to his lips, and that reminded her of the earthshaking kiss they'd shared.

No. Not. Now.

"Okay," he said once more, and she contemplated screaming at him. "I can help you with your third issue, though. Let me watch Leonora."

Thoughts of his sexy kissing drained away.

"Do you know anything about kids?"

Geno shrugged. "Yes, I think I do. I volunteer with the scout troops. Those boys and girls certainly are serious about earning their badges. I help with woodworking, and sometimes with the outdoors programs."

She shook her head, unable to process this. She'd always assumed he'd have kids of his own, a whole houseful. He'd said as much many times when they were growing up. He envied her the brothers who were such pains in her ass.

"And I help out each May with the fourth graders throughout the county. It's a program where they get to try out different art forms. They do carving with me." He looked slightly embarrassed.

"I know the program. Leonora's class will be in it this year. I wasn't sure it was a good idea for her."

He nodded his head vigorously, and she suddenly wondered why his marriage hadn't worked out. He was such a dedicated, quiet, and lovely man. Who loved kids, lots of kids.

"She'll love it, I promise. All sorts of kids with," he hesitated, blushing slightly, before continuing, "with issues enjoy it. I'll watch out for her. She's special."

She didn't want to have her heart do a little flip-flop, but it did.

"Mother, I can't find it. Are you sure it's here?" Leonora's voice rang out with a decided screech to it. She closed her eyes before responding.

"Keep looking. I'll be there to help you in a minute."

When she opened her eyes, Geno was smiling at her. "Offer still stands. I'll be next door for a while. If you'd like to bring her by, I'd be honored."

"How much do I need to pay you?" She wasn't sure why she blurted that out. It only seemed fair. He wouldn't accomplish as much with the child underfoot. She knew that from experience.

His smile faded, his gaze growing more intense from dark pools of green. The transition made her heart race and her woman parts stand at attention. It had been a long, long time since they'd even wanted to do more than steal a quick look from behind the curtain.

"No payment required, *Agnese*." And he disappeared out the door. before she had a chance to question his stern tone.

>>>>>

It had been a spur of the moment thing. He probably hadn't thought it through.

"I might be an idiot."

Behind him, Lucky thumped his tail on the exposed subfloor in apparent agreement.

But this would give him a chance to insert himself more fully in two lives that mattered to him. First Agnes, and now, Leonora. He'd never forgotten that day, the only time he was allowed to see her.

Agnes had her wrapped up tight, against the breeze, she said. But it wasn't chilly in the deepest, darkest corner of the restaurant.

"Geno, please. Will you consider it?"

He'd shaken his head to tell her no, his voice choking on the word. Disappointment flooded her eyes.

"Can I please see her?"

Agnes looked a little maniacal at that request. If everything he'd heard was true, she kept the child away from everyone, doing all the baby needed by herself. Her parents wanted nothing to do with their grandchild anyway. He wondered how they could be so cruel.

"Please, Agnese. I promise to be gentle. No one will see us here."

His old friend started to cry, not big noisy tears, but slow rolls of continuous water down her cheeks. She lifted the baby from the carrier, holding her close and cooing to her as she started to fuss. The baby's face was red, probably hot from the heavy blankets in a room that felt cozy to him in his shirtsleeves.

He reached for the bundle, and Agnes gave another hesitant shake of her head, but she finally handed the child across the table. He'd had only limited experience holding babies, but he thought he knew how to do it. A hand under the head, another under her body. She was so small that his hands looked more like a made to order cradle.

The baby started to fuss, and he bounced her and rocked her as he'd seen Agnes do. She started to reach across the table, but the child suddenly quieted, and when she looked up at Geno and smiled, he was sunk.

But he still couldn't do what Agnes asked of him.

"It's okay, I guess. Maybe if you see her, you'll understand."

He nodded, his heart in his throat. He undid the yellow knit bundle the color of sunshine, and the baby cooed at him, gurgling as if happy someone finally let her free. And by the time he'd unwrapped her completely and examined her tiny features and her madly waving feet and hands, he'd done something he rarely did, and never in public.

He cried.

"Yes, I am definitely an idiot. Then, and now."

Lucky thumped harder and rose to his majestic height. The dog must have some Great Dane in him, because he could set his chin on a table while seated without stretching. He ambled over, plopped down, and extended a paw to Geno.

"Yeah, congratulations on realizing it? Is that what you're trying to tell me?"

Lucky woofed once in doggy agreement, then his attention moved to the front door of the empty suite as if zeroing in on a raw steak.

Outside, Geno could see two shapes through the glass. One he made out immediately to be Agnes. At her side, a small shape, smaller than he thought she should be for her age, must be Leonora.

Lucky woofed again, accelerating in a race to the door and giving a few more barks for good measure.

Geno ran after Lucky, grabbing his collar before he could place his big paws on Agnes and knock her to the ground. As big as the dog was, he'd probably be eyeball to eyeball with her. He'd completely crush her daughter.

The door swung open, and Agnes called, "May we come in?"

He dragged Lucky back, intent on getting him under control. If he'd known he'd be hosting a child today, Lucky would be at home. The dog whined unhappily, associating any company with scratches and love. He really was a sappy goofball. If only he wasn't such a grand-sized goofball.

"Mother, I told you, this isn't nece-, necessa-," a small voice said in a prim tone.

"Necessary, and yes, it is. Mr. Altimari is very nice. I've known him for a very long time, longer than I've known you. It's very nice of him to offer to let you visit today."

Glancing over her daughter's head, Agnes locked eyes with him, sending an electric charge into the air. Then her eyes fell on the dog and widened. "Is that a dog? Or is it a pony?"

"He is kind of cute, but he looks funny," Leonora said.

Agnes rolled her eyes at her child's remarks. Funny, but it reminded him a lot of Agnes herself at that age. "That isn't very nice to say about Mr. Altimari, sweetheart."

But he thought it was hysterical, and he laughed, a full belly roll that had Agnes staring at him strangely.

"I meant the dog, Mother. Yeesh." Leonora looked Geno up and down, then settled her eyes on the dog, moving forward slowly. "What's his name?"

"His name is Lucky. He's very friendly, so brace yourself. He likes to give big wet kisses."

Leonora's haughty nine-going-on-thirty face slipped a little bit.

In Agnes's hand, a phone rang, and she looked down at the screen and back at Geno, a hint of desperation in her expression.

"Go on," he assured her, "we'll be fine."

As she ran out the door with the phone already to her ear, she glanced back once, and Geno had no trouble reading the expression. She was grateful.

He wanted her to be a whole lot more than grateful.

"Can I pet him?"

Geno started to tell her he'd hold the dog so they could get acquainted. It wouldn't do to have the child bombarded with a hundred-plus pounds of dog flesh when he doubted she weighed anything close to that herself. But Lucky had other ideas.

The dog slipped out of his collar and gave an overjoyed woof, bounding across the room. Geno couldn't get his feet to move fast enough, contemplating scooping the child up and her probable screams at the act. He'd have to hold her up in the air until the dog calmed down. The fact that Lucky liked to jump and could hurdle high wasn't going to help.

But he didn't have to do any of that, because the dog did a curious thing. He came to a scrambling stop a foot from the little girl, put his big butt on the floor, wagged his tail, and extended his nose to sniff her feet.

When she reached out for him, he sniffed her hands, licked them, and raised a paw of his own.

"He wants to shake." Leonora's voice was enchanted. As if to show what a great dog he could be, Lucky sat a little taller and whined until Leonora fist-bumped his paw. Then the dog dropped down at the tips of her shoes and rolled over, exposing his belly.

"He's nice." She gave him enthusiastic belly scratches, and Geno watched in wonder as girl and dog obviously fell in love.

It was probably five minutes later, precious time as he stared in silence, when Leonora stood up and looked at him solemnly. She walked across the room, the gait a little awkward and stilted, and stopped in front of him. If he'd had to say a word at that moment, he doubted he could.

She extended her left hand to him, inviting him to shake it. "My name is Leonora Amendola. How do you do?"

He took a very deep breath, extended his right hand and said, "Geno Altimari, Geno to you. I'm very pleased to meet you, Leonora."

The clumsy meeting of opposite hands didn't go smoothly. Geno extended both his hands, palms up, in the customary position for a palm slap, and Leonora regarded him thoughtfully. Her hands snaked protectively behind her. She had that same tilt to her head her mother used as she examined him. The eyes were the same too, a rich brown that probably appeared almost black when she was riled up.

"I don't do that."

He pretended not to understand her. "Don't do what?"

She pointed with her chin at his upturned palms. "That."

"Why not?" He copied the tilt of her head.

She wiggled a little, rocking from side to side. "Because I can't."

He exaggerated the puzzlement on his face. "Can't, or won't?"

She took a step back and crossed her arms, hiding both hands in the folds against her sides. "I can't, so I won't." She looked mad enough to start crying at any minute.

He stood, copied her posture again, and said, "Okay."

Then he turned back to the worktable and picked up a piece of scrap wood and his carving knife. If there was one thing he knew for sure, no kid could help but be drawn in when an animal started appearing out of a stick. Seating himself in a folding chair and pulling another even with his, he gestured to the empty seat.

"Have a seat. I was just going to do a little carving. Do you carve?"

She shook her head. He could see her inner argument on her face. Turn into the haughty little princess again, or give in to her natural curiosity and come closer to see what he was doing?

Lucky picked that moment to get up from his prone position on the floor and walk over to Geno too. He took one delicate sniff of the wood in Geno's hand as the work of the knife paused, then took three tight turns in a circle next to the open chair. Heaving a huge sigh, he curled up there, eyeing the little girl as if in invitation.

Damned if the dog wasn't better at this than he was, not that Geno regarded this as a contest. Whatever got Leonora to open up and relax was fine with him.

She flipped her head to get her long hair over her shoulder, then stomped across the room and huffed into the chair with much less grace than Lucky had shown. She pretended to examine the ceiling, but Geno caught her glancing at the work in his hands more than once. Finally, she decided to let him off the hook enough to ask, "What are you making?"

Geno fought the urge to smile. He'd bet every tool in the place that her bravado hid the fact that she knew she was different, and it made her uncomfortable. But calling attention to it would only make it worse for her.

"I'm brainstorming, actually."

She frowned, a deep furrow forming between her eyebrows. The word was probably unfamiliar to her. He doubted it was one that came up in conversation at her age.

"That means, I'm looking for ideas, and I'm thinking hard about them. You see, your mother wants to have some fancy carving around the doors and windows, and I'm trying to come up with styles that will work."

She still didn't look enlightened, so he tried another way of describing it. "Kind of like daydreaming, except with something specific in mind. Or meditating. Do you know what that is?"

She nodded then, her face brightening. "You're noodling."

The word surprised a quick laugh out of him, and he covered it with an energetic nod of agreement. "Who calls it that?"

"Momm-, I mean, Mother does."

This isn't what they used to call noodling when they were in high school, but if it worked for Agnes now, so be it.

"What does she noodle about?"

Leonora started to kick her feet, exciting Lucky enough to raise his head and try to grab her shoes in his big, slobbery jaw. Her arms remained folded, but she seemed to be losing some of her bravado.

"Oh, you know, this and that. The other day, she was thinking about this place, about how to make the spa bigger. A while back, she noodled about buying us a house. That didn't get too far." Leonora nodded her head as if he should know exactly why this wasn't an idea that would work.

He didn't ask anymore, giving her the chance to decide if she wanted to talk with him or not. Lucky made random grabs for her feet, encouraging her laughter. It was a delightful sound, the kind that made his heart a little lighter.

How much time went by, he wasn't sure. The wood in his hand began to take on the shape of a lizard. Leonora watched him for a while, finally clearing her throat and saying, "Mother isn't going to like that. She doesn't like snakes and bugs and stuff."

"Oh. Well, I guess I'll finish it up and use it for something else." He kept carving.

"You should know that, because Mother said she's known you longer than she's known me, and she's known me for a long time. She must know you for a very, very long time."

He nodded his head to agree. He wanted to tell her that he knew her, too, since she was a little baby, but that would require a lot of explaining.

"How long have you known my mommy?"

He didn't miss the slight shift in her tone, changing from pseudo-adult to young child.

"A long time. Since we were younger than you, first grade, in fact."

She said nothing in response, and he could almost hear the wheels turning in that sharp little mind.

Leonora reached down and petted Lucky's head absently, and the dog moaned in happiness.

"Did you know my mommy when you were older too?"

He nodded solemnly, his eyes focused on the carving. Stealing a glance her way, he saw the question forming before she even said it.

"Did you know my daddy?"

He nodded again, feeling his heart crack wider and shake like a troublesome drill on a bite of steel.

"Mommy never talks about him. Whenever I ask, she changes the subject. Why is that?"

He suddenly wished he'd thought to ask Agnes what the child did and did not know about her birth. It was important to maintain whatever reality had been set, and he couldn't do this without information. Now wasn't the time to ask that question, though. Agnes had only begun to trust him again. He couldn't afford to lose that precious gift.

Geno stopped carving, setting the wood and knife on the table behind them and turning to Leonora fully. He rested his forearms on his legs, settling his hands palms-up again, in case the girl was willing to extend a hand to him. Her expression wavered between seriousness and sadness, her eyes widening.

"I don't know why, Leonora. Sometimes, adults do things for silly reasons, and sometimes, it's because we feel hurt or scared inside."

She regarded him without blinking, and he tried not to squirm under her measured stare. It broke his heart to see how quickly she'd grown up. For a young child, she seemed ages older in terms of wisdom and understanding, even if she didn't understand the reason behind his words. She unwrapped herself slowly, settling her left hand on his arm as if to comfort him.

"Don't worry, Geno. It's okay to be scared sometimes."

Out of mouth of the proverbial babes. He doubted he could hold in the flood of emotions much longer. This precious child deserved to be treasured, and to be able to do whatever she set her hopes on in life.

"Thanks, honey. That makes me feel better." He patted her offered hand in return, unwilling to break the spell of her solemn eyes on his.

They sat like this for a while, until she slowly began to move her other arm. At a pace that would make a turtle seem like a racecar, she brought her right hand around, settling it on his knee without breaking his gaze.

"I get scared sometimes too." She still hadn't looked away, and Geno realized she was probably braver than he was, allowing him into the intimidating part of her life.

He nodded in response. "And why is that?"

She frowned, the look again so much like her mother's than Geno had flashbacks to times when they were kids and Agnes wore that same expression.

"Because I'm different. Some of the kids don't like me because of that. And sometimes, adults stare at me too. I want to be able to do the things normal kids do."

He couldn't help himself then, reaching out slowly so he didn't spook her. He let his big left hand lay on top of her much smaller right one on his knee. She didn't pull back, watching him as carefully as a frightened bird that wasn't sure if it should take wing and escape. He lifted her hand in his, letting his thumb glide over it, back and forth, getting as much comfort from the gesture as Leonora seemed to receive from his motions.

"It's always been like that, since I was born, Mommy said. I used to have funny feet, too. Club feet. They fixed those. But they can't fix my hand." Her voice sounded sad, but accepting. She gave a huge sigh, watching their joined hands for a while, before adding, "I wish I could do more things."

He lifted their hands, making a point to nod at Leonora in agreement. That's what everyone wanted.

"What kinds of things would you like to do?"

She shrugged, stilling his hand. "I don't know. Play games. Play music. Do things in art class that look pretty, pretty enough to give to Mommy and have her look really happy. I mean, she always looks glad I gave them to her, but I can see she's still sad. You know, because I'm disabled."

She said it so matter-of-factly that Geno had to work hard not to gasp in surprise. Lucky helped him out by choosing that moment to whine and place his big head in Leonora's lap as if he understood her dilemma, and the girl disentangled her hands from Geno's and started petting the big dog's ears. Lucky gave a happy moan and his eyes dropped half-closed.

Geno wasn't sure how to respond. The child knew she was different. She knew it made some people uncomfortable and others sad. If he was wiser, maybe he'd have better words to say.

"Everyone has issues, Leonora. Everyone has a disability, sometimes on the outside, like yours, and sometimes on the inside where we can't see them."

She raised her eyes from petting the dog and stared at Geno. He could almost see her processing the idea, weighing his words as if determining how much of what he said was true. Finally, she seemed to reach a conclusion with a little nod of her head.

She said, "I can see yours."

He jumped at her words. "My what?"

"Your disability, silly. Geno, hair doesn't grow on your head. But it does grow all over your face and down to here." She gestured to a point a few inches below her chin.

Leonora was a delightful kid, full of sass that reminded him of her mother and odd wisdom she'd clearly accumulated all on her own. A laugh burst out of him. He wasn't sure what she'd gotten from her father, an idea that sobered him again as fast as his laugh had erupted.

The door opened behind them, and he heard the rapid tapping of heels that he recognized immediately.

"Hey, sweetheart, are you behaving for Mr. Altimari?"

An exasperated sigh blew a little breeze across Geno's face as Leonora rolled her eyes and met his gaze. Her expression seemed to say it all. *You see what I have to put up with?*

"Mother, it's Geno. And yes, we're having a pleasant discussion. We're talking about his disability."

He glanced up in time to see Agnes's mouth drop open and her eyes widen. She stared at her daughter for a moment, then looked up at Geno. He doubted he'd ever seen her so surprised. Then her eyes narrowed and a thundercloud dropped over her face.

"Leonora, why don't you take the dog to the back of the room and see if you can get him to do any tricks. I'm sure he does tricks, right, Geno?" Agnes drew out his name in a parody of the little girl's voice.

The child rose and said, "Come on, Lucky. That's Mother's no-nonsense voice, and you don't want to be around when she gets mad." And she led the dog to the back, where she asked him to sit and shake. He obeyed without hesitation, seemingly content to be the center of the child's attention.

"How dare you patronize her?" Agnes whispered the words with fury in her voice, and Geno blinked away from watching the girl and dog to watching the incensed woman. He didn't say anything. He knew from experience that the less he said, the better, because no matter what he said, it would be the wrong thing.

"What kinds of foolishness are you putting in her head? It's bad enough that my clients fawn over her and talk behind her back. It's worse when the kids at school mock her. Tolerance isn't something practiced at that young age. But I expected better from you, of all people. Your disability."

Agnes snorted the last words with disbelieving derision. She paced back and forth so fast that the staccato beat of her heels reminded him of a drum solo. She got in his face then, one finger pointed at his nose and so close, he had to cross his eyes to look at the brightly painted tip. Today, it was blue.

"Be kind to my daughter, *Genovese*, kinder than you were with me when you had the chance to something more. Be kind, or you will know just how mean I can be."

Chapter 17

The man sitting across from her regarded her with enough interest to make her think he didn't feel sorry for her. Too many people did, and she was tired of it.

Bliss had had enough of that from Geno yesterday. She'd been so ticked off with him that she ignored his jumbled words about final plans. She tried to shake off the last view she had of his face as she glanced over her shoulder before slamming the door. It was sad, a deep well of sadness, the kind that came from the heart. It served him right. He had his chance years ago. She'd take her chances with others now.

She focused back in on the man sitting across from her and the conversation, one that made her only marginally happier.

"I'm not sure Leonora and a gym are a good combination." She stirred her coffee with its little silver spoon, glancing at their daughters to make sure they hadn't gotten into any trouble – yet.

Noah Kinkead looked their way too, and in his face, she recognized the overwhelming love and concern of a parent feeling a little out of his depth. When he looked back, sympathy filled his eyes and he nodded in understanding.

"I understand that. But there's no reason she can't participate in the activities program. It boils down to an active day care program for kids during school breaks. The health club offers swimming and different kinds of team and individual sports, but they also offer quieter games."

Compassionate eyes regarded her steadily, set in cover-boy features that looked much younger than his years. His body was buff, like he spent as much time as possible in that gym working out. And then there was his profession, an emergency room doctor. A nice single man with kids, who understood both her challenges as a single parent and the special needs of someone like Leonora. Pleasant to talk to, a nice friend, and he didn't seem to need fixing. But –

There was no zing. Like, zero. Zero zing was not the place to start a relationship.

"Tell me about Leonora." He wore an expression of genuine attention as he took a sip of his plain black coffee.

Bliss sighed, not because she felt this was an intrusion, but because some days, she didn't want to talk about it. She wanted to pretend, for a little while, that she hadn't ruined her daughter's life before it began.

But this man would understand. She said, "She was a full term baby, a normal pregnancy, and normal delivery. It wasn't until the doctor and nurses were cleaning her up and checking her over that they all became silent, and I knew something was wrong. I'd never heard of amniotic band syndrome. When they tried to explain it to me, I got hysterical. I thought it was something I'd done, that somehow, I'd broken my daughter."

Noah grimaced and reached out a hand across the table to cover hers. He leaned a little closer, his eyes shining and his voice soft, when he replied, "You know it isn't your fault, right? There wasn't anything you did or didn't do that brought this on. It's a condition we don't fully understand. It happens spontaneously."

He was very attractive in his intensity, and she bet he had a terrific bedside manner, next to it or in it. But still, zero zing.

"How extensive was it?"

Bliss pulled her hand away, not feeling good about holding hands with a man in public, a man with whom she shared nothing past parental challenges.

"You see her right hand. They say the band stopped her hand from growing, and at first, I thought they meant her fingers would fully form once she was outside of me and away from the band. They had to explain it to me. I didn't even notice her club feet at first. I thought those would straighten with time as well."

If Noah was disappointed that she'd drawn away, he didn't show it. He leaned back in his chair, watching the girls giggling at a table in the corner of the bakery. His eyes still on them, he asked, "What did you choose for her treatment?"

Her eyes followed his, happy to see Leonora laughing like any other girl her age. "Non-surgical. It seemed the outcomes were better. The Boston doctor used an advanced treatment that wasn't available generally at the time. I'm amazed how much they were able to repair."

Her daughter picked this moment to look at her, her eyes full of mischief as she arched an eyebrow and flicked her head toward the nice doctor as if telling her mother to be paying attention to him, rather than her.

Bliss turned back to find Noah staring at her again. If he felt something between them, he must have super powers.

"So what brought you to Flynn's Crossing?" She asked the question and drained her fancy coffee, wishing she felt her waistline could stand another one.

"I had a job offer from the company that provides staffing services for the emergency room at the local hospital. I worked for them in LA too. After my divorce, I concluded that the Southern California lifestyle wasn't a positive influence on my girls. Plus, my brother lives up here. I thought it would be good for them to get to know their uncle."

The flash of irritation across his face was interesting, and she suspected there was more to his back story than he was willing to share. She was curious, but not enough to push him into telling her.

He turned the tables back to her again when he said, "What about Leonora's father? Is he in her life?"

Bitterness mixed with longing, feelings that always accompanied thoughts about him, rushed through her, and she lifted the empty coffee cup to her face as a delaying tactic. She didn't want to think about that time in her past. Of course, her past had a way of sneaking up on her present and reminding her that she might never fully escape the shame and trepidation of those times. She didn't want her child to feel tainted by what had happened to her, by what had happened to them both. She talked about it as little as possible.

Her sensors must have been occupied thinking about the past, because she missed her daughter's movements until the girl put her good hand on Bliss's arm and asked, "So Mommy, can I go?"

Her best friend of the last three months, Charlotte, stood next to her dad and put her head on his shoulder as if she was a little shy around Bliss. The truth was, she seemed shy around everyone. Leonora made up for it by talking a mile a minute when they were together, taking Charlotte under her wing, broken or not. Maybe she recognized another wounded spirit. Bliss suspected Noah's divorce had been exceptionally hard on this young child.

"Dr. Kinkead and I are still talking about it, sweetheart."

If the good doctor was put off by the fact that she hadn't answered his question, he let it go with remarkable ease. Noah leaned toward them both, his eyes on Leonora. "What kinds of sports do you like to do?"

Leonora shrugged, her face getting red at the edges as a blush started to rise. Bliss knew that look. It was the feeling of shame, which the girl tended to cover up with an emotional outburst, followed by a meltdown. She had mere seconds to ward off the scene that was to come.

Charlotte beat Bliss to it. "How about swimming?" Her gentle question held no censure or pity. She appeared to be honestly interested in what might fit her friend.

Leonora lost some of that beet color and shook her head. "I don't know how."

And that, Bliss figured, was probably her fault too. She didn't want her daughter to take on things at which she would fail, so she kept her back from trying.

Noah, however, didn't appear to be fazed by any of this. "Well then, I guess it's a perfect time to learn. Summer's coming, and you'll want to be able to enjoy the city pool, right? It's much better when you know what you're doing." He winked at Leonora, who seemed to be considering this with some gravity.

Bliss tried to get Noah's attention, to shake her head so he would know it wasn't the best thing to get the girl's hopes up. But if he saw her worry, he chose to ignore it. He didn't meet her eye, and for a moment, she wondered why men felt compelled to make grandiose statements without consulting her first.

He continued, "They have swimming classes at the club this week. You can learn the basics and decide if you like it. If you do, maybe you can take the city's classes during the summer. What do you think?"

Leonora frowned at him, watchful and wary. Bliss knew the girl liked him, and if the little minx had her way, Bliss and Noah would be dating and a couple and then, well, you know.

But there was no zing. And now he appeared to be deciding on things that were none of his business.

"I guess I could try it. I might not be any good at it." Leonora swung her attention to Bliss. "Mother, I think I should do this." Her young voice was firm and demanding.

Back to Mother. She was Mommy when her child felt lost and Mother when she wanted to be in charge. But in this case, maybe letting her make a choice would be good. If Leonora became involved in an activity she liked, something she could do with other kids, all the better.

"I guess you can try it. I wonder where we can get you a swimsuit quickly?"

"She can wear some of mine. I have tons. We used to have a pool in the backyard." Charlotte delivered those words quietly, and her face fell into an instant funk. When he father tried to wrap an arm around her, she crossed her arms over her chest and stepped away.

Ah, so his daughter blamed Noah for changes she didn't like in her life. And in the middle of the school year, too. It was no wonder she was quiet, and also no wonder Leonora saw it as her mission to befriend her. She probably saw Charlotte as an outcast like her.

"It's settled then. If your mom can drop you girls off at the club in the mornings for the rest of the week, I'll pick you up at the end of the day." He delivered that information to the girls before turning his movie star face to Bliss and quirking an eyebrow. He didn't expect her to argue.

Anger perked up and made her want to narrow her eyes at him. He didn't make the decisions for her. She made them, and only her. The men in her life always let her down when it mattered.

The picture of Geno on that fateful day years ago, his face crumpled and tears leaking from his eyes as he stared at baby Leonora, slid into her mind. It had been years since she'd seen him cry, since before they were teens, actually. It shocked her into silence that day, right before she raged at his continuing denial.

"That will be fine. Thank you for the help. Leonora, what do you say to Dr. Kinkead for coming up with this great idea?"

Her daughter responded with a mechanical thank you. Her face was a puzzle, part exhilaration and part trepidation, and Bliss bet she was already rethinking the wisdom of her choice.

But it was her choice, and she made it, and Bliss would support and encourage her. Maybe it was time for both of them to step outside of their comfort zones.

>>>>>

"No, she hasn't signed off on the design changes yet. I'm sorry, Powers, but I tried. Someone in the shop didn't show up to work and she was pissed off, then I had Leonora for a while as Bliss tried to cover additional appointments, and then Bliss was mad at me."

Geno saw Powers' interest shift. His stance relaxed and he wiped a hand over his short hair as if trying to figure things out. Finally, he asked, "How did you piss her off?"

There was no way to explain this, now without telling stories from the past that should stay in the past. Besides, they weren't his to tell. That decision needed to belong to Agnes.

He shifted his eyes away as he said, "I don't know."

"Well, kiss and make up with her, would you? Howard wants her okay on the changes before we go to the city. This holds up the project and we had a tight timeline as it is."

Another voice sounded from the front of the old house. "That means more time for our house, though, right?" Mac walked into the library and stopped, taking a slow turn in a circle as he studied the newly installed shelves.

"Man, this is amazing. You gave Roxy the kitchen of her dreams, and now I get the office of mine. You do incredible work, Geno. No one else would take the time and the care to get everything right."

Powers slapped Geno on the back in congratulations, and Mac walked over and shook his hand, pumping it hard enough for Geno to feel the stretch in his shoulder socket. It was moments like this, when his hard work was recognized and appreciated, that made the rest of his life worth it.

"I think I should buy another place to fix up, just so that you can work on it," Mac said, running a hand over wood that was smoother than satin. Geno knew it was, since he'd sanded it by hand.

"Great idea, Mac. But how about one that isn't falling down around our ears next time?" Powers joined Mac's hearty laugh as the two men agreed this transformation had been nothing short of a miracle. And Geno was at the center of that.

Too bad he couldn't create more miracles. Like some for Leonora. And if her daughter was happier, the miracle would spread joy to Agnes too. He only wanted to make her smile at him again, like she had when they were young.

Powers said his goodbyes and headed for the door, giving Geno a final nod as he reached it. He said,

"Whatever you need to do to get Bliss to approve those plans, do it. We can't move forward without it."

Whatever it took might mean just that, ambushing her on her way to work or parking on her apartment doorstep. Geno felt the ill ease awaken the acid in his stomach and reached into his pocket for antacids. Was it any wonder his insides were tied in knots when he had to break through Agnes's distrusting blockade?

Chapter 18

He hadn't heard from her all week, not since she'd all but punched him in the nose for an imagined slight to Leonora. He stopped in the spa a couple of times, but she always insisted she was too busy to talk. He offered to spend time with Leonora again, but Agnes declined his help.

And Powers leaned heavily on his case about getting the design changes approved. Time was money. Was it any wonder he felt stressed out?

Desperation brought him to her door on Saturday night. Geno rocked on his heels, looking up at Agnes's windows. They were lit, all of them, contrasting with the darkened retail shops below. He thought he saw a curtain shift, and he wondered if Leonora watched the view. It was a window to the world, and it sat at Leonora's feet.

If only her life wasn't limited in any way. It wasn't the first time he'd had this wish, but it had become more urgent and more real now that he saw her growing up. But, as Agnes pointed out, he'd had his chance, and he'd blown it.

What he wouldn't give to turn the clock back and make a different decision. Still, he firmly believed that you made choices at each crossroads in your life, and if you had do-overs and made different selections, you would be a different person from who you were today. Would that option be better or worse?

Behind him, Lucky huffed noisily in the truck, hanging his big head out the passenger window and whining a high-pitched and mournful chorus.

"You can't come up, boy. I shouldn't be long. Take a nap. You always need another one."

The dog sighed again and scratched his nails against the seat as if trying to make it into a comfortable bed. Then he exhaled strongly enough to raise the hairs on the back of Geno's neck. Lucky always had a flair for the dramatic, and that usually made Geno smile. But not tonight.

Deciding hesitation would get him nowhere, he lifted his hand and pressed the bell next to the door. He couldn't hear anything, and he wasn't sure if it worked or not. Knocking probably wouldn't, since the door at the top of the stairs was closed. He gave Agnes a few minutes to respond, and when she didn't, he pressed again, holding it down this time. Then he stepped back and watched the windows for a reaction.

He saw a shadow move behind the curtains, and by its height, he guessed it was Agnes. But no one opened the door at the top, and the stairway stayed dark.

She was avoiding him. She saw the truck out front and she didn't want to talk with him. On a personal level, he couldn't blame her. But this was business. One more time, and he would leave her alone. Maybe Powers would have better luck.

He put his thumb to the doorbell and left it there, holding on to it for a good five seconds. Releasing it, he stared through the clear glass door up into the darkness.

Someone hurled the door to the apartment open and sudden light glared in his eyes. A figure appeared outlined in the brilliant light, standing still at the top of the stairs. Then it began marching down in rapid steps, a long skirt flowing around legs that seemed determined to pound through the wood in agitation.

Agnes threw open the outer door and stared at him, one hand on her hip and the other holding the door open a crack.

"What do you want, Geno?" Animosity heated her words and irritation showed in her tense posture.

"I'm sorry to bother you at home, Agnes, but I need you to sign off on the design changes. The owner won't move forward until you approve them. We're at a stalemate."

"Now? We have to do it now?"

She still sounded angry, though it took him a minute to realize she didn't appear to be directing her wrath at him.

It was then that he looked down, seeing bright red toenails peeking out of fuzzy slippers. The long skirt wasn't a skirt at all, but a robe of some kind, and it looked soft and warm. Agnes had pulled up her hair in a sloppy knot on the top of her head, and her face was devoid of make-up. Her skin glowed almost as much as her eyes, and she looked years younger.

She sighed, a resolved sound that told him he wasn't winning any extra credit points by trying to do this on her evening off.

"It won't take long," he assured her, though his thinking was getting a little vague as he noted creamy skin showing where the robe slid a little lower down her shoulder.

She sighed again, and opened the door wider. "Come up. I'm getting ready for a bath, but I haven't filled the tub yet, so that's the only thing saving your ass right now. Give me the designs and tell me where to sign."

He glanced back at Lucky and commanded the dog to stay once more.

"You brought the dog? You can't leave him out there by himself. He could run away. Someone might dognap him. Bring him up."

He spun again in surprise, and she stood three steps above him, her hands lifting the bottom of the robe out of the way of her feet. Shapely calves carried goose bumps where the colder air from outside swirled through the stairwell.

"Are you sure?"

She gave him an exasperated sigh. "Yes, bring Lucky along. The more the merrier."

He hadn't been thinking about the dog when he asked. His blood pounded loudly inside his head, and he wondered if she could hear it too. But she turned away and continued up the stairs, and he watched her graceful sway until she reached the top. When she looked back over her shoulder as if wondering what took him so long, he fumbled the papers in his arms and turned away, unwilling for her to catch him staring.

God, she was beautiful. Up until they were about twelve, she was gangly and precocious, a tomboy through and through. She had more skinned knees and bruises than he did, because she took more risks. He always envied her that ability to try anything simply because it was there.

In their teens, she'd blossomed. Her petite height accentuated her curves as they formed, until she was one of the best-stacked girls in their high school class. Even on the fringes of the popular crowd, she had a following of her own. Most times, when she crooked her little finger at a guy, he came running.

In contrast, Geno had been clumsy and shy and lacking in social skills. Girls tended to go out with him because they lacked other choices. Agnes went out with him a few times out of pity. He was sure it was pity, because why would a girl who could have anyone settle for him?

"Are you coming, Geno? I don't want this to take all night."

He shook his head to clear it, turning back to the truck and grabbing Lucky's leash. The dog was only too happy to have a new adventure, and he leaped out of the truck window and landed on the pavement with a grace that belied his huge size. With Geno in tow, he proceeded up the stairs as if he did this every day of his life.

At the top, Agnes held the door open, dropping a hand to Lucky's head as he entered the apartment. After Geno walked through the door, Agnes shut it with a decidedly deliberate crash. The dog never glanced back, simply walking to a rug in the middle of the living room, spinning in a tight circle, and lying down with a contented sigh. He was snoring before Geno had a chance to blink.

"Where's Leonora? Is she sleeping already?" He scanned the room for the little girl. He longed to see her again. It scared him how much.

Behind him, Agnes gave a huff of emotion he couldn't identify. "I doubt she's sleeping. She's over at her best friend's house. When they get together, there's a lot of giggling and laughing and movies and popcorn, and very little sleep. She loves it. But she never comes home rested."

Geno turned slowly, taking in the space decorated in bright colors and odd combinations. Chaos reigned supreme, from fanciful fabrics in bold prints to mismatched pillows on the furniture. Every space had stuff on it, thought what everything was, he wasn't sure. Framed posters filled the walls, and the small kitchen off to the side held counters crammed with appliances and jars and bottles. It looked like Agnes and Leonora had barely moved in, except he knew they'd lived here for at least a couple of years.

"Geno? The plans?"

He started, remembering why he was here. There was so much color here, so much Agnes, that he felt overwhelmed. He didn't want to feel this swamped by violently mixed emotions. He'd had enough of them nine years ago to last him a lifetime.

He pulled the roll of blueprints out from under his arm and slid off the rubber bands holding them together. Unrolling the pages, he looked round for a flat surface to display them. The only space remotely vacant was the dining table, and he crossed the room in a couple of strides to try to clear enough space.

Agnes came up next to him and helped him move napkins and condiments and a stack of books that looked like Leonora's schoolwork.

"She has to carry that many books?" The load looked enormous, almost as tall as the girl herself. "How many hours of homework does she have a night?"

"It isn't too bad. And she loves most of it. She's very smart, much smarter than you'd think, given her genes."

Geno remained silent, wondering if she meant the remark as a taunt, waiting for him to comment.

"She could probably skip a grade this year, but I don't want to set her up for failure. She's already smaller than most kids her age, but the fact that she's smart makes up for it a little bit. In an older class, she'll stand out even more because of how she looks. Kids can be so cruel. I don't want to push her and have her get hurt in the process."

She continued moving items out of the way. A pink flamingo coffee mug. A salt and pepper set in the shape of dancing yellow pigs. Zebra striped paper napkins. Crayons, pencils, and pens, along with colored construction paper and wooden sticks that probably belonged in frozen desserts. It was a mishmash of items and colors, similar to the chaos in the rest of the apartment.

How did they live like this? The dish drainer by the sink was stacked high with mismatched plates in bright colors. Two doors leading off the main room stood open, and through one, Geno could see towels hanging askew on bars, each of them in a different primary color. A glimpse into the bedroom indicated similar vibrant hues. And clothes were everywhere.

"You know, there are larger apartments in town. I've renovated a couple of them over the shops, and they're much more spacious than this. You two don't have to live on top of each other."

He wasn't sure why he said it. It wasn't as if he had the right to influence Agnes's actions. He'd lost that privilege a long time ago.

She frowned at him, settling her hands on her hips as if she was about to lecture him. Her eyes flashed and she tapped a foot on the floor, the fuzzy slipper bobbing up and down like an agitated pink rabbit.

"If you must know, those places are expensive. We're fine here. We're saving to buy a house. I want Leonora to have a yard to play in and a swing, if she still needs it." Her fury faded into worry so quickly, it was like a curtain drew across her face.

"I bet it will be a great house." He didn't know what else to say. If he apologized to her, she'd probably boot him out the door, and he'd again have missed an opportunity to spend time with her. He missed her. Oh, and the plans. They needed to go over the plans.

His gaze slipped down to the robe, gapping a little lower than before. In the shadowy opening, he could see the edges of her breasts. Agnes at sixteen had been built. Agnes at almost thirty with the substance bearing a child brought was voluptuous and abundant.

And she smelled good, like spices and something he couldn't name, something bright and fresh like new sap in old pines. The scent of her took him back, back to school bleachers and fast food runs and movie theaters where the darkness allowed him the luxury of leaning closer for a sniff.

Of course, as they got older, she started dating, and their fun times were reserved for the nights she didn't have a guy on the hook. She never seemed to realize she'd caught one and held on to him from the time they were six years old.

"Can you believe we made it? I had my doubts, you know. If you hadn't helped me with algebra, I bet I'd be held back this year."

Agnes played with the fabric fringing a skirt that was, in his opinion, too short. Her sweater was a multicolored marvel of yarn that her grandmother knitted for her. Nothing matched, not her boots or the skirt or the sweater. And she looked amazing. If he swallowed his tongue, he wouldn't be surprised. The way she sucked on the milkshake through the thick white straw made his ears burn. He was sure he blushed, because his thoughts about his best friend were anything but chaste.

"Oh look, there's Conrad with his friends. And that cheerleader. God, don't you hate them? She's so plastic, so fake, and he doesn't see it. He needs a real woman to take care of him. He needs me."

She swirled the straw in the shake, but her eyes were glued on the group across the diner. Geno thought his insides would burst from her actions. She didn't notice his distress, though. He didn't think she ever did.

"Agnes, you're a girl. He's two years older than you. He's graduating and going to that big name college. What would you two have in common?"

When her eyes swung to his, he saw the flash of anger on her features. If smoke started wafting out of her ears, it wouldn't have surprised him.

"I'm tired of being compared to kids our age. I'm much more mature than they are. The guys in our grade don't have a clue how to treat a lady, and they certainly don't have experience. You know, the kind of experience that makes a relationship special."

She emphasized the last word with a sly grin that didn't include him. It was just as well, he supposed. He had little experience, but he doubted Agnes had any more.

"I'm going to be his girlfriend someday, just you wait. Conrad's the one for me. Why, I might even lose my virginity to him. I'm sure he knows how to treat a woman right."

He avoided covering his ears by sitting on his hands. Trying to block out the words was already a lost cause, because the picture in his mind of Agnes locked in a torrid embrace with Conrad, the kind of clinch you saw in the movies rated R, already played in his mind.

"Yeah, he's going to be the one. Then we'll get married and have a wonderful life, Conrad and me."

She returned to circling the straw in the milkshake, and this time, when she pulled on the straw with a knowing smile on her face, he closed his eyes to block out the image of her lips pursed and full.

That was a dozen years ago. He'd learned about life and relationships since then, not that all of this knowledge was useful. His ex-wife made sure he knew about every one of his shortcomings. He'd worked on those too. He had things he could show Agnes, though he doubted he was in her league.

"I like what you've done here with the design. I hadn't thought about reconfiguring the space and putting the entrance in the new suite, but this works much better. In fact, this puts the services that deserve a peaceful environment out of the way of the hustle and bustle. And look at that great atrium area. I can see how I could decorate that for the holidays, or even seasonally."

Geno blinked his mind back into focus. Agnes bent over the prints, humming in a low tone he remembered. It meant approval. When that kicked his heart up faster, he was powerless to slow it down.

"Geno, are you paying attention? I like this. My only concern is venting the hair stations. They will be open to the area above. How can we make sure everything doesn't stink like chemicals?"

He shifted on his feet, thinking of the obvious answer. "Don't use any chemicals."

She stared at him like he'd grown a second head.

"What do you think perms are, or hair color? They're chemicals. The nail products are more of the same. So how are you going to vent this area?"

Her finger tapped the paper, and her foot tapped along with it. He sensed her growing impatience. Her lips parted and her tongue darted out to run over them.

His body acted before his mind caught up to it. His hand reached out and captured her finger, stopping the impatient tapping. It surprised her enough to make her foot stop tapping too. And he pulled her into his arms so that he could settle his mouth on those lovely lips.

The shock of contact rivaled the jolt he'd received from that live wire a few years ago. It was so good, better than his dreams, even better than last weekend when he brought her home. It was everything and nothing like what he imagined, and he had a very vivid imagination.

Agnes shifted and made a mewing sound. He was acting like an animal, and it distressed her. What was he thinking? Whatever they'd once had or might have had, it wasn't who they were today.

He released her lips gently, though it cost him every ounce of willpower to do it. His desire raged against the sudden loss. He wanted to pull her back tight against him and plunder her mouth for hours, if not days. But if he'd learned one lesson very well over the past few years, it was how to tell his body no.

With eyes tightly closed, Agnes seemed to hold her breath as he gripped her upper arms. She might fall if he let go completely, he reasoned. If this allowed his fingers to linger and stroke oh-so-subtly, that's the price he'd have to pay. She finally blinked open with a wide-eyed look that had him confused and flustered and more than a little horny. Bleary eyes met his and held.

She cleared her throat with a whimper, and he wondered how close that sound would be to her moans of pleasure. He was sure she'd moan. She was vocal about everything, even things that didn't require noise to express an opinion. Would she scream his name if he made her come?

Her eyes rounded further, giving her face an owl-like expression as her lips parted on a slight pant of air. She stepped back, and as she did, her face fell into a sadness he recognized. He'd disappointed her again. It wasn't the first time, and he doubted it would be his last. It pained him to admit it, but he didn't know how to please her, not like he could when they were young and life was simple.

Her face shifted away and he lost sight of her expression behind waves of disheveled hair. She smelled good, too good, like promises and sins and yes, sexiness. It must be his overactive imagination. He tried a silent meditative chant to clear his mind, but he couldn't hear himself think when he was this close to an almost naked and tousled Agnes Amendola.

"Thanks Geno."

She confused him. Was she thanking him for kissing her? As if he needed any excuse or provocation to do that.

"For what?" His voice sounded strange, rough and uneven to his own ears.

"For being nice to me. For caring about Leonora. For everything. Just, thanks."

She dropped down to the couch, picking up a green and yellow tie-dyed pillow and holding it front of herself like a shield. She looked miserable. He took a hesitant step closer over the sleeping dog.

"I do care, you know. About you. About Leonora. That's never changed."

If she heard his words, she gave not sign of it. Hugging the pillow tighter to her middle, she stared at the pictures on the shelf, the ones of Leonora growing up. They cataloged years of new beginnings he'd missed, and all because he'd been a selfish ass who was too proud to see the beauty in what Agnes offered to him.

Another cautious step brought him to stand in front of her, but she didn't look up. He thought he noticed a glint of tears on her cheeks. He hated it when she cried. Nothing could turn him into mush faster than the sight of her unhappiness.

"I know you've always cared, Geno. Even when I was angry with you, I knew."

Her distant words were spoken so softly, he wasn't sure at first that she'd said them. Did he image them in his head? But she lifted her face to his, her eyes swimming with wet droplets clinging to her lashes. One hand let go of the pillow and reached out to him, and he took it, pressing it gently. She tugged, and he sat down next to her.

Her hair smelled like the banks of flowers draping over an old stonewall in his yard. She snuggled against him, and his blood pulsed in an increasing tempo. This wasn't good. He had his arms full of Agnes, and all he wanted to do was turn her face to his and let his lips take over for his turbulent mind.

"Thank you for being such a good friend to me, Geno. It's good to have you back in our lives, mine and Leonora's."

She nestled into him, wrapping her arms around his waist and hugging him against her. And there was nothing he could do but put his arms around her body and pull her in tighter as well.

And he sat like that, his cheek resting against the crown of her head, giving her an occasional whisper of a kiss, as her breathing slowed and leveled off. She trusted him enough to fall asleep in his arms, and damn if that wasn't the most amazing feeling in the world.

Chapter 19

As kids, this is how they'd often end up when one of them felt upset. As teenagers, those clenches were heavy with tension because of that undercurrent of energy she now knew was sexual frustration and hormones. When she awoke Sunday morning from the most refreshing sleep she'd had in years, his arms hadn't loosened, and he snored in counterpoint to the dog on the floor.

She didn't want to move to break the spell. She snuggled closer and drifted, alternating between contentment and worry. He held her in sleep like that for two more hours, until she realized the time and shot up for the shower, mumbling her thanks and slamming the bathroom door. She winced even now, thinking about his astonished face and his confused questions.

"Mother, I think Geno is very nice. I think you should go out with him."

How the child knew the direction of her thoughts was a mystery. Leonora sat at the small table, a book propped up in front of her and her eyes on the page, even as she shredded Bliss's heart with her words. Next to her, colored pencils lay across a pad of drawing paper. As the mood struck her, her daughter doodled on the pages. Bliss had to admit the drawings were good, but maybe she was prejudiced.

"It's Mr. Altimari, young lady." Though she knew he'd already invited the child to use his first name.

"Or you should go out with Noah. He likes you too."

"Dr. Kinkead, Leonora." Bliss tried to make her correction sound offhand, not like she was aghast at her daughter's matchmaking activities.

"He said I could call him Noah." She lifted the spoonful of cereal to her mouth and chewed it, her eyes giving an exaggerated roll. When she finished, she added, "You need to date someone."

Emphasis on the last word made Bliss roll her eyes, only catching herself when she realized she probably looked exactly like her little girl. She didn't say anything, continuing to stir the sugar and cream in her coffee as if her life depended on it.

"Let's see, who else could you date? There's that man who owns the shop with the olive oil. I'm not sure he's as nice as Geno or Noah, but he's single. I think there's a teacher at school who's single too. Or maybe one of your clients has a brother. Who do you like better, Noah or Geno?"

At this pop question in the stream of other distractions, Leonora's eyes locked on Bliss's face with laser precision. Knowing that any response would generate a long discussion with no good conclusion, Bliss went for a distraction of her own.

"Would you and Charlotte like to go to the movies today? There's that new dog adventure, or we could see something scary. You like scary movies. Does Charlotte?"

Leonora frowned at her and put her spoon down with a distinct clatter of metal against dishware. "You're trying to change the subject," she said with obvious disapproval. She picked up a blue pencil and added the color to the drawing, before setting it aside with a satisfied shake of her head.

Bliss gave a putout sigh of her own. "Sweetheart, I don't need to date anyone. I'm happy with my life as it is. I have you, I have my shop, and that's enough." Even though it wasn't. If she gave the idea honest consideration, she was lonely. And it wasn't the kind of lonely that could be filled with a nine-year-old child.

"Charlotte doesn't like them," Leonora said, jumping around between topics.

"Okay, the dog one then." Bliss took a restorative sip of her coffee and wondered how long it would be before she couldn't keep up with her daughter at all.

Leonora shook her head, toying with her cereal again. "No, we're going to the club to swim. Then I'm going to stay over at Charlotte's for a sleepover. Noah's going to cook us burgers, like an early birthday present for me. I bet he'd be happy if you came over too, Mommy."

She ducked behind her book, but not before Bliss saw the sly smile on her face.

"I doubt that very much, Leonora. I wasn't invited. Besides, I have plans." Yeah, plans to curl up and ponder why her life wasn't enough the way it was.

"What plans? Are you going on a date and you didn't tell me?" Leonora all but jumped out of the chair and raced over to hug Bliss's waist. The fingers on her good hand dug in and held on tight, and the fist of her other hand tried to do the same.

Yes, that was one of the reasons things weren't enough anymore. Her daughter was growing up, and there was little Bliss could do to shield her from the disappointments that being different would bring. She could do some things to make her daughter happy, even if it meant exposing her to the possibility things wouldn't work out.

"What do you want for your birthday, sweetheart?" She ran one hand over her daughter's hair, long and wavy as her own had been at that age, the only difference being the little girl's blonder color. If only that was the sole difference between them.

Muffled against her body, Leonora's small voice held sadness. "I want you to be happy, Mommy. And I want to be able to do everything."

Those were two things Bliss couldn't promise. But there was something she could deliver. It had been all her daughter talked about for two long weeks, when the art teacher at school sent flyers home to parents.

She rocked her daughter a little before the girl pulled away and turned back to the table, resignation in the carriage of her body and slow dragging steps. It still broke Bliss's heart to watch her sometimes. She'd walk with a little unevenness for the rest of her life.

"I know I can't do everything. I'm different, and that means I can't do things."

She dropped back into her chair and put her head on her book with true dramatic flair. The girl should try out for a school play. Or go to art camp to feed that creative energy. Taking chances and trying new things didn't need to mean risk and danger. They could result in triumph and happy beginnings.

And Bliss needed to pull up her big girl panties and try the same.

Geno remembered the story on the evening news last fall. Robotic hands for kids like Leonora, made by their parents. They linked up with computer specialists through some kind of network. The results weren't advanced and their movements were limited, but it gave the children a chance to use both hands to eat a meal or play sports. The beauty of the design, though, was in its inexpensive materials and the ability of someone to build one in their own home.

He'd hit a gold mine after only a few hours of online research. A website offered designs for simple robotic hands made with a 3D printer, and the instructions were available to anyone. He scrutinized the descriptions and realized he'd found exactly what he wanted to give Leonora for her birthday. If that curried favor with Agnes as well, all the better.

It took him two evenings to order all the components, the software for his computer, the 3D printer, and the special plastic that would be layered by the printer. Other supplies came in a kit, and he ordered that too, unwilling to waste time in finding local sources when Leonora's birthday was so near.

The Cyborg Beast. He loved the name. It made him believe a kid would think this was cool, like becoming part bionic. The plastic to make it came in a rainbow of colors, and he thought he'd ask Leonora what her favorite colors were, so he could make the hand in those. Once he had the fitting right, he'd make her as many as she wanted. And when she outgrew it, he'd print her another.

What Agnes would make of this, he wasn't sure. He heard her agonize over Leonora's inability to do everything other children did. She had a right to try, though. Who knew what talents she might discover? It would be the perfect tenth birthday present.

The place to start, though, was the difficulty. He needed to measure Leonora's good hand to program the software, but he wanted the gift to be a surprise. When Agnes was only too grateful to have Leonora come next door for a while, he knew he'd have his chance. Settling the girl at his worktable, he retrieved his tape measure and hoped he could engage her in the process.

Leonora watched him for a time, chattering about her friend Charlotte and the spelling test they both aced. She wasn't fond of math, but she was good at that too. When she ran out of school topics, she quieted, and he let the silence sink in.

"Can't you remember things?" Her question popped out of the blue.

Leonora frowned at him when he turned around, the wrinkling of her forehead so like her mother that Geno almost had to laugh. When she tilted her head to the side as he delayed his response, he thought she looked prettier than any almost-ten-year-old had a right to be.

"Why do you say that?" He set the end of the tape measure in place against the wall and pulled it out of the spool with a metal rasp.

"You measure something, then you go back and measure it again. You must not remember what you measured before. See?" She flattened her hands in the air in front of herself as if this explained everything, and he thanked karma for presenting him with an opportunity.

"That's a logical conclusion to draw, based on what you see. But what if the real answer is something different?" Now that he had this chance to put his plan into action, he wasn't going to pass it up. "I bet you never heard the old saying, 'measure twice, cut once'."

She shook her head, and he read her curiosity as she leaned closer.

"In olden times, like very, very old times, English carpenters thought it best to measure something twice, to double check things, before they cut a piece of wood. That way, they wouldn't waste material because the cut was wrong, and they wouldn't waste time by having to do things a second time."

She sat quietly, watching him transfer his measurements to the wood he planned to cut. When he returned to the wall to double check the numbers, she walked across the room to watch his actions more closely. She followed him to the wood set on sawhorses and inspected his verification of the measurements. When she nodded with apparent satisfaction, he nodded back.

"You see what I mean? I could have put the first number down wrong and then the board wouldn't fit."

She nodded solemnly. "That's smart. You don't want to waste things. That gets expensive." She picked up the marking pencil in her good hand and toyed with it.

"Thank you for the compliment. Do you want to try it?"

She glanced at the wall and back at the board, frowning once more.

"We'll start with something simple. Here, put your left hand on the paper with your fingers spread out."

She dropped the pencil on the big sketch pad he'd left open on the table, and put her hand down, setting her fingers in an exaggerated spread. "Like this?"

"You don't have to spread your fingers so wide. Like that. Okay, now, I'll trace your hand and your arm."

He ran the pencil between each finger, around her hand, and down her arm on both sides. It gave him an almost perfect set of measurements to create her super-hand. Marking the location of her wrist and knuckles with small dots, he nodded to her that he was done.

"Now, let's measure things. How would you measure the place where your wrist would be?"

Leonora took the straight ruler he casually pushed toward her and accepted the pencil back. She set the ruler in place with deliberate care, the tip of her tongue poking between her lips in concentration. When she had the ruler where she wanted it, she looked up.

"Now what?"

"Write the measurement down next to the wrist. Perfect. Now how about doing the same thing for where your knuckles are?"

She looked at the tracing, then at her hand. With a puzzled pout to her lips, she put her hand back inside the lines. Her face cleared and she smiled, repeating the careful measurement process.

"This is fun. Maybe I can be a carpenter one day."

Her simple statement tightened around his heart in a fierce grip.

"If you want to, *amatissimo*." The grip squeezed harder.

She cocked her head and glanced at him, one eyebrow higher than the other, mimicking another of her mother's favorite quizzical expressions. Playing with the ruler, she asked, "What's that mean?"

He gave her a big smile. He hadn't earned the right to initiate a hug with her, much as he wanted to. "It means precious, because that's what you are."

She stared at him, still playing with the ruler. Then she set it down carefully and put her left hand on his forearm. "You're precious too, Geno."

The sudden stab of pain he felt as his heart burst open bordered on exquisite pleasure, and he wondered if she could see the tears in his eyes.

Chapter 20

Lucky sat at his feet, panting in anticipation. It wouldn't do him any good, but he tried it every time. Geno had long ago decided the dog had a stomach bigger than his body, and a brain the size of a pinhead. He'd fed the dog an enormous bowl of kibble an hour ago, and he'd begun begging for human food almost immediately.

"None for you, and you know that." Geno added seasonings to the last chicken breast, pushing the plate to the back of the counter, out of doggie reach. Lucky wasn't above standing on his hind legs and swiping something when his human wasn't looking. Granted, he never touched the counter, so Geno had to hand it to him for resourcefulness.

Turning back to the cutting board, he pulled an onion forward and grabbed his favorite knife. It was one of his guilty pleasures, cooking an elaborate meal on Saturday night. He'd enjoy it as much as leftovers during the week as he did the first time. Tonight, the medley of vegetables played the starring role alongside twice-baked potatoes and chicken. The cadence of his knife matched the tempo of operatic voices soaring from the stereo. If he hadn't been a finish carpenter, he might have tried his hand at being a chef.

That was something Leonora might never get to try. He wasn't sure why she popped into his head. His time with the girl had been limited, but even with those short hours together, he was hooked as he'd been when she was a baby. The child clamped on to his heart tighter than any vise grip.

It wasn't only the girl, either. Her mother was never far from his thoughts. Morning meditation tended to be distracting, specifically as memories of Agnes's scent seemed to fill his deep breaths. And that created other pressing issues. Cold showers dispelled the physical ache, but not the mental anguish.

He could have handled things differently years ago. He should have. It wasn't that he owed Agnes, but she was his best friend, and when she'd needed him the most, he let her down. She had relied on him, and then she cut him loose when he hadn't stood up to the pressure. Tears burned his eyes, and he couldn't blame the onion.

He concentrated on making his cuts uniform and thin, the protest of produce beneath the blade blending with Rossini's notes in the songs. Lucky still panted, examining the space for any stray crumbs. Then he suddenly shifted to a sitting position, his panting forgotten as he ears pricked up and he tilted his head to stare out the window. Dusk had almost fallen as Geno prepared the food, but there was still enough light to see a car pull in the driveway and disappear into the parking area in front of the balcony.

"We didn't expect any visitors, did we, Lucky?" The dog sounded a loud whine in response.

Washing his hands and wiping them on a paper towel, Geno blinked rapidly to turn off the faucet of tears. It wouldn't do to answer the door crying like a child, but the onions gave him a good excuse. Emptying his mind of thoughts of Agnes was harder.

Lucky gave a delighted bark as the brisk tattoo of a knock sounded on the front door. Friend or foe, it was the same. The knock sounded again, louder this time, as Lucky gave another woof and sniffed madly at the bottom of the door. His big tail swished from side to side, picking up speed until it knocked against the wall.

"Hold on," Geno called out, taking a pass at his eyes with the towel.

He put a hand on the door, considering the foolishness of having no peephole in the solid wood. He didn't recognize the sound of the car, and in the darkness, it was impossible to see who it was behind the glare of headlights. He was unprepared, and he hated that feeling.

Lucky, tail still wagging, gave another joyous bark and scratched a paw at the door. Heartened by the dog's response, Geno pulled the door open and nearly got rapped on the chest by a hand raised for another round of knocking.

Big brown eyes looked up at him in sudden surprise, like she expected him to be someone else. Her hair hung down her back, pulled back with a single big clip. Agnes dropped her hand, grazing him below the belt as she did so, and every nerve ending not already on full alert by thoughts of her came to stuttering life with her sudden presence.

"Geno, sorry, you startled me." She snatched that wayward hand to her own chest as if to hold in a fast beating heart. He swore he could hear it. No, that was the pounding of his own crazed heart he heard, the pulse picking up in tempo in his ears.

"Did you expect someone else?" He didn't intend to make it sound like a joke, but his brain wasn't working right. Agnes was here, at his house. On the inventory of the people unlikely to be at his door, she was high on the list.

Her hand guided his eyes to someplace he shouldn't be staring. Hiding inside a warm coat, her curves were tucked into a sweater in a rich color of blue, her jeans were filled with precision, and the heels on her boots only brought her height up to his shoulder. She was perfect in every way.

And she was frowning at him.

"No, I expected to see you, but I didn't expect you to yank the door open like I was an intruder. Am I disturbing you?" Her hand dropped to the strap of the big purse hanging off one shoulder.

"How did you find me?" Why couldn't he get control of his voice?

Agnes's frown deepened as she tilted her head to one side, and in it, he saw the echo of the gesture Leonora used.

"I'm sorry, I didn't know your location was a secret. I asked Serena, and she didn't have your address, so she called Tess, who looked it up in Powers' computer. Satisfied?"

She sounded as out of sorts as he felt. He blinked rapidly, willing the remnants of tears to dry up. If he thought he could fool her, the idea didn't last long.

Her face softened and her expression changed into one of concern. "Are you crying? What's wrong?"

Her hand reached out and closed on his forearm, and the sudden contact sent a bolt of lust through him. It shouldn't be this way. He wasn't supposed to want Agnes, but his body had other ideas. Attempting to set up a distracting chant in his brain did nothing about the pulsing of his body.

Unable to form a coherent thought, he mumbled, "Onions."

Confusion washed over her face and she stared at him more closely. Then she sniffed, and the confusion cleared on a wave of enlightenment.

"Sorry, I didn't think about the fact that it's dinnertime. Are you busy? Can I discuss something with you? I need advice."

She brushed past him, and he didn't want to inhale the spicy aroma of Agnes. He thought he wouldn't be able to over the onions. But he did, and he could. Even the most casual of touches made his heart race fast, and he swore his eyes crossed.

She stopped to give Lucky a brisk rubdown, and the dog rolled over to expose his belly in delight. He was such a dog-whore. Of course, Geno didn't think he himself was much better. He'd expose his vulnerabilities to Agnes in a heartbeat and with pride, if she seemed the least bit interested.

Straightening, she examined the produce on the counter and scanned the rest of the kitchen.

"You have company coming. I'm sorry. I should have called." She started backing toward the door.

He wasn't sure what gave her that idea. Then his glance landed on the meat.

"No one's coming. It's just me and Lucky."

He felt slow and stupid, standing in the gaping doorway, and he reached out to make a blind grab for the door to shut it. Once it closed, he turned the lock. As if she'd noticed he hadn't needed to unlock it to open it for her, one of her perfectly shaped eyebrows raised in question.

She walked slowly through the kitchen, her glance moving from the flames dancing in the stone fireplace to the big picture window overlooking the forest. Her purse still hung on her shoulder and her coat remained on. This registered slowly in the thick sawdust of his brain, and he realized he hadn't asked her to stay.

"Where's Leonora?" His throat felt parched and he wondered if his face betrayed the riot pumping through his mind. At least with the girl around, he had a barrier. Without that, his thoughts turned racy and wild.

Facing the pines and newly budding trees, Agnes said, "She's at a sleepover again. I'm beginning to think she likes Charlotte's house more than ours. Of course, Charlotte has her own room and a father who indulges the girls in whatever they want. If I didn't know better, I'd say that Noah is trying to woo me through my little girl." In the window, he saw the distorted reflection of her wry smile.

Wait, Noah was trying to woo her? No way.

He stepped forward without conscious thought, his mind on denial and his body slipping into protective mode. His hands closed on her shoulders as he pressed against her back, and if the move surprised her, the expression on her face didn't give it away. In fact, she looked as heated as he felt.

"You shouldn't date Noah." The words screeched out of him like hard wood through the table saw. He made an effort to loosen his fingers and let go, but the move turned into a caress before he could stop himself. His body seemed to have intentions all its own.

She looked honestly puzzled, her head tilted to the side in consideration as she watched him in the window's reflection.

"I'm not dating anyone."

Relief flowed through him, a pure and simple river of emotion. It made him spin her around to face him, and he dropped a lightning kiss to her mouth as she opened it to say something more. The taste of her rivaled the best meal he'd ever eaten. And he pushed her away before he gorged himself.

Stepping back, he waved his hands like a clown and stuttered a meaningless response. "That's good, really good."

Agnes stared at him, her gaze traveling the length of his body until it came to rest on his bare feet. If she wondered about that in the chilly April evening, she didn't comment, but he noticed her focus sharpening. He had the sudden urge to hide his toes. And if she noticed the tent formed by the pulsing arousal in his sweatpants beneath the white of his apron, well, he wasn't sure what to do about that give-away either.

He turned around slowly, trying to focus on anything to make sense of thoughts that were out of control. His eyes fell on Lucky, sitting patiently in the middle of the small kitchen with his head tilted like Agnes as if he too was trying to figure things out.

Damned if Geno knew. No, that wasn't true. He knew exactly what was wrong. Agnes was here in his house and he didn't have any defense against the raging need to grab her and hold on. This time, he wouldn't screw it up.

"Have you eaten? Want to stay for dinner? There's plenty of food."

When she said yes and he heard her purse hit the floor, he wondered how he'd have the endurance to resist her.

This situation confused her. She'd rushed over here, intent on asking for Geno's advice. Okay, not exactly completely rushed, since she'd taken time to change her clothes into something more stylishly casual, and if she checked her make-up and fixed that too, who wouldn't? And maybe she wasn't completely honest about the advice for Leonora, because she also wanted some of Geno for herself.

What she didn't expect were sucker punches of emotions he brought out in her. Seeing his face wet with tears nearly undid her. It brought back memories she'd rather avoid thinking about.

Then his unnerved confusion. She could see it in his face and hear it in the wobble of his voice. Telling her not to date Noah was absurd. No one told her what to do. But in her heart, she felt a little twinge of satisfied excitement that he would try.

And those bare feet. What was it about his feet that heated her through faster than her best blow dryer? If the pounding of her pulse was any indication, she was more turned on than she had a right to be. Geno was off limits. He'd told her so nine years ago, and she never forgot his words.

"I can't do it, Agnes. I can't. You need to stay away from me."

She begged him to change his mind, if not for her, then for Leonora. Who could resist a vulnerable little baby? With tears streaming down his face, Geno did.

"I can't take care of the two of you. I'm barely making ends meet the way it is. Hell, I'm still living with my mother. Do you want to ruin our friendship forever? Because that's what it will come to. You and I will end up hating each other because of the struggle."

Yes, he'd told her so nine years ago, but he'd kissed her now. He seemed to have no problem inviting her to stay. In fact, he looked eager, if she read his choppy motions and waving hands correctly. Geno never got flustered, and yet he certainly was now.

"Can I take your coat?" He reached out for her shoulders, and she swiftly shed the jacket to avoid his potent touch. It felt like an electric shock, like the time she boggled a hair dryer into a sink full of water. Sputtering arcs hissed and fizzled, snapping off the power in the salon faster than the switch by the door. Her fingers stung for days afterwards.

He took the jacket from her and crossed the room to a door hidden in the paneling. When he turned inside the closet, she had a chance to admire the way the apron ties crossed his back at the waist and the white fabric framed his butt. No man had a right to a rear end that looked this great.

Of course, what was hidden under the front of his apron was borderline illegal too. She remembered the game they used to play before they knew any better.

"I'll show you mine if you show me yours." She taunted him with her best singsong voice, the one that made her brothers yell in frustration because she was usually teasing them without mercy. On this scorching hot summer day, she and Geno had played in the open fire hydrant at the end of the next street, one of hordes of kids trying to stay cool as the sun beat down.

Finally bored and feeling the burn of too much sun, they retreated to his house. His mother had left them cookies and juice and wasn't due home from work for a couple of hours. Agnes voted for his house over hers because the constant din of her brothers fighting and yelling made her mad. Her wet clothes itched, though, and she didn't see anything wrong with stripping in front of her best friend, even if he was a boy.

Besides, what did she have to show off? She was thirteen and her chest was still as flat as her mother's ironing board. Her knobby knees sported scrapes and cuts, since she never backed down when it came to playing dodge ball or climbing the few trees in the neighborhood park. It wasn't like she hadn't seen it all before, after all. She had big brothers, and they had no problem sporting wood around the house. See, she even knew what it was called when they got that way.

"Agnes, do you know what you're saying? You'll have to confess that to Father Mark. Getting naked if you're not married is a sin."

She laughed, thinking what a wet blanket Geno could be sometimes. The kitchen windows faced the untended little patch of backyard, and no one could see inside. Turning her back on him as her laughter grew louder, she pulled off her tank top and training bra and tossed them over her shoulder at him. He didn't say anything, and her laughter faltered a little. But she was never one to back down, not ever.

Pulling off her shorts, she sent them flying, hearing a wet plop as they hit the far wall by the closed door to the dining room. Putting her hands on her hips, her bravado nearly failed her, but she spun around, ready to call Geno the biggest coward in the world.

She stood alone in the kitchen. No Geno. Her clothes lay in growing puddles on the linoleum. Where did he go? He was such a coward, and she was going to call him that as soon as she found him. But she couldn't go racing around the house almost naked.

She wasn't sure who she was madder at, Geno for running away from her dare, or herself for even doing it. Now that she considered her actions, she was a little embarrassed. The girls in her class and even some of the younger ones had boobs already. What if he told everyone there was no need for her to wear that training bra?

As she reached for her shorts, the swinging door to the dining room opened a few inches, and a towel appeared in the crack. With a swing, it flew across the room and hit her square in the face.

"There, you can dry off." Geno's voice cracked from high pitch to a sudden rough low before he cleared his throat. "I'm going to my room. Don't follow me. I'll come back downstairs."

She sighed on the memory of his gruff tone. She hadn't seen anything that day. By the time Geno came back downstairs ten minutes later, she'd dried her body roughly and wrung out her clothes over the sink before putting them back on. He'd changed clothes, and hers were damp dry. He asked her if she wanted to go get an ice cream bar from the corner store, and she readily agreed. It was as if her taunting had never happened.

It wasn't until three years later that either one of them ever brought up the dare again. But this time, it was his turn.

The city pool was crowded with teenagers. It was the annual picnic at the end of their second year in high school. The blue bikini she wore wasn't a garment her mother even knew she owned. She'd snuck off with a couple of girls from her class to buy it at Filene's bargain basement downtown. Her mother would tan her behind, send her to confession, and ground her for years if she knew about it.

She had to flaunt her assets, though. Anything to capture the attention of Conrad Walsh. He starred in every sport he played, and he had a different girlfriend for each one too. Or more like one each night of the week for each sport he played. He was the best looking boy in their school and soon he'd be going to college. If she could just get up the courage to drop her cover-up, Conrad would fall in lust instantly, and then he'd fall in love as hard as she had.

"Agnes, your mother will drop dead if she sees you in that."

She glanced over at Geno standing a few feet away. He braced his back against the side of the pool, uncaring about the commotion around them. He didn't fit in with any specific crowd, but everyone seemed to accept his easy-going ways. He'd outgrown his shyness, but he didn't make a statement. He was the guy everyone liked.

He'd grown in other ways too. Even as they completed their sophomore year, he was already six feet tall, one of the tallest boys in their class. His shoulders filled out a little, and while he didn't play sports, he had the body of a lean athlete. If she hadn't known him since she was a kid, she might think he was cute, in a laid-back kind of way. His long swim trunks and soaked t-shirt left little to her imagination, and the little she couldn't see made her curiosity poke at her. But this was Geno, after all. He was like a brother to her, and she shouldn't be the least bit curious about his equipment.

She clutched her long shirt tighter around her, knowing that if it got the least bit wet, it wouldn't hide the blue underneath or her burgeoning curves. Because she'd filled out too. And thank god, it was going to all the right places. She had boobs, and she loved them. Her wider hips, not so much, and she dieted like every one of her peers to be model slender.

Geno lounged closer in the water, a lazy expression in his eyes and a smile on his face. His voice, deep and husky now, sent a shiver through her when he said, "From my vantage point, though, it's a great view. You fill that suit out in all the right places, Agnes. You look hot." And his knowing smile grew as he shifted positions and leaned his arms on the edge of the pool.

She was glad someone liked her in this damned suit. She'd paid almost twenty dollars for it. It was probably last year's style, but it was all she could afford. Babysitting didn't earn very much money. Her mother only let her work as the clean-up girl at the local hair salon on Saturday. She sat down on the edge of the pool and let her legs dangle in the water, staring at Conrad once more.

"So, are you ever going to take off that thing and strut your stuff? I bet Conrad would love to see you in all your glory. I know I would."

Geno sounded a little disgusted as he glanced in Conrad's direction. The superstar stood in the middle of a big circle of admirers, and at least four of the older girls were vying for his attention by blatantly flirting. He took turns swinging an arm around each one's shoulders and giving them a kiss.

Damn, she wanted to be on the receiving end of Conrad's kisses. But she'd never worn anything this revealing in public. Hell, she'd even blushed in the privacy of the fitting room at the department store when she tried it on. And besides, Geno was watching, and his attention made her feel a little shy.

"Agnes, you're not getting any younger." Geno's teasing tone sounded closer to her ear, and she turned to find him standing next to her, giving her knee a shove with his elbow. "Show me yours and I'll show you mine. Shirt for shirt. Go on, I dare you."

She looked down into his laughing brown eyes, realizing he would completely do this if she said yes. He had her back, per usual. With a rush of gratitude, she knew he was there for her, even if he didn't understand her crush on the high school hero. If something looked a little put-off in his expression, she couldn't figure out what it might be. She and Geno were just friends.

She reached for the buttons on her cover-up, and Geno chuckled in response. His eyes sparked with good humor and he stood straight, reaching for the hem of his t-shirt.

"Hey, what are you two doing over here? Looks like you need to get wet and join the party."

Agnes felt a flush of annoyance at the sudden appearance of her brother Luke and kept her face turned away. He was part of Conrad's class, and while he wasn't that much older than them, he lorded his advanced years every chance he got. In fact, he delighted in letting Geno and Agnes know they were still fair game for pranks as far as he was concerned.

Luke dove across the few feet of water, splashing as hard as he could. Agnes felt the water hit her front, turning her shirt into transparent tissue and making the bright blue underneath shine like neon. Geno, his head still stuck in the t-shirt as the waves hit, uttered a curse and started to lower his arms.

"Oh yeah, this is too good to pass up." Luke splashed again, diving underwater, and Agnes watched his movements, unable to look away, like seeing an accident about to happen, as he yanked Geno's trunks down around his ankles.

A string of curses spewed from Geno's mouth as he struggled to get free of the shirt. The tight cotton twisted, and she thought about helping him. That is, she considered it until she looked down into the water and her eyes froze.

It was long and pointed upwards like a challenge. Thick at the base, she only glimpsed the flared head as the water distorted her view. Distorted the clear view, that is. She could still see plenty, and all of it made her gasp. She knew every slang word for this particular appendage, and yet she couldn't think of even one. Geno's thing looked grand, and happy, and maybe even a little scary. Woosh.

"Shit, Luke, I am going to kill you." Geno spun around, taking away her great view and offering her another one. His ass. There, she could think of a name for that. It flexed as he reached down, ducking under the cover of water to reach for his trunks and pull them up. It was almost a shame he covered up so fast. He swore some more as he righted his clothes and dove after a crowing Luke, dunking him underwater as they wrestled across the pool.

She shouldn't care, but she sat rooted to the spot by what she'd had a chance to see. He was like a brother to her, and it shouldn't matter. But she hadn't felt this surge of heat when her brothers clowned around the house with things showing. Front or back, Geno Altimari was one fine looking guy. Why hadn't she ever realized that before?

Bliss shook off the memory. How much would he have changed over the years? They were older now. He was even taller, his body filled out and muscles sinewy from years of physical work. His wife must have been nuts to leave him. From Bliss's limited experience, she assumed he'd be a hell of a lover.

"Agnes, is something wrong? Your face is flushed."

Geno leaned back against the counter, his ankles crossed and his bare feet looking as sexy as they did before she took that trip down memory lane. His pose was almost identical to his slouch at the side of the pool, too, except his hands propped against granite instead of concrete and the only heat in the room seemed to be coming from her.

"Sorry, I was thinking about something else. Work, you know. Things pop into my mind at the strangest times."

If he wasn't completely convinced by her explanation, he had the good grace to give her a simple smiling nod and turn back to chopping food. She drew in a quick breath as his sexy rear view filled her vision again and slammed her eyes shut. She had to get a handle on her hormones. When she opened her eyes, he watched her with that same sidelong stare, but this time, missing the smile.

Bliss felt her tension rise like a teased out hairdo under his careful consideration. Geno didn't say anything, but fine lines appeared at the edges of flared nostrils and his sexy lips settled into a tight line. She watched the rise and fall of his chest as his breathing exaggerated.

"So, would you like to stay for dinner?" The fingers clutching the chef knife loosened and he placed it on the cutting board with slow movements, his eyes still locked on her.

She glanced at the food on the counter. A pile of vegetables in various stages of preparation surrounded the board. On a plate pushed against the backsplash, chicken breasts swam in liquid and spices.

"Oh no, I couldn't. I'm so sorry. I'm interrupting." She flapped her hands in agitation, then stopped abruptly once she realized what she was doing. She probably didn't look that different from the chicken at one time.

Geno shook his head, glancing at the food as well. "I prepare extra food on the weekends for lunches or dinners during the week. I don't always have time or desire to cook after working all day. Making extra gives me no excuse to hit the fast food joints. Meals are ready."

He picked up the knife once more and continued chopping and slicing. His measured movements, the blade hitting the board in a steady rhythm, hypnotized her. His hands seemed almost too delicate for the work he did, and yet she knew the tough skin on his fingers could probably pluck a nail out of wood without the help of a tool. Lucky spread out on the floor behind Geno, his eyes glued to the work too, and his tail beat in harmony, if not exactly in tempo.

"You're good at this, aren't you?"

Bliss wondered why such inane things came out of her mouth around him. It didn't used to be like this. When they were younger, she never had to watch what she said. Now she sounded like a fool.

"I like to eat good food, and I can't afford to go out all the time, so I learned to cook. When I was married, it was a point of contention between Mary Margaret and me. She wanted to fix premade whatever, even though she was home all day and she had time to cook meals from scratch. She just never wanted to."

That was surprising. Bliss always assumed Mary Margaret worked too, since they didn't have children. The woman had been raised in an old school Italian household and should have learned to cook like all of the girls in their group did, at the knees of mothers and aunts and grandmothers. She should have been eager to show off her talents for her husband. That's what good Italian girls did in their old neighborhood.

"Didn't she know how to cook?" Bliss moved forward and picked up a piece of red bell pepper, biting down on the crisp flavor and chewing. Her curiosity about Geno's life after they parted ways overcame her desire to run.

Geno shrugged. "I assume she did, or at least she said she did. She said she didn't like it and she was an adult, so she could do what she wanted. That included not cooking. So if I wanted something that hadn't been frozen or came out of a can or box, I had to cook."

"But that wasn't fair. You worked all day, and I know it wasn't easy labor. I heard about the extra hours and jobs you took on to support the two of you. I just assumed she worked too."

Geno shrugged again as if it didn't matter. And maybe it didn't anymore. He always had been much more forgiving.

"Do you cook?" He pulled a second cutting board from a hidden slot and set it on the counter, grabbing another knife from the block and setting it on the plastic.

Bliss nodded, her motions on autopilot as she pushed up her sleeves and washed her hands.

"No, let me do the onions. I don't want you ruining your pretty eyes crying. Here, can you slice the mushrooms?"

He pushed a pile on to the board in front of her, seemingly content to take her probable response for granted.

Bliss began the methodical process of cutting the ends of the stems and slicing through the soft flesh. "Is this okay?"

He looked over at the single one she'd finished and nodded. "So you do cook."

As if slicing mushrooms was evidence of cooking skills. "I have a child and I want her to be healthy, so of course I cook. Actually, I love it. It's a great time to socialize with Leonora. She talks, and I listen."

Geno glanced at her sideways, that easy questioning smile on his lips once more. "I bet she cooks up a storm too, doesn't she? She seems like she wants to be part of everything."

Bliss froze, the knife hovering two inches over the final mushroom. Geno's knife kept moving, making fast work of the last onion and tossing it into the hot pan where it sizzled provocatively. Usually the aroma alone would distract her and take her to a happy place. With her brain snagged on his comment, she blamed the onion when tears came to her eyes.

"Agnes? What's wrong? It's the onion, isn't it? Why don't you sit on the sofa and let me finish everything." He closed fingers around hers to remove the knife from her grasp and turned her with gentle hands toward the living room.

Bliss wanted to kick herself. She never should have come here. Something about being with Geno made her all soft and mushy inside, and she didn't know what to do with the feelings.

But when he gave her a gentle shove and she felt herself crumple to the sofa, the years melted away.

This was the person she'd run to when the world didn't resolve itself the way she wanted. He'd done the same, and together, they'd weathered storms and celebrated triumphs. At least they had until she'd spoiled it all.

She felt the cushions dip at her side. "Here," he said. He placed a box of tissues in her lap, patting her back as he leaned away and started to rise.

"Geno, I'm sorry. I'm just such a mess. You don't know how hard it's been, raising Leonora by myself. I didn't realize it would be like this."

His surprise at her outburst was written all over his face, and he paused in his seat. Then she surprised herself by reached out and clutching his arm with both hands.

"Agnes? Are you having problems? Is Leonora sick? Is it money? What can I do for you?"

And bless the man, he looked like he'd do whatever it took to make things right. But he'd had that chance, and it would be best to remember that. She let go as if his arm burned her fingers, and it brought a frown to his expression.

"No, it's none of that. I'm being stupid. Sorry. I'm saying that a lot, aren't I?" Just to be sure he believed her, she forced a watery chuckle out as she mopped her face.

He patted her back again and rose, walking to the kitchen and pulling something out of a cabinet. "Would you like a cup of herbal tea? I find it calms me. I have several kinds."

And damned if he didn't. She laughed through her tears, with more feeling this time, as she looked at the basket in his hand piled above its rim with individual tea bags in various colors.

"Now what's funny?" Geno watched her with the same look she imagined wardens gave people at the funny farm.

"Nothing. Or rather, it's me, not you. Yes to the tea. Do you want some too?"

He shook his head, a relieved movement with a little too much enthusiasm. Setting the basket on the corner of the counter, he returned to dinner, stirring the vegetables in the pan and picking up the knife once more.

"What I meant was, I get overwhelmed like any parent does every once in a while. I want Leonora to be able to have whatever she wants in life. But she isn't going to be able to do some things that other kids can, and it's hard to watch. Like cooking. I can't expect her to handle a knife in the kitchen. She wants to help, but I only give her tasks that I know she can do."

He chopped and stirred and she opened cabinets until she found a mug. Turning to fill it at the sink, her gaze fell on his bare feet once more. He had the sexiest feet, and she had no idea what to do with the fact that they turned her on.

"Can I ask you something?"

He nodded at the pan, his expression absent as if he was thinking about something a million miles away.

"How can you stand to be in bare feet when it's thirty-five degrees outside?"

Chapter 21

He'd forgotten how much Agnes could make him laugh. Not a tentative smile or a gentle chuckle, but a deep belly laugh. Of course, she argued with equal passion. Geno kept his stronger opinions to himself.

Instead of calling Agnes on her change of subject, he suggested she lose the high-heeled boots and base her answer on personal experience. His heated floors delighted her, and she danced around the room giggling like she had when they were kids. He slid the chicken into the vegetables and put the pan in the oven, joining her on the sofa with a beer as she sipped her tea. And for once, his ulcer wasn't screaming at him.

In fact, it was the most relaxed he'd felt in a long time. Even if Agnes changed the subject whenever he veered too close to discussions about personal topics, he was content to let her lead the way. There was something fundamentally troubling about her fears that Leonora would never be able to do everything. No one could do everything. He knew she was only trying to be a protective mother, but someday, her daughter might not agree this was the best path.

"That chicken was delicious. Can I have the recipe? I think this would be something Leonora would enjoy."

He tapped his temple with his index finger, giving her a suggestive rise of eyebrows to add humor to his point. "It's all in here, so unless they've perfected the mind-meld, you'll have to come back when I make this dinner again and take notes. Bring Leonora. I'll teach her how to prepare the vegetables. I think she'd enjoy it too."

He watched her expression shut down as the humor left her face. She didn't meet his eyes, toying with her fork. When she stood up abruptly and reached for both of their empty plates, he closed his fingers around her wrist without conscious decision.

"Leave the plates. I'll take care of them later. Sit. You wanted my advice, but you haven't asked me anything."

She didn't release her hold immediately, looking everywhere around the room but at him. When Lucky whined from his place under the table, she blinked a couple of times as if a spell had been broken. Tension crackled between them with new energy when her eyes met his. She settled the plates back on the table, but remained standing.

"I have to apologize for the way I treated you that night. I should never have asked, back then. It was selfish of me. You had a life to live. You were already seeing Mary Margaret. And I expected you to drop everything and save us. Have I apologized enough tonight for us to consider it a blanket for all current and past stupidity?" Her stammering voice turned to pleading, and he felt the pressure build.

She tried out a smile, and he wondered if she realized how her beauty threatened to stop his heart. Her eye make-up had long since been washed away by her tears, and she'd tucked her rich-hued hair behind her ears. If he had any doubt about how much he loved her across the years, the rapid race of his heart settled the question.

"You don't have to apologize, *Agnese*. We were best friends. Who else would you go to when you needed a favor? I was honored, even if I couldn't help."

She smiled, though it didn't reach her eyes. Sinking back into her chair, she tapped the back of his hand before lacing her fingers through his.

"You know one of the best things I remember about the old days? You were always there for me. Even that day, you still tried to find a way to help me. I was embarrassed afterwards for what I put you through. You could have told everyone what I asked, but you never did. Why is that?"

He loved the thoughtful tilt of her head, loosening strands of hair behind one ear until they cascaded over her shoulder. When he reached out to tuck it back once more, he found his fingers lingering on her soft cheek, and her eyes widened slightly. He had to force himself to lean away from her, dropping his hand to his beer bottle to grip, even though it was empty.

"*Genovese*?"

Her use of his Italian birth name felt intimate. She'd never liked her own, but he thought it was magical. When he'd used it for her as a youngster, it was only partly as a tease. The other reason was because he often thought of her like some kind of princess. Its meaning fit her. Pure. Holy. And she was both to him.

She continued to stare at him, and he fidgeted. He said, "It wouldn't have been fitting to share a private conversation, especially one like that. You trusted me with a confidence and a request. Just because I couldn't help you with the request didn't mean I would betray your trust."

His heart swelled when she broke into a big smile, grabbing his hands as she jumped up and pulling him with her.

"I always knew I could trust you. I have to admit, I hated you for a while after that. But again, it wasn't you. It was me. I'd gotten myself into a mess and I should never have asked you to fix it for me. It's taken me years to become wise enough to see that. Come over to the couch with me. There's something about those big feet of yours that's so mesmerizing. I want to give you a foot massage. Do you have any lotion?"

His mouth opened and closed, because once again, Agnes surprised him. After knowing her for twenty-five years, you'd think she'd run out of ways to do that. But there it was. A foot massage was the last thing he considered doing at the moment.

But she pulled at his hands, sending him tumbling into the sofa. She laughed that wonderful up the scale and down sound of hers and picked up his feet, pushing him back against the arm of the couch. Twisting with agility he remembered from games of tag, she headed for the bathroom and re-emerged short seconds later with a bottle of lotion in her hand while he gawked at her. He never felt so stupid. He wasn't sure he'd ever felt so in love, either.

Plopping down and lifting his feet to rest in her lap, she gave him a wicked sideways grin. "Now, tell me if this tickles. I won't promise I'll stop if it does, though. Your big sexy feet deserve a little attention after feeding me such a marvelous dinner. And as a bonus, you can ask me one question that I promise to answer. That is, if you can think while I do this. I'm pretty great at foot massages."

She waggled her eyebrows and winked, pouring lotion into her palms and rubbing them together vigorously. When she ran her fingers down one foot from toes to arch to heel and back again, he thought he might pass out from the exquisite pressure.

Instead, he groaned out loud, and he wasn't ashamed about it. "God, that feels good. You can keep doing that for about a hundred years."

"I know, great, right? Now, your question, sir?" Her thumbs dug into the bottom of his foot and he felt the pressure all the way up his legs into his groin.

Everything in his pants twitched against confinement as she pressed more deeply.

He spoke before thinking. "Why do you have the nickname of Bliss?"

She paused, her fingers pushing into the soft tissue on the side of his foot. Her expression turned blank, and he knew he'd strayed into risky territory.

"Never mind. I don't need to know."

Her fingers began moving once more. "I could tell you the story I tell everyone, about a rich man who said my massages took him to a land of bliss when nothing else could. I embellish that with tales of sexual exploits, adjusted for the shock value to my audience. I could tell you that story, but it's simply that. A story. Fiction."

She kneaded his foot with absentminded motions. He let her words settle around him, content for the moment that she didn't feel she had to spin a tale with him.

"Do you want the real reason?" Her serious eyes locked on him, and he could only nod.

"I wanted happiness, for Leonora, for myself. Bliss. I decided to use that whole power of intention thing you started talking about when you took that college philosophy course. I wanted bliss. Therefore, I would be Bliss. I used it, and it stuck, and when it came time to name my spa, it seemed obvious."

He nodded once more, torn between thinking through the implications of her words and the more than pleasant distractions her movements caused.

"I'll give you another question. That one was boring anyway. I'm tired of searching and tired of thinking about being happy. I'd like to just be happy. Ask me another question, *Genovese*."

He shouldn't think about her motions, the press and release of knowing fingers and the little smile she wore when her eyes met his, as if she knew exactly what this was doing to him. Her pace slowed, and if anything, that made it even more sensual. If she let her hands glide up his legs to his crotch, he would be powerless to stop her.

Even though he should. This was *Agnese*, after all. She should be like a sister to him. After all, they grew up together, best buddies and all that. But somewhere along the way, the childhood best friend had grown into a desirable woman, and he wasn't sure he could back away.

And there was the promise. Shit, the promise.

"Focus, Geno. The question, remember?"

Easy for her to say. Her blood wasn't racing from brain tissue to another soft organ that was rapidly getting rock hard. She was only rubbing his feet.

"A question. Right. Here's one. How did you get from Boston to Flynn's Crossing?"

Her fingers paused a fraction of a second, then resumed their deep pressure on the instep of his right foot. "You asked a biggie, didn't you? How much time do you have?"

For you, babe, the rest of my life. But he realized it was too soon to say that, or maybe too late. He bit his tongue hard enough to draw blood and barely avoided an audible groan as she found another amazing spot at the base of his little toe. Who knew a foot massage could be so destructive?

As she started explaining, pacing her words to her slow movements, he could envision the movie of their journey. As soon as Leonora completed the treatment for her club feet, she and Agnes left town. Boston to Philadelphia. West to Columbus. Chicago, a big push to Denver, Salt Lake City. At each stop in their journey, she worked at whatever jobs made sense. When she thought they would stay someplace for a while, she earned her state license and worked in a salon, until she felt the urge to move.

And through each mile of her journey's tale, she kept massaging his feet, changing to the left one when she hit Omaha. People who made a difference in her life, or people who disrespected Leonora, got honorable mention. But nowhere did she mention special friends she kept in touch with, and if there had been men, she didn't bring them up either.

Geno praised his luck, because the idea of *Agnese* with another man would have made the constriction in his pants wither away. He was enjoying the agony, because it meant Agnes had her hands on him and she didn't seem inclined to let go. Each run of her thumb along a nerve made him hotter with longing. He couldn't move if an earthquake rumbled through and shook the house off its foundation.

"As Leonora got older, I realized I needed to settle someplace before she started first grade. It wouldn't be fair to uproot her. I was working in Sacramento. Jobs were plentiful and the schools were good. But I wanted my own shop, something I could grow, something that offered a stable life for my daughter."

Sadness tinged her gaze as she looked up at him. Geno didn't need her to say more. A more stable life, because she was a single parent. On the floor next to them, Lucky whined.

"Ah, that's his signal. Time to go out before bedtime."

He extricated his feet and rose, turning away so she couldn't see the by-product of her ministrations. He could walk to the door with his back to her, but what the hell was he going to do when he had to turn around?

"Wow, it's late. I guess I gave you a very long explanation. Clever of you, Geno. There's no way I could have answered that briefly without sounding catty and snide. But I should go."

He watched her reflection start to rise from the end of the sofa, and he swung behind a tall chair to face her. "No, sit, stay."

She glanced up at him in confusion, and at his feet, Lucky dropped his butt to the floor obediently and thumped his tail. Then he whined again.

"Not you, goofus. Agnes. You go out, and get done fast."

Behind him, Geno heard Agnes giggle as the dog shot out the door on a woof of happiness.

"You have us both well-trained. See? I sat too."

She laughed again, her eyes sparkling. He suddenly didn't care if she saw the power she had over him. If anything, it might break the ice in the one area they hadn't ventured in their discussions.

Intimacy.

Geno settled back on the sofa, close enough to Agnes to reach for her feet and bring them up into his lap. He pulled off one sock and threw it at her, bringing out that laugh again, and made a show of placing her foot carefully on his thighs. If she wiggled her toes, he'd be bursting like a firecracker on the Fourth of July. Did she notice his predicament?

"Ah, Geno, you don't have to give my feet a massage. Really, you don't."

But her words bit off on a groan as he pressed at the spot where her heel met the bottom of her foot.

"You've done this before." She closed her eyes and rested her head on the back of the couch as she spoke.

He shook his head, pleased with himself. If this got him hot and bothered, it must do the same for her.

One eye opened to stare at him. He smiled, putting every bit of innocence he could muster into the expression. "I'm a quick learner."

And he wanted to learn every secret she had. The ones she'd spent the last nine years accumulating, not trusting anyone enough to share them. He chose to believe other men hadn't made her moan or sigh as she was doing now. She shifted back and forth as if she was getting uncomfortable, and in response, his cock twitched and his balls ached.

A gentle woof sounded outside the door, followed by a thud against the barrier. Another woof, louder this time, brought Agnes out of her bliss. Her eyes met his, and uncertainty darkened her expression.

"Don't move. I'll be right back."

He slid out from under her feet and strode across the room fast enough to make papers blow on the notepad on his counter. Lucky nearly fell into the room when the door opened fast, recovering and trotting out of sight into the main bedroom. Another thud let the world know he'd settled in for the night, completing the action with a loud sigh of contentment.

There wasn't another sound in the room. The fire had long since stopped crackling, its logs glowing low and warm. Usually, dirty dishes on the table and the mess of food preparation on the counter would make him crazy. But tonight he barely noticed it. Tonight, he had Agnes to look forward to.

When he turned, he found her eyes traveling down his body, the exploration stopping when she reached below his waist. He heard the gasp, barely disguised as a clearing of her throat as she suddenly made a big show of looking at her watch. She stared at it for a long time, longer than she needed unless she was taking her pulse. Her chest rose and fell in rapid rhythm, her breasts pressing against the sweater until he could see the outline of every curve and bump.

Her body couldn't lie. She was as turned as he was, though she didn't seem to be inclined to do anything about it. Maybe their decade apart scared her. Hell, it scared him, but not because he was afraid this would change things. He wanted that change, now more than ever after spending hours talking with her. Agnes was the one for him. He only had to prove it to her.

"Well, thanks for dinner and everything. You were great – I mean, it was great. You were nice too. I mean – oh hell, I don't know what I mean."

She staggered two steps forward, close enough for him to look into her eyes and see the pupils dilated, near enough to note the slight flare of her nostrils and hear the pants of her heavy breathing. He couldn't let her leave like this, not if he ever wanted their friendship to be the foundation of something more.

"*Agnese*, stay. What are you running to? Your daughter is safe and the night belongs to you. I'd like you to share that time with me."

Stricken eyes met his, her mouth forming a perfect circle as if his words startled her. Crossing her arms only emphasized her agitation. She was like a frightened deer, frozen but trembling in the light of his gaze.

He wasn't doing much better. His feet felt like they'd adhered to the floor, skin stuck to wood and unable to move. Only a few feet separated them, but he couldn't make his body respond to commands. Take her in his arms and whisper his intentions in her perfect shell of an ear. Better yet, take her in his arms and show her.

"You don't mean that, *Genovese*. You don't know what you're getting into with me. We're better off as friends. I'm not even sure I know how to do that very well. Look at the mess I made of it years ago."

Her shoulders hunched protectively and her eyes drifted away from his to stare into the inky night outside the window. He couldn't see her face at this angle, and her reflection was hidden too. He could still tell what she was feeling, though. It was in every uptight line of her body.

"You didn't make a mess alone. I should have been more willing to take a risk, to take on you and Leonora. I was scared, plain and simple. And if we're being honest, I was hurt too. I wasn't sure I could raise another man's baby, particularly a man who hurt you so much."

She didn't turn back, but he thought he saw a relaxing of the tension in her shoulders. He wanted to reach out and caress them, easing her worry. She had nothing to fear from him.

"And now? What's changed now?" Distance made her voice quiet. She could have been asking him about the price of a cabinet for all the emotion she showed.

"I've changed. I'm not that frightened boy. I'm a man, and I know what I want. And that's you, Agnes, you and Leonora. Simple as that."

She barked out a rude laugh, spinning to face him. "There's nothing simple about it, Geno. I'm not asking for everything like I did before. I don't want to get married. I don't need help supporting my child. I'm interested in sex. Are you man enough for that?"

Prowling the distance between them, she stopped when they were almost toe-to-toe. Her head tilted back to continue to meet his gaze, unblinking in the muted light. If he was going to guess about the feeling she was trying to project, he'd have called it a dare. And he was no longer one to back down from a dare.

He stepped forward, his body pressed against hers so that she couldn't help but feel his arousal. She did this to him, and she wasn't even trying. God help him, if she turned on her feminine powers, it might kill him. But he'd die happy.

"What are you doing?" Bravado laced her question, but she didn't step back. Geno knew he was about ten seconds away from grabbing her and settling his mouth on hers for the next few hours.

"I'm getting close to you. And I want to be closer still." He brushed stray tendrils of soft hair from her cheek, watching her eyes grow wider and her expression become unsure.

"Maybe I don't know how to do this." Her rough words sounded almost desperate with doubt.

"I do." Or at least, he thought he did. It never mattered as much as it did with Agnes.

Cupping her chin and tilting her face, he lowered his head until his lips hovered over hers. When his mouth closed over hers, she sighed and parted her lips. He sampled gently, afraid to spook her. The flavors and aromas of dinner did nothing to mask her sweet taste. If nothing more than this happened tonight, he'd consider it hours well spent.

But Agnes evidently had other ideas, because her fingers traced his chest as her hands began a slow ascent. When she reached his beard, she paused and ducked out of his grasp enough to break their kiss.

"It's so soft," she said, her voice low and husky.

"What?" The mush that usually passed for his brain didn't currently work, and he stared at her, confused.

"Your beard. I wondered what it was like on an everyday basis. I expected it to be scratchy, but it's soft. Most men usually don't have soft facial hair."

He frowned. He didn't like the idea of her spending time with her fingers wound in any other men's beards, or anywhere else on their bodies for that matter.

"Don't get all gruff on me. In my line of work, I see a lot of hair, and not all of it is on someone's head. I'm merely making an observation. I like it. Your beard is kind of a turn on."

He'd take that as a compliment. He caressed the base of her spine as he leaned back to look into her eyes.

"What else turns you on?" He ran the pad of his thumb over her plump lower lip. Her eyelids drooped and her gaze lost focus. "Do you like this?"

She nodded, barely moving her head. Satisfied, he lowered his head and started a string of kisses on her neck below her ear. A shiver ran through her body, stirring an echoing shake in his. He heard a growl and thought he'd have to lecture Lucky on his timing, until he realized the sound came from his own throat. He pushed the fabric of her sweater to the side and continued the kisses along the soft skin of her shoulder.

"I'll give you about ten days to stop that."

He chuckled at her words, enjoying her closed eyes and dazed expression when he paused. She responded to the interruption by wrapping her arms around his neck and pulling him back down for another kiss.

He wished he hadn't wasted years to get to this point. He could have spent the last decade worshiping her every day, but he'd said no when she needed him the most. He would never make that mistake again.

Walking her backwards, he got them to the sofa without any mishaps, and he turned to sit, taking her with him and settling her on his lap. The torture was exquisite, made even more so when she wiggled into place and settled her head on his shoulder while never breaking her lock on his mouth. Her fingers curled into tight fists in the material of his shirt.

When she finally broke the kiss, she leaned back against his circling arms and smiled up at him. "You kiss great, you know that? What else do you excel at, Mr. Altimari?"

He smiled down at her, pulling her closer. "I'm pretty good when it comes to slapping meat on the grill. I'm kind to small children and animals. And I know how to make women squirm when I do this." He shifted a hand under her sweater and ran a light touch up Agnes's belly to stop right below her breast. He wasn't sure who he was teasing anymore, her or himself.

She shivered again, pulling away slightly. "That tickles."

"It tickles? I take that as an affront to my manhood. I never knew you to be ticklish, Agnes. Must be old age."

"I'll give you old age. I have a few moves of my own," she said, as she reached between their bodies to stroke the length of hard flesh pressed between them.

The feel of her fingers was no less exciting with the clothing blocking her full access, and even slight pressure made him throb harder. She gave him a wide-eyed stare of faked innocence as she stroked a second time, and then a third.

He wanted her to stop, because he didn't want to embarrass them both by coming like a boy in high school. He wanted her to continue, because it was the most exquisite torture he'd ever endured. Instead, he gave her a lazy smile and said, "I'd say I'll give you about ten days to stop that, but if you don't stop in the next ten seconds, I won't be responsible for my actions."

She chuckled, and he felt every rumble through their chest to breasts contact. When the sound escalated to a full-fledged laugh, he joined in. They hooted loudly enough to rouse Lucky, who gave a moan of complaint from the next room. That just made them laugh harder.

She stroked then retreated like a game of tag, and he brushed his fingers over the peaks of her nipples, straining the knit of her sweater. That game continued until he thought he'd go crazy with agony, and Agnes groaned and arched her back to push a firm breast into his hand.

Their sounds cut off in unison as they stared at each other. He waited for her to say or do something. Even though he wanted her more than his next breath, he wanted her to have the choice. Stay or go.

Tracing his face with fingers that might be shaking a little, she said, "What do you want, Geno?"

Another woman might be fishing for compliments or wishing for a declaration of devotion, but he knew Agnes was asking a different question. This had to be her choice. Instead of answering directly, he said, "I want to see if you still have year-round tan lines."

"I can't believe you still remember that. I'm not sure why they never faded. It wasn't like we took a winter beach vacation or anything. But I remember that you tanned just as dark. So let me see." And she reached for the edge of his shirt and pulled it up, covering his face and blinding him as she ran greedy hands up his bare chest.

He pushed the shirt out of the way and grabbed her hands, unwilling to end this game prematurely. "My turn," he said, as he reached for the knit and tangled it up in her hair on the way off.

Muffled, her words were garbled when she gave a little shriek of mock indignation and tried to free her hair herself. With both of them trying, the tangling got worse before it got better, and they were both breathless and giggling when her head popped out like a whack-a-mole.

Unable to stop himself, he traced the lace edging her bra. Toying with the strap, his eyes met hers, and laughter died out until the room was silent. The desire he saw in her face matched the flood he was feeling, and he knew what came next was as inevitable as the sun rising in the morning.

Knowing and doing something about it were two completely different things, though. Would this step strengthen their revived friendship or ruin it forever?

As if she read his thoughts, she turned away, though her body remained pressed against him. Since he knew it pleased her, he dropped his lips to the tender skin under her ear and wrapped his arms around her curves. Her body felt lush and warm against him. He hoped his kisses down the line of her shoulder produced a quaking through her body.

"This might be a mistake," she said, putting her hands over his just below her breasts.

"Do you want me to stop?" It would come at a price, but he'd pay it if it was what she wanted. He struggled in preparation to clear the pulse of emotions running through his mind, even as the craving for her ran through his body.

She didn't say anything, but pulled against his arms to move away from him. He bit back the ache her separation caused. It was probably for the best. He valued her as a friend, and sharing that would have to be enough.

But she surprised him again when she only leaned far enough to link her fingers on the clasp of her bra. When the edges parted, she shrugged out of it and let it fall to the floor before nestling back against him.

Skin to skin, with nothing in between them, was the most amazing sensation.

He wasn't going to second-guess things any longer. He ran his fingers over the tender flesh above her waistband and felt tremors in the muscles underneath. He couldn't resist sliding up and cupping the full weight of her breasts, loving the way they filled his hands. As he caressed her puckered nipples, she arched into his hands on a small moan of pleasure.

His lips repeated their course on her neck and shoulders, lost in the subtle scent of her skin and the restless movements of her body. When she tried to twist to face him, he held her in place, loving the way she filled his arms and cradled his erection against her butt. She fit him in all the physical ways that mattered, as completely and as deeply as she filled his mind and heart.

"You have an amazing body." He whispered the words in her ear, following with a teasing poke of his tongue. She shivered, even as she shook her head in denial.

"I have an overweight and under-exercised body." Then she moaned when he toyed with her nipples again.

"I disagree. You have a curvy, lush body and I can't wait to explore all of it."

His fingers run down her belly to the button on her jeans, and he felt Agnes hold her breath. He chose to think it was in anticipation, and he fingered it to give her time to get used to the idea. When he popped it open, she sighed and raised her arms to clasp his head, pushing even closer to him.

The metallic grating of her descending zipper filled the room with sound. Now he held his breath, intent on unwrapping the best present he'd ever received. When his wandering fingers found lace inside, he felt a little lightheaded and giddy. The woman was wrapped up like Christmas, and he couldn't wait to see what was inside the rest of the package.

He slipped his fingers under the lace and caressed her hot, soft cleft, the moisture growing stronger as he stroked. Agnes fidgeted against him, and each time she did, she brushed against his swollen cock. Much more of this and he'd explode.

"Come for me, Agnes." He stroked faster, pressing deeper, and she churned her body against his.

"I don't – I can't – Geno." The stammering words halted as her body tightened and froze, and he kept his one arm wrapped firmly around her body, his palm filled with a mound of quivering breast. Her pleasured moan filled him, more satisfying than anything he'd ever experienced.

She went suddenly limp, panting and grasping his hands. She held on tight, as if she was afraid he'd leave her. Didn't she realize that now, he only wanted to hold her closer? He couldn't resist caressing her gently, dropping lingering kisses on skin that had become moist and dewy. Her breathing slowed and her head fell back against his shoulder.

"That was amazing," she said, her eyes still closed.

He chuckled. "I'm glad you think so."

"What can I do for you?" She began to move with her question, as if to pull away. He tightened his arms. He wasn't ready to let her go, not yet and not for this night. Maybe never.

"You can come to bed with me. I want to make love to you all night long, and watch the sun come up and light your smile in the morning."

This time she did pull away, far enough to turn and watch him cautiously over her shoulder. He couldn't tell if she was pleased with what he proposed or confused by it. She pushed against his arms, and he dropped them with reluctance. It felt like part of him had been severed, the amputation painful and abrupt.

She examined his face carefully, like she was weighing his words. He let the silence drag on. If she had questions, he'd answer them as honestly as he could. She might not like his answers, though. It might be too soon.

She stood in front of him, and he couldn't resist the quick kiss to her belly button, framed as it was by the gaping jeans. Her fingers clasped behind his head, cradling him against her body as if she too was unwilling to let go. She stroked his balding head and toyed with the fringe of hair, occasionally running that gentle touch down his neck. He wrapped his arms around her back and returned the gesture, exploring the dip at the base of her spine and the feel of her spine beneath his fingers.

They stayed like that as minutes ticked past, and Geno wondered if she understood how deeply her gentle moves shook him. He wanted to show her more care, so much more. Finally, he loosened his arms and she stepped back. He ran his hands down her arms until he reached her hands and their fingers linked. When he stood, she smiled, letting a seductive gaze wander down his body to the place where his sweatpants strained.

He smiled back. It was so easy to be tender with her, even if he couldn't act on the full extent of his feelings. It was too early, too soon in this rediscovery of who they could be for each other as adults. When he tugged her toward his bedroom, she didn't hesitate.

The room was dark, lit only by the glow from the living room. The dog snored gently in the corner, undisturbed by their entrance. When Geno settled on the bed and pulled Agnes in front of him, he kissed that belly button again. It was a cute little shell, half in and half out, one she'd been teased about as a child until she swore she'd deck the next one who said a word about it. That didn't mean it wasn't very kissable, and he wondered if she remembered he'd never been one who said a teasing peep about her body.

She didn't give him much time to linger, reaching for the elastic waist of his sweats. Her fingers wrapped around him before he had a chance to prepare himself mentally, and the sensation of her smooth caress made him throb harder. As if she felt it, she moved her hand faster.

He grabbed her strong fingers and stopped her before his eyes crossed and he lost it altogether. "Hey, slow down. There's no rush. Do you have a hot date to head to or something?"

She giggled, her eyes sparkling in the pale light. "I think I'm on it already."

He gave her a big grin in return, shifting only enough to push his sweats and briefs down his legs and off. She kicked them away, reaching for her jeans as she did so.

"Allow me," he said, hearing the strain in his voice.

Trailing open-mouthed kisses over the skin her descending jeans exposed, he had to admire the lacy panties that were a match for the bra on the living room floor. Her undies showed off her assets to maximum advantage, and he'd tell her that, as soon as he remembered how to speak.

Because she robbed him of that. Words couldn't describe her beauty. As a child, she was all gangly angles and sharp corners. As a teenager, she'd begun to blossom. Carrying Leonora had brought generous curves to her frame, and if anything, the years had made them more appealing. He wanted to savor every inch of her body, but he didn't think he could last that long.

He pulled her down on the bed next to him, and she leaned her head on his shoulder and closed her eyes, much as she had when they were kids and she needed comforting. And he knew just how to comfort her now. Wrapping one arm around her and pulling her into him, he reached into the nightstand drawer with the other and grabbed a condom.

The wrapper crinkled in his palm and her eyes opened. "I'm on the pill."

He didn't want to think about the implications of that. He didn't want to consider her with any other lovers. The consequences of her night of unprotected sex when they were twenty had stayed with him as a valuable lesson in life. He'd never had a woman without latex in between, not even his ex-wife. Now wasn't the time to risk changing his standards.

"I always use a condom. You taught me that."

She nodded, her face falling into a sad grimace as she glanced away. She seemed to be watching Lucky, his feet twitching as he chased some quarry in a puppy dream. With her eyes still on the dog, she plucked the condom from his fingers. She stared at the package for a moment, then opened it with a decisive rip and reached for him. Her fingers might have jerked as she rolled it on him, or it might have been him. His pulse raced at a speed unknown and there was little opportunity for him to think clearly.

Rolling them both on to the bed, Geno rested his legs between hers and felt the furnace of her heat burning against him. Her eyes watched his face, and the tips of her fingers traced his features. He held himself above her, wanting to savor prolong this moment. There would never again be this first time, and he wanted to remember each and every second of it.

But Agnes had other ideas. She wrapped her legs around his and pulled him closer, rubbing the apex of her thighs where it counted most. Soon, too soon, he was notched into that heat. Before he was too far gone to think, he put a hand between them and found her core, fondling the bundle of nerves until she panted along with him and twisted her body as if to get closer. Their rhythm sped up until they rocked the bed enough to send the headboard banging into the wall.

He was lost in her, in this. Her face held both pleasure and astonishment. He celebrated the first. He'd consider the ramifications of the latter when he had brain cells working. As his balls pulled up in anticipation and he felt himself prepare to explode, Agnes moaned and went rigid underneath him. Her body squeezing him tight was all he needed to lose himself in the most shattering orgasm of his life.

Chapter 22

Light teased her eyelids, demanding that she open them and check out the day. But she didn't want to. She wanted to burrow deeper under the blankets and inhale the aroma of Geno and a night of hot, incredible sex.

On that thought, Agnes's eyes bolted open and she sat up, looking around quickly. Finding the other side of the bed empty was something of a relief, and she flopped back and pulled the covers over her head. She'd had sex with Geno Altimari last night. Not once, not twice, but three times. Her toes curled as she thought about it. Each time had been an amazing discovery, the additional orgasms even more so.

She'd never known. All these years, from the night she lost her virginity and got pregnant and through the scant men she'd shared a bed with for brief periods in between, she'd never felt it. The big O. Now she understood what all the fuss was about. She always assumed she was frigid, and she'd perfected the art of faking it. Or she took matters into her own hands and rushed the men along so they never guessed. But she, Agnes Amendola, had five big ones last night, and she was greedy for more.

She lowered the covers a couple of inches and blinked at the angle of the sun. It was high, meaning she'd slept later than she had in years. Her body felt heavy and sated, but if Geno walked back through that door, she'd jump him.

Of course, she couldn't stay here all day. Leonora would expect her by noon, and there was no way she could pick up her daughter without a shower, hair and make-up. The child would immediately know something was different.

She stretched, letting her hands drift down to the indentation in the pillow on the other side of the bed. When she'd awoken in his arms, he made tender love to her, slowly and deliberately as if they had all the time in the world. That time, he'd showed her new pleasures that had her eyes crossing as she stuttered out his name. When she woke him a few hours later, she returned the favor.

Her eyes settled on her clothes, neatly folded and stacked on the dresser. A plaid bathrobe draped over the top of them. Considerate man that he was, Geno had placed her purse on a chair next to the clothes. A stack of fresh towels shared the space. He'd thought of everything, except a bag of make-up and hair styling products. And a hair dryer. He probably didn't have much need for that, she thought with a sudden grin.

She'd thought the balding head and full facial hair would be a detraction, but instead, she found she loved the rough but gentle feel of his beard caressing her skin when he kissed her. And he kissed her everywhere, including some places that had only been visited by her gynecologist. She probably blushed when he explored those places, but the overwhelming sense of intimacy and comfort she felt with Geno made any embarrassment evaporate.

She heard the murmur of his voice, followed by a thump that was probably Lucky's tail. Master and dog were well suited, two laid-back guys with easygoing manners and ready smiles. But who knew Geno had those moves in him? She'd never have pegged him for sex machine. Mary Margaret must have been out of her frigging mind to leave him.

Agnes had heard the stories, courtesy of her brother Luke. Word was that Mary Margaret made a big production out of the divorce, claiming Geno wasn't a good provider and didn't meet her needs, wink-wink.

That should have been something left in the privacy of their own home, but the woman had made it public knowledge. She'd even petitioned the church to have the marriage annulled, just in case she wanted a church wedding again the next time around. Before she found Mr. Next, she spent her days and evenings telling her cronies what a lousy lover Geno was and how he never knew how to satisfy a woman.

Any more satisfied and Agnes would need physical therapy. Either Mary Margaret had lied, or Geno had done some studying in the years since. That concept brought her thoughts to a screeching halt. It was one thing to consider Geno with his virgin bride years ago. It was another to think about the other relationships he must have had over the years.

Feeling her mood shift and take a nosedive, Agnes pushed back the covers and grabbed the robe. She wanted to see him. He'd bring back the elation she felt when she first opened her eyes.

Pushing her arms into sleeves that were miles too long for her, she heard her phone ping in her purse. She'd almost forgotten about Leonora, which made her feel guilty. What kind of mother was she, forgetting her only daughter because she had a night of good sex? Okay, mind leveling, cell killing, fabulous sex. Maybe she could be forgiven for the lapse.

'Morning Mommy. We're having pancakes.'

Agnes smiled. Mommy again, so Leonora must be happy. She fingered the keys to reply.

'Morning Sweetheart. Hope you slept well.'

Not that she expected the girls to sleep for a sleep over.

'I hope you didn't miss me too much. Maybe you should get a cat.'

That made her smile wider.

'I missed you something terrible, but I kept busy. And no cat.'

The response took longer this time.

'Love you – bye.'

Agnes responded in kind and stared at the phone. What would her daughter think if she knew how Agnes had spent her night? Of course, there was no way Leonora would find out, and it was only one night. It wasn't like this was going to become a habit or anything. She could get addicted to Geno and his loving ways, so she should stay away.

What had they done? Why wasn't he coming back to bed? Was it that awful for him? Was he hiding out to give her time to get dressed and leave? Damn, why had she ruined a friendship, a perfectly wonderful one she missed? She didn't realize how much she missed him until he was back in her life.

She couldn't wait any longer. She'd always been one to face the consequences of her actions, and she needed to set the record straight with him. If he was embarrassed, she'd swear to him that she would never breathe a word of this to anyone, and they never needed to speak about it in the future. But she needed to know they would be okay, because he'd knocked her stable world off its foundation in more ways than she could count.

Pulling open the bedroom door, she paused at the sight in front of her. Geno was dressed as he had been last night, down to the sexy bare feet, damn him. There was something about his feet. Hell, the whole package turned her on.

But she couldn't love him. She had to remember her obligations. Once Conrad came to his senses and decided to be a father to Leonora, everything would change. She had to be prepared for that.

Not that she couldn't appreciate a fine male specimen until then. And now that she knew about the magic Geno hid in his sweats, she wanted to rethink celibacy during that interim. If the thought of using her friend so coarsely gave her pang, she tried not to dwell on it. She doubted he had any expectations of her, she wanted more intimacy, and she wanted it with him.

She looked around the room, expecting everything to have shifted as much as she had overnight. But the place looked the same. Geno had cleaned up the dinner dishes, and the counter was now spotless. A kettle sat on the stove, and next to it, two mugs and that damned basket of tea bags. She needed caffeine, preferably intravenously, to figure out how to fix this.

He glanced up, smiling as his eyes swept over her from head to toe. She'd rolled up the sleeves as much as she could, but her hands barely peeked out. Belting the waist had been a challenge, as she'd gathered up fabric to shorten the robe so that she didn't trip over it. That made a big balloon effect that she was sure added the equivalent of twenty pounds to her heavier curves. But what the hell – it wasn't as if she needed to impress him. He'd gotten an eyeful more than once last night.

"Good morning. Did you sleep well?" He waggled his eyebrows as he asked the question. Sleep? There was a little of that, and a whole lot fun in between.

"I did. And you? I didn't expect to see you up so early."

He nodded to her question and pointed at Lucky. "Big guy needed to go out, and then he demanded breakfast. Then he had to go back outside and now we're having lesson time. I try to train him a little each day. It keeps both of us on our best behavior." He motioned at her with an arm. "Come here."

She frowned at his natural acceptance of what they did. Didn't he realize this changed things? She couldn't even look at him without remembering all the pleasure he brought her last night. She hoped she gave him some of that back. He acted as if he didn't have a care in the world.

"Geno, fuck, what did we do?"

He quirked a questioning eyebrow at her, resting his hands behind him on the edge of the counter and crossing his ankles. He was the epitome of relaxed. She was a wreck.

"Agnes, my skills must need work if you don't know that is, in fact, what we did." His emphasis wasn't lost on her. The Big IT, and three times. Plus those other orgasms of hers. She had to stop thinking about them. They made her hot and itching to go another round.

He gave her a lazy smile, as if he knew what she was thinking about. He probably did. The last few hours were all she could think about, and she assumed his thoughts probably weren't far from it either.

Stretching out his arm again without another word, he invited her closer. This time, she went, as she assured herself it wasn't because she couldn't stand to be this far away from him. When he folded her against his lean body, she marveled at the powerful muscles hidden there. He'd held himself off her last night like it was nothing. Even when he'd bucked into her like his life depending on it, she sensed something held in reserve, like he was being careful not to hurt her. He'd never do that intentionally. Even years ago when she blamed him for refusing her, she knew what she asked was unreasonable.

"*Buongiorno, Agnese.*" He kissed her lightly on the lips, resting his forehead against hers.

"*Buongiorno, Genovese.*" And it was a good morning.

>>>>>

Even after using his soap, Agnes retained her unique scent, one Geno would recognize anywhere. She sat across the table in her clothes from last night, inhaling the eggs and vegetables he'd placed in front of her like she was afraid they'd disappear. And who could blame her? He had a larger than usual appetite this morning too. Only some of it was for food.

Pushing away the empty plate, she said, "That was amazing. I still can't believe you're such a great cook. I'd gain ten pounds a month if I ate like this all the time."

"You'd work it off, somehow." He'd make sure of it, if he cooked for her all the time. And he knew the best kind of exercise they'd both enjoy.

As if she read his mind, she blushed. The steady stroke of her fingers on the handle of the mug reminded him of other strokes throughout the night. If she seemed shy the first time, she made up for it later. As if to prove he could do it again, he felt the swell of blood rushing south. Now was not the time. Taking deep meditative breaths and telling his mind to blank out, he felt only minor relief.

From his post under the table, Lucky suddenly rose and lumbered to the window, barking his gruff greeting. Moments later, Geno heard it too. A car crunched on gravel, coming to a stop in front of the closed gate.

"Is someone here?" She followed his gaze outside and they both stared at the late model high-end car parked behind hers. No one got out, and the windows were tinted too dark to see inside.

"Do you know who it is?"

He shook his head slowly at her question. She rose when he did, and together they moved out to the balcony, examining the car.

"Why don't they get out? Do you have a bell or something for them to ring?"

He shook his head again, realizing he'd have to go down and see who this was. Lucky continued his low woofs, fogging the glass and slobbering on the window. When the driver door pushed open, he gave a joyous bark, as if to say, finally.

Beside him, Agnes recognized the driver at the same second Geno did. Her gasp was loud enough to let the man know where to locate them, and on cue, he looked up.

"Oh my god, my brother cannot find me here. I have to go." And she began rushing around the room, grabbing boots and purse and whirling in a circle.

"Agnes, relax. It's just Luke."

But she didn't respond, and when he turned away from the window, he found her on the sofa, yanking hard on her second boot with a panicky look in her eyes. She popped up as soon as the boot was in place, grabbing her purse again and looking around wildly.

"Where's my jacket? Never mind. You can bring it to me the next time you come into town. Keys? Where are my keys? You have to get me out of here, Geno."

He didn't understand her panic. It was only her brother, and the one she was closest to at that. Luke knew they both lived in the same town. What was wrong with her being here late on a Sunday morning? If he didn't know better, he'd think she was ashamed.

Thought of the promise slammed into him about the same time she dumped her purse out on the counter, searching frantically through its contents. The irony of the situation wasn't lost on him.

"Hold on. You can't go anywhere. There's only one driveway. His car is parked in it. You have no way of getting out."

"Then I'll walk. It's not that far to town. You can bring me my car later, after he leaves." She stopped to stare at him, as if this question just occurred to her. "What's he doing here anyway?"

Lucky's barking grew riotous, and a moment later, a knock sounded on the door.

"Geno, do something." Her stage-whispered command only added to the mayhem.

From outside, Luke called, "Hey Geno, you home?" The knock came again.

Agnes stomped her foot and waved her arms in frantic circles before diving into the bathroom and slamming the door.

Geno grabbed Lucky's collar with one hand the lock with the other. If Agnes felt the need to hide, so be it. It would only be a matter of time before Luke figured it out. Geno wasn't going to let Agnes wander far away, not when he'd finally connected with her at the most elemental level.

When the door swung inward, Luke leaned with one hand on the frame, a smile on his face. "Hey man, surprise. How are – whoa, that is one big ass dog. It is a dog, right?" He dropped the pose and took a step back as Lucky gave a yelp of excitement.

"Hey man yourself. This is definitely a surprise. When you said you were thinking about a visit, I didn't expect to see you on my doorstep a couple of weeks later. How are you?"

Still holding on to Lucky, the men fist-bumped and bro-hugged, slapping each other on the back. Not wanting to be left out, Lucky whined for attention.

Luke put out a tentative hand. "It won't bite it off, will it?"

Geno chuckled, releasing the dog, who immediately stuck his nose in Luke's crotch in welcome. "It's a he, Luke. Lucky, down. Shake."

The dog immediately dropped his butt and lifted a paw in welcome.

"Wow, he's smart. He didn't learn that from you, did he?" Luke took the proffered paw and shook it with caution. As soon as he let go, Lucky raised the other one and they repeated the process. Niceties completed, Lucky left them to sniff at the bathroom door and whine again. He pawed it a couple of times, and finally lay down in front of it.

"Does he have to go out or something?" Luke took a quick look around the room before turning to look back at Geno.

"No, that's the bathroom. Listen – " But he never got a chance to finish as Luke broke in.

"Bathroom, perfect. That's a long drive on a few cups of coffee, so I'll start my house inspection there." And he reached the bathroom door handle and pushed before Geno could stop him.

Luke's "What the fuck?" coincided almost perfectly with Agnes's "Damn it." Sister recovered faster than brother as she sailed past him, purse in hand.

"Geno, thank you for the use of the facilities. As I said, Leonora's friend's house is so far out of town, and I wouldn't have made it there comfortably. I'll continue on my way now." When her overly loud words stopped, she widened her eyes and mouthed the word 'keys' to him. Behind her, the door slammed on a cursing Luke.

"I need my keys. I have to get out of here." She flapped her arms as if she was going to fly out the window.

He'd almost be enjoying this if it didn't make Agnes so agitated. He couldn't let her leave like this. She'd have a wreck on the first turn. Besides, Luke had eyes, and he used them. He probably already noted two sets of used plates and cutlery on the table, with the mugs still steaming. With a quick nod of his head in the table's direction, Geno emphasized the obvious to her too.

Her gaze followed his lead, and when she noticed the evidence on the table, she closed her eyes with a look of resignation on her face. Then she opened them and became a blur of motion, grabbing the dishes and silverware and shoving them in a drawer. He cringed when she almost did the same with the mugs, liquid slopping. She seemed to think the better of it and poured them out in the sink, leaving them there. Then she composed herself again as Luke reappeared.

"So, Sis. Long time no see, because I don't count Skyping. How are you?" He stepped forward and wrapped his arms around her for a hug, and over his shoulder, Agnes shot Geno a panicked stare.

"You smell different. New perfume? And I like the naked face look. It suits you." He held her at arm's length as if assessing her features. Geno appreciated her forced smile as she stood still under the scrutiny. When her gaze slipped to his, he read the agony of embarrassment in her eyes.

Geno couldn't stand to see her crushed like this, so he let her off the hook. "Agnes was just leaving, Luke. It's a strange coincidence that you ran into her here." He opened the closet panel and took her jacket from the hangar. "Text me when you get back, okay? And tell Leonora hello for me. I'll see you both tomorrow."

She pushed her arms into sleeves as he held the jacket. She slapped her pockets once, relief flooding her face with the jingle of keys. Her polite smile dropped back in place and she put out her hand as if she planned to shake his.

Forget that. Too much had happened for them to part company on a shake, whether she was embarrassed or not. When he grabbed her hand, Geno didn't give her time to think. He pulled her in close and dropped a kiss to her lips.

"Drive safely," he whispered in her ear, and she backed away quickly with a little shake of her head. That wasn't going to chase him off either.

"Luke, you'll need to move your car. Back down to the main road until Agnes passes you, then come back in." Geno walked behind Agnes to the door, giving the dog a command to stay as all three humans made their way outside.

Agnes turned when she almost reached her car and said, "Luke, give me a call while you're in town and we'll get together. Leonora will love to see you." And she slid behind the wheel and started the engine before either man could respond.

Chapter 23

"Ma sends her love." Settled in the chair on the balcony, the steam rising from his coffee mug obscured part of Luke's face. Geno hoped his face appeared equally blurry, because he hadn't been able to control his chaotic thoughts about Agnes. Her exit sucked the energy out of his refuge. He never noticed how monochromatic and dull it appeared.

He took a sip of tea to stall, searching for a benign topic. "I miss her marinara sauce. Despite following her recipe to the measure, I can't duplicate it."

A genuine laugh boomed out of Luke, scaring up a few birds in the process. "She'll tell you it's because you don't put enough love into it."

Geno's throat tightened in response. Yes, that sounded like Sophia, though how she could talk about love but not be accepting of her own flesh and blood was beyond his understanding.

"You always had a way with Ma. The bros all say hello too and Papa said he expects you there for the holidays. They all consider you one of the family." But no word about their daughter and sister. No such invitation for their niece and granddaughter. How could they be that cruel? He couldn't stand to think about it, not without taking his anger out on the messenger.

"So, you and Agnes." Luke took a sip of his coffee as he shot Geno a speculative look.

Geno took a cleansing breath. "So, you and – wait, what was her name again? The latest one, the scion of a branch of the Kennedy clan or something. What are you doing here, and where is she?" He mirrored the sip of his tea.

It wasn't like Luke to show up unannounced. It wasn't like him to leave his work behind either. His caseload at the law office was huge, and he rarely took time off without months of prior planning.

"Breena. Her name was Breena, and she's a has-been in my book. Too much baggage. Too pushy. She wanted me to run for office. She dropped hints about a big flashy wedding and starting a family, ready to grow a dynasty. I'm not into the whole marriage thing." Luke shifted deeper into the chair to underscore his discomfort and ran an absent hand over the carving on the balcony railing.

"How long will you be in town? I'm sure the guys would love to meet you, with whatever time you have left around visiting with Agnes and Leonora."

Luke gave a little frown, staring at his coffee for a moment before taking a long drink. When he looked up again, he said, "I'm staying indefinitely."

That was more of a surprise than him showing up in the first place.

"Did you win a big case, making the senior partners so grateful they gave you a long vacation?" Within the ranks of one of Boston's oldest prestigious law firms, making partner before the age of thirty was unheard of. In the usual way of things, Luke would still be waiting. But he did it at twenty-eight. The man never rested.

He shook his head again. "I quit."

Geno snorted tea through his nose and coughed in response. Luke gave him a few rough slaps on the back, and Lucky whined and put his head in Geno's lap until he could again speak.

"You quit? Did you tell your parents? Your father must have had a stroke and your mother is probably saying continuous rosaries."

Luke shook his head, leaning forward and glancing around as if he expected spies to overhear them. "The truth is, I was tired of the mega-practice, and criminal defense is draining. I'm ready for a change, and I'm damned tired of the winters, so I decided to come west, to become reacquainted with my little sister and niece."

Geno took a long sip to avoid an immediate response. Something was not adding up. Luke might hold his family in esteem, but he held himself in even higher regard. He was a city boy, and he celebrated the frequent heavy Northeast snowfalls by cross-country skiing to work. Luke was also the only brother who kept in regular contact with Agnes. The story he was telling was more warped than rotten wood.

Luke continued, "Though I'll have to work hard not to get all twangy like you. You don't sound like the North End anymore, boyo. Or should I call you dude? And I should probably talk about the vibe of this place being groovy or something." His thick Boston accent made everything sound foreign.

"Don't change the subject. I don't believe you. You and Agnes and Leonora talk on the phone and on Skype. You and I talk regularly, and you've never given any indication of wanting to quit your job. You've often said you didn't want to live anywhere other than Boston. Why the sudden change of heart?"

Luke stared at him for a moment, then raised his hands in mock defeat. "Okay you're right. I was ready to leave the firm and Boston, but I hadn't settled on a location. Then I heard something through the rumor mill that had me concerned, so I decided to do something about it. You remember your promise to me, right?"

Geno nodded with sudden sickness about where this was going.

"Conrad Walsh is now sizzling hot stuff in the football world. When his team went through their first and second-string quarterbacks last year, Walsh did a fair job of helping them to a wildcard slot, even if they didn't make it to the finals. The team upped his salary in exchange for a contract extension. He had months to grow up and into the job, but instead, he turned into a real shit-head. You and I both know he was always that way, but when he spent most of his playing days on the bench, it didn't matter. Now he's in the spotlight, and it isn't all for good reasons." Luke stared into his coffee mug in apparent disgust.

Conrad Walsh, the man who was Leonora's father in sperm only. A one night stand he claimed not to remember, a lifetime of changes for Agnes. Nine months later his daughter was born, and he never bothered to see her. His family wealth insulated him, and his parents laughed when Ma and Papa Amendola demanded Conrad make an honest woman out of their daughter. It sickened Geno then, and the feeling had only grown stronger with time.

"This post-season, Walsh has something of a public relations issue. He's been accused once too often of using and abusing young women. In a couple of cases, this included paying for abortions. It's hush-hush, of course, since the women received payments on the premise that they keep things quiet. There have been a couple of allegations, charges, and investigations into domestic violence, but none of it sticks. The team's owner and management are getting jumpy and fed up with his nonsense. They're playing hardball, expecting him to clean up his image."

"How do you know all of this?" Luke and Walsh had been in the same grade in school, and while they weren't part of the same crowd, the gossip lines strung across all clique boundaries. Besides, Luke was someone with a capital S now, and that meant money in Walsh's circle.

"I heard it from some buddies of mine who are closer to his action. On the surface, none of this would matter, except for one important thing. Walsh seems to think the best way to clean up his image is to show he's an upstanding guy who does right by his past mistakes."

"And Agnes and Leonora suddenly fall into that category." Geno didn't need confirmation. He felt his anger rise to the surface. No one should use a child that way, and Agnes had been through enough. He couldn't stay on the sidelines, not when they could be hurt.

"Yes, and Walsh is on the hunt for them. He figures he can sweet-talk Agnes into being his image of redemption, and the fact that Leonora is disabled doesn't hurt his cause either. He'll be kind and considerate until the furor dies down. Then he plans to dump them."

"And that's why you're here."

Luke nodded, a frown of concentration on his face. "I have to sit for the bar in California to practice here, so I'm in a holding pattern, business-wise. I figured I'd watch out for Walsh and try to deflate his little scheme. But I need your help with Agnes. She will be hard to handle."

It didn't sound like there would be much difficulty in getting her on board to hold Walsh off. Agnes would never stand for anyone using her daughter, and she had too much self-respect to be a doormat.

"I can't see her doing anything other than giving Walsh a kick in the ass."

Luke stared at him with a look of surprise. Then he shook his head. "Oh man, you don't know, do you? You know why she went with him in the first place, right? Puppy love, a crush, or so I thought. But she let something slip a few months ago. She's never gotten over him. Agnes still considers herself in love with Conrad Walsh, the asshole."

Now it was Geno's turn to stare in shock.

Luke added, "You promised me you'd watch over her, but neither one of us thought it would be difficult. Well, I think the time is up. Walsh is sniffing in the wind. Whatever you have to do to insulate her from him." He leaned forward as if to emphasize his point, his gaze hard. "Geno, whatever you have to do to protect Agnes and Leonora."

He set the nails with more force than necessary, preferring the hammer to the nail gun as a way of working off his simmering aggression. On Sunday, Luke had stayed for another couple of hours, filling Geno in on more gossip from the old neighborhood as well as continuing snippets about Walsh.

While he could separate all of this in his mind and consider Walsh a threat that would be neutralized, he couldn't shake the fact that Luke believed Agnes was still in love with the jerk. The man had done nothing to earn her love or her trust over the years. Luke had to be mistaken, but there was only one way to know for sure. He had to ask Agnes, and the idea of what he might hear petrified him.

But a conversation was proving to be harder to arrange. Monday, Agnes had been busy catching up with Luke, and then Leonora wanted to spend time her after-school time with the only uncle she knew well. Agnes politely declined Geno's invitation to dinner. On Tuesday, she was busy with work – and with Luke again. Today he expected something of the same, and trying to find inner peace wasn't working for him. He and Agnes needed to talk.

"You're going to put a hole through the beam with a hammer throw like that."

While he clutched the tool reflexively, he was glad he wasn't up on a ladder, because he'd have jumped and landed on his ass. He spun around, ready to lift the hammer and take on any comers.

"Whoa, just me, Geno. What has you pissed off? I've never seen you look so mean."

Powers stood inside the front door, hands raised in surrender. That he was curious was evident, not only in his statement but his expression. And it was probably true. Geno rarely felt this angry, and Powers had likely never seen him worked up over much of anything, other than mildly annoyed over an uncooperative wood joint.

"It's not a good idea to sneak up on a guy with a hammer," he said, turning back to finish setting the offending nail.

"I'm surprised you didn't hear the street noise when the door opened, but whatever. So what's going on?"

Geno took a final swing and replaced the hammer in his tool belt. "We're in the queue for the plan change. No issues."

Powers nodded, wandering the space and examining the framing Geno had completed. He nodded approvingly. Then he turned that curious gaze back to Geno.

"Are you sure there's nothing you want to tell me? Because if you have a problem, you know the wolf pack has your back."

Powers was too perceptive by a long measure. This was something the wolf pack might be able to help him with, but not until he talked with Agnes. If, as Luke said, she considered herself to be in love with Walsh, there was no reason to even bring it up to his friends. Walsh would be in the picture, and Geno would be out of it.

What he couldn't wrap his mind around was why she was willing to share a night with him if she was in love with another man. Likewise, why hadn't she told him about her feelings? Was it all simply sex? And what was with her confusion and surprise afterwards? He added it up multiple times and couldn't get a consistent answer.

He would dwell on it further, but for the moment, he had to get Powers off his back. If his friend sensed something was seriously off, he'd pick at it like a scab until he drew blood.

"I don't think I had a chance to tell you one of Agnes's brothers is in town. Luke Amendola, the brother closest to us in age. We were fairly tight growing up and we've stayed in touch. I thought a guys' night might give him a break from the intensive time with his sister."

Powers nodded, his scowl clearing. "Yeah, let's get as much of the wolf pack together as we can and have a beer. How long is Luke staying?"

"Indefinitely. There's a story behind it, but I'll leave that for him to tell. You'll get a kick out of his Boston accent. I didn't realize how much of mine I'd lost. When I talk with him for a while, I start gutting my consonants again."

Powers chuckled as he pulled his phone out, already texting. "I'll let Tess know. She and Serena have been trying to get Agnes to come out for a drink with them. They want to get her more involved with the girl tribe. I think they mentioned the word lonely. You know how determined they can be if they get an idea like that."

Chapter 24

"This is all very peculiar. You're hovering, brother dearest. I'm fine having a night apart from you. What are you worried about?"

The truth was, Luke was being both mysterious and overshadowing, and she didn't like either of those things. He wouldn't say how long he was staying. There was no room for him in her tiny apartment, so he stayed in a bed and breakfast in Flynn's Crossing, but every day, he showed up early and hung around late. He even sat in a waiting room chair at the spa for most of yesterday. Frankly, she was getting tired of having him underfoot.

"No, I don't think I should go out with Geno and his friends. I mean, Leonora has a play date and you'd be by yourself."

All by herself was something she'd like to be, to figure things out. She'd successfully avoided Geno all week, and if he was with Luke and the wolf pack, he wouldn't be trying to contact her. That would be good, since she was too confused to attempt to explain herself.

She'd seen the expression in his eyes the few times he'd tried to get her alone. He was upset. He'd been hovering almost as much as her brother, and between the two of them, she felt smothered by testosterone overload.

"I have things to do. Tess and Serena want to have drinks, so I'm going to go out with them." While the invitation was real, she didn't plan to act on it. In fact, as soon as she got Luke on the road, she planned to call Tess and bow out.

The apartment doorbell rang, and Leonora burst out of the bedroom, tote bag in hand and jacket in place.

"I promise we won't be late, Mommy. Noah has to work in the morning, so he'll bring me home at eight. Bye." Her quick kiss was almost a drive-by. "Bye Uncle Luke." And she sped out the door before Agnes had a chance to issue a cautionary word.

She scrambled to the window, followed by Luke. Both of them watched as Leonora tumbled out the door and into her friend Charlotte's hug. Linking arms, they turned to the SUV at the curb, with the good doctor standing at the driver's door looking up and waving. When everyone settled inside, he pulled away and disappeared down the street. The whole scene took less than a minute.

"What do you know about this doctor?"

Agnes fought the urge to punch Luke in the arm. Given that he was buff and muscled, it would mean bruising her hand before she made an impact on him. Besides, they were no longer children.

"He's a nice guy. Single parent, two girls. Charlotte's the younger. He's an ER doc at the hospital. He moved here around Christmas to get the girls away from messy divorce memories. He's asked me out."

"Oh really? I'll have him checked out. Can't be too careful about any guy you're dating."

Okay, that was enough. "Luke, first of all, I'm a grown woman with a good head on my shoulders. I make my own decisions. I date who I want, and if you think you can do something about that, you'd better go back to Boston right now."

He settled on the sofa and crossed his arms, glowering at her under lowered brows. When she didn't continue, he asked, "What's the second thing?"

She didn't want to give him the satisfaction of saying she wasn't dating Noah. Which was worse, your brother lecturing you because you were dating, or because you weren't?

The doorbell sounded again, saving her from further explanation. She made a production of checking the contents of her purse, as if preparing to leave herself.

Luke didn't move. When he didn't say anything either, she finally gave him a pointed glance, then turned her stare to the door.

"Go. Geno will be waiting, and it's impolite to sit there like a dumb ass once you've accepted. I have plans, I told you. I'll be leaving on your heels." Or not.

Luke gave a deep sigh, as if having a younger sister was the heaviest cross he had to carry in this life. He kissed her on the forehead, much as he had when they were older teenagers and on good terms. This felt – nice.

"Call me when you get home, and when Leonora gets back. I want to know you're both okay." He paused with his hand on the door's handle. Concern showed in his gaze as he turned back to look at her. "Be careful, all right? Be very careful out there."

She barked out a laugh. "Luke, this is Flynn's Crossing, not big, bad Boston. It's a very safe place. And I've been on my own for a decade now."

He didn't reply, simply frowning before opening the door and heading down the stairs. His behavior was definitely strange, like he expected to find monsters behind every light post and hiding in the bushes. Something was up.

Curiosity had her walking to the window once more, pulling the curtain back enough to stare down at the sidewalk. Where Noah had parked moments before, Geno's truck now stood. He and Luke argued on the sidewalk, with her brother gesturing up toward the apartment while Geno crossed his arms and shook his head in disagreement. Finally, Luke threw his arms up in the air and moved to the truck's passenger door, wrenching it open and climbing in. Geno's gaze rose to meet hers, and she dropped the curtain, even though she knew it was a dead giveaway. Let him think what he liked about it. She wasn't sneaking a look at him.

All right, maybe she was. She couldn't get Saturday night out of her head. Geno, playful, sweet Geno, was unlike any man she'd become intimate with before, not that the list was long. The surging emotions were something she didn't expect. This was her childhood best friend, after all, and she felt way more than friendship when she thought about him.

She picked up her phone, scrolling through contacts to find Tess's phone number. She'd call and make her excuses. Marinating in her feelings would be a much more productive use of her time.

Just as she found the entry, the doorbell rang. It would be just like Luke to come back, second-guessing his night out with Geno and company a third time and coming home to check on her.

The bell rang once more, and she pushed the curtains aside to see something unexpected. Tess and Serena waved at her, motioning her down with big gestures. She sighed, because dressed as she was for a night out, costuming designed to placate Luke, she wasn't going to fool the women when she pleaded exhaustion and a plan for an evening with her feet up. Besides, they probably expected her to back out, and she already had a taste of how persuasive they could be.

There was no escaping it, but the restaurant was only a short walk away. She could go for a drink, fake a headache, and come home in short order. Come to think of it, the headache might not even be faked based on how she was feeling. Locking her apartment door and descending the stairs, she met the smiles of the women with an over-bright one of her own. If they noticed it was forced, they had the good manners to let her get away with it.

"Girls' night out, here we come," Tess said, by way of greeting, as she linked arms on one side.

"And Bliss, we can't wait to get to know you better," Serena added, linking on the other.

She wasn't sure why she felt compelled to say it, but when it popped out, she felt sudden relief. "It's Agnes. Please, call me Agnes."

"Are those real?"

Geno glanced up at the stuffed animal heads mounted high on the pub's walls. He'd had a similar reaction the first time he came here, but after so many visits, the unique features faded into the background. Mallory's was a singularly unusual institution in an area filled with them.

"Yes, they're real. The guys are back there."

Geno watched Luke swing his attention with apparent difficulty, glancing over his shoulder as if he expected the animals to charge. When they reached the table in the corner of the bar, the seated men rose as one.

"I'm Powers. Good to meet you, Luke."

Powers lounged to one side, Dane to the other, and Mac was across from them. Two chairs were kicked back, expecting them. Introductions completed all around, they sat and poured beers from the pitcher in the center of the table. A toast, a round of first sips, and the men stared at one another.

"So, you're going to fill us in on the stories about Geno growing up, eh Luke? Was he always so laid-back? It's like nothing rattles him." Dane took another sip of his drink after completing his pointed questions. How Luke might respond had Geno's gut do a sudden roll. Maybe beer wasn't such a good idea.

"Laid back? Hardly. He was a nervous kid, always the one trying to keep Agnes in line. That was nearly impossible, so he got in trouble along with her."

"Agnes? Who's Agnes?" Mac crunched on a handful of pretzels and stared between the men.

"My sister, Agnes. You might not know her. Back then, they were Altimari and Amendola, the inseparable."

Geno considered keeping his mouth shut, but eventually, it would come out. If it came from him, perhaps he could control the damage.

But Powers already knew and felt compelled to enlighten the others. "She's Bliss, at the day spa on Main Street. She and Geno go way back."

Mac shook his head in recognition. "I know Bliss. I met her at Roxy's kitchen unveiling party. Great woman. Roxy says she has a cute little girl, too. She's what, seven or eight?"

Luke jumped in before Geno could form the words. "She's almost ten. Born in Boston, though you can't tell by listening to her. For that matter, Agnes and Geno don't sound like the North End anymore either. And those two," he pointed at Geno and circled his finger, "were tight. For a while, we thought they'd get married."

Powers put his glass down slowly. Dane grew still and watchful, and Mac didn't bother to hide his curiosity as he leaned in. Geno fought the urge to squirm under their scrutiny. All eyes settled on him, and he realized they waited for him to say something. The thought occurred to him about the time Powers narrowed his eyes as if sizing him up and finding him lacking.

They thought he was Leonora's father.

Chapter 25

When Tess, Serena and Agnes arrived, Roxy was already holding court with the owners of the new restaurant, seated at a table on the courtyard patio overlooking the river. Agnes hung back as the other women exchanged enthusiastic greetings. Then Roxy turned to her, pulled her into a hug, and said, "Welcome to the girl tribe."

And as simple as that, she was enfolded into their company. No one asked her disturbing questions or quizzed her on her past. Conversation flowed around Roxy's remodeled kitchen, Tess's issues with challenging pricing for flowers from foreign growers, and the upcoming donor drive for Serena's nonprofit. Agnes had promised herself she'd leave after a drink and a polite amount of time, but by the time she'd ordered sparkling water to keep Serena company for the second round, she realized she didn't want to go.

She'd never been part of the cool girl clique, growing up. In her neighborhood, they'd known each other from the cradle and boundaries were formed before most of them hit puberty. She'd had Geno, though, and she hadn't minded.

Until he didn't want to hear about her everlasting love for Conrad Walsh, or her plots and plans to attract his attention. She discovered make-up and hairstyles, and she never looked back. Geno hadn't pulled away, exactly, and he was always there for her when she needed him. But they never were as close after that.

Tess said, "So, Agnes, you and Geno go way back, don't you?"

She nodded automatically, her head in the past before she realized she'd responded.

"It must be nice to have a friend who's known you since childhood." Serena squeezed lemon into her fizzing water as if the question was casual conversation.

Except for her, it wasn't. Agnes wondered if this was the time to leave, pleading a need to be home for Leonora's return. But it was only seven o'clock.

"Oh, and your brother's in town. He's out with the guys tonight. Luke, isn't it?" Roxy swung her eyes to Agnes as she asked.

Now all three women stared at her. None of their questions were more than the simple getting-to-know-you things people commonly shared. But for her, it felt like a threat.

As if sensing her distress, Tess put a hand on Agnes's arm and changed directions. "Tell us about your family, Agnes."

This she could do. They already knew she had a brother, and by the time Luke was done shooting his mouth off tonight, the rest would be known too.

"I have five brothers, all older. Peter, Paul, Matthew, Mark and Luke."

"Wow, Catholic, I'm guessing? Were your parents hoping for John next?" Serena smiled in jest, and Agnes felt her lips curve in response.

"I was a disappointment, so I got Agnes, as in pure and holy. I think my mother was praying for a miracle, or maybe a nun. She gave up on that idea by the time I reached middle school. I was a tomboy through and through. I didn't discover boys were for something other than beating up or competing against until I was in high school."

The women laughed, and Agnes felt her tension lessen. That lasted for only a moment, as Roxy said,

"Geno's quite an amazing guy. Was he your first love too?"

Another innocent question, but Agnes didn't know how to answer it. She'd never thought of Geno in those terms, at least, not until last weekend. Her first love had been Conrad, and since then, no one else competed. She was beginning to think she'd had it wrong all along.

Her silence must have lasted too long, because when she looked up, the others stared at her with worry. Roxy said, "I'm sorry, I don't mean to pry."

Agnes waved it off. She really had to think about this. If Conrad walked back in the door tonight, what would she do?

"We're making you uncomfortable. Let's change the subject. How is the remodeling of your new space going?" Tess patted her arm again.

But they'd given her more to consider. For once, maybe listening to the input of others would be better than trying to work it out by herself. These women were smart and compassionate and had faced their own demons along the way. And they embraced her as one of their own now.

"Geno's doing an amazing job. He had perfect design ideas. It seems whenever it matters most, Geno is looking out for me."

The table stayed silent when her words faded out. She decided to be brave and rip off the bandage to reveal the truth.

"I know what you're all wondering. Is Geno Leonora's father? No, not by birth. But he could have been by marriage. If only I'd found a better way to spring that on him."

The small restaurant wasn't crowded, both a blessing and a curse. They had privacy in the darkened booth.

"How are you? You and Leonora, I mean?"

His attentive tone, caring and gentle, made her eyes prick with tears. He'd always been like this, worried when something hurt her, ready to protect her against all comers. If only she'd listened to him when he warned her what a prick Conrad Walsh was.

"We're okay. I found childcare so I can go back to work. Leonora's therapy is going well. The doctors say she'll be able to walk almost normally once she's been through the full treatment."

He nodded, a pinch of worry pulling his forehead tight over his green eyes. They shone brightly, as if he too fought tears. Opening his mouth, he paused, an unsure expression crossing his face. His mouth closed, and he stared at the baby in the stroller.

"I found a doctor who's willing to take payments, did I tell you that? Leonora qualified for state assistance, but there's still a balance I have to take care of. It will take me some time, but I want to make sure she never has to suffer in the future because I didn't do everything I can now."

She heard his gasp as if in sudden pain, and his lips thinned into a line. When his eyes rose to meet hers, she read the anger easily.

"Isn't he helping?"

They both knew exactly who he spoke of.

"No, he laughed when I asked him. He didn't even want to see her. His parents dismissed it too. We would need blood tests to prove he's the father. Then I'd have to hire an attorney and sue him for support, and if I do that, I won't have any money left for Leonora's specialists. Besides, in this town, the Walshes are

royalty and I doubt I'd find anyone who'd be willing to go up against them."

He nodded, but his anger didn't seem to lessen.

"Walsh is an asshole." Geno slapped his open hand on the table, drawing the few eyes in the place to them, and in the stroller, the baby fussed a little before settling back to sleep. He looked immediately contrite. "Sorry, I don't mean to wake her."

Agnes frowned at him. He didn't understand. Conrad had a big career ahead of him. The NFL courted him on a daily basis. If his father didn't insist he finish college first, he'd be drafted and playing in the lucrative spotlight. His skills were rare among college quarterbacks. Plus, he didn't remember that one night last summer, much as she would never forget any detail of it. Most of it wasn't pleasant, but it was her first time, after all.

Geno, on the other hand, was already settled. Okay, not completely settled, but his professional path was clear. He was a carpenter, a good one, and while a college degree would help him advance someday, it wasn't a necessity. She tried not to think about how she might be screwing up his future. His future was more like hers, working class, blue collar, easily transportable. Plus, they were Altimari and Amendola. They were destined to be together, friends forever.

And someday, when Conrad came to his senses, Geno would understand and step aside. Why this thought brought a sudden desire for a good cry, she wasn't sure. She could blame her post-pregnancy hormones. They were still out of whack.

She cleared her throat, suddenly parched despite the coffee in front of her. Taking a fast sip, she choked on it, tears squeezing from her eyes. He could assume they were from her liquid inhale. Geno came to the rescue, as usual, slapping her back and offering her a stack of napkins.

"Thank you." She sniffed and blew her nose in the paper, embarrassed that people around them looked at her in sympathy. They had no idea. Geno handed her another napkin, and she repeated the process. Onlookers lost interest or took pity and gave them privacy again.

"Geno, I have a favor to ask you."

He stared into her face, his eyes flicking across her features. His smile came easily, as if he thought whatever came next would be something simple. It wasn't going to be, not by a long shot.

"Ask away, Agnes. You know I find it impossible to deny you anything, even though sometimes I should. You're my best friend."

He hadn't approved when she wanted to party with Conrad. He never said I told you so when she found out she was pregnant, though something between them broke and she hadn't been able to fix it. Since he'd rescued her after Conrad's party, their relationship had been strained. He treated her with the same kind of laid-back distance he used with casual acquaintances. But he still called her his best friend.

She burst out the words before she could rethink it. "Will you marry me?"

He went completely still. Not even his eyes blinked. All background noise faded away and time seemed to slow down as she waited. She counted his breaths, matching hers to his. His face closed down and became so neutral, it looked like an empty mask.

Agnes cleared her throat again, grabbing the coffee mug for a sip. It was empty. Reaching for the carafe on the table, she refilled it in continuing silence. The next sip blistered her tongue, but the pain felt welcome. When he still hadn't said anything, she lifted her chin and stared at him.

"Did you hear me, Geno? I want you to marry me and help me take care of Leonora. We don't have to have a church wedding. City Hall is fine. We can make it quick. It will be platonic. Don't worry, it shouldn't be for long. Just until Conrad is ready to settle down and he and Leonora and I can be a family."

She realized she was babbling, nervous energy making her say things before she thought them through. His expression didn't change, staying more distant than China.

"I don't expect us to have a real marriage. I just think Leonora deserves a man in her life, a good man. You know, just until."

His anger came on so suddenly, she thought she was looking at a different person.

"You want us to get married?"

He bit off each word, his voice low and yet strong and brutal in his disbelief.

She lifted her chin higher, flicking the blanket off Leonora as if emphasizing how important this was. Not for her, but for her child.

The child picked this moment to open her big brown eyes, gurgling with joy as she saw two big people staring at her fixedly. She was blessedly unaware of the drama surrounding her. She pulled her arms free and waved her little hands at them, gifting them with a piercing laugh.

Agnes couldn't help but smile back at her. Her light in the darkness. Despite her disability, Leonora was perfect, and Agnes would protect her every single second.

Geno's hand drifted out as if it was a waft of smoke. When a finger came within reach, Leonora latched on with her good hand, unconcerned that she couldn't with the other. That would come later. Her grip was tight, and Agnes watched Geno's face transform into something soft and gentle. A single tear traced down his cheek.

"Let me get this straight." He inhaled deeply, his eyes staying on Leonora. "You want me to marry you, but in name only. And only until Walsh is ready to take over."

When he put it like that, it sounded incredibly stupid. Not only that, it disrespected him as a person and as her best friend.

Leonora cooed and batted her eyelashes at him, as if she knew it was an important time to be charming and precious. More tears followed the first on Geno's face as he moved his caught finger back and forth. Agnes didn't dare glance around the room to see if they were making a spectacle of themselves. And frankly, it didn't matter. She'd do whatever it took, make herself into whatever kind of exhibit she needed, if it convinced him.

"No."

His single word stilled her, and while a hundred arguments to convince him raced through her head, she found she couldn't say a word. Geno shook his head, his shoulders hunching deeper into his body and tears flowing freely down his face. When he looked at her, the despair and sorrow in his eyes killed any idea she had about trying to change his mind.

"I can't, Agnes." His voice sounded tired and defeated, as if her request broke something irreparable inside him. "I can't be your stopgap measure while you wait for another man."

Around the table, Tess, Serena and Roxy were silent when she ended the story. Agnes thought she saw a tear in the corner of Tess's eye. Serena cleared her throat and said, "Wow. That was intense."

Roxy nodded, taking a rapid sip of wine before saying, "Damn, that was one ballsy move, girlfriend."

For some reason, that didn't make Agnes feel better. She waited in silence for Tess's verdict, but the woman stayed quiet.

"I know what you must be thinking. It was stupid, but I didn't think so at the time. It seemed like the ideal solution. But Geno was right. I gave my virginity to a man who was an asshole. He didn't even remember me when I drove to Dartmouth and told him I was pregnant." She choked on the memory. And boy-oh-boy, what a way to let the women get to know her better.

"I get the feeling there's still more to this." Serena's words matched the sympathy on her face.

Agnes nodded. "I kept asking, begging, pleading. He kept saying no. Even after he held Leonora, he said no. I couldn't believe he'd turn away from a helpless child. Finally, I had enough. I threw my coffee in his face, grabbed the baby, and raced out the door." She paused, ashamed of her actions all over again. "I didn't realize until much later how it all sounded. I asked him to raise another man's child, as a temporary placeholder." Closing her eyes, she could still see the pain in Geno's face. "I disrespected my best friend. I'm surprised he talks to me today."

The touch of Tess's hand on her arm felt soothing, more than the gentle stroking should have been. Agnes felt like her spirit was being soothed too.

Tess said, "It's okay, Agnes. We're all capable of desperate things in the name of love. Now, it's time to leave the past in the past. You and Geno are destined to be together, and the future will happen."

Agnes glanced at her, skepticism warring with a strange hope inside her.

Surprised, Agnes said, "That's what our first grade teacher said."

In response, Tess gave her a big smile.

Chapter 26

"It's not what you think."

Geno knew he should probably feel grateful for Luke's clarification. But he hated putting Agnes in the spotlight like this. Every protective bone in his body jittered in response as the men regarded him with obvious questions in their expressions.

Luke continued, "Unfortunately, Leonora is the product of a major lapse in judgment on Agnes's part. I love my sister, but she was a little wild back then. And don't get me wrong, I love my niece. It's a shame she has her disability to deal with, because she has big dreams."

Thankfully, the wolf pack took another look at Geno's face, rigid in anger and embarrassment, and let the matter drop. Sudden discussions of sports teams didn't lessen his tension, though, not when Walsh's name came up and Luke explained the rest.

"You had to give them the full story. Couldn't you have kept it to yourself? What is Agnes going to say?"

Geno hit the steering wheel in frustration. The only part Luke left out was the one he didn't know about. Only Geno and Agnes knew he'd turned her down. But the rest of the story would be enough to set her off.

Glancing across the truck cab, he noted that Luke seemed to be considering that same fact with more than a little trepidation. Neither one of them forgot how Agnes could be when her temper was riled up. In middle school, Luke had half his head shaved bald while he slept by a vengeful sister.

"I'll stand by my decision. I thought they should know, in case Walsh actually finds her in this off the map little town. The fact that she uses a fake name for her salon helps, but I wouldn't put it past him to have someone searching government databases and public records. As a business owner, Agnes is in the system. She'll be visible."

Geno could see the practicality in Luke's argument, but that didn't mean he had to like it. Leonora deserved privacy. And it was Agnes's story to tell, not her brother's.

"Besides, you heard what the guys said. She's part of the girl tribe now. That means they'll all protect her. Those men seem tough, so they're good to have on our side. Hey, why are we stopping here?"

The spot in front of Agnes's apartment was filled, but parking a little up the street on the other side was even better. As he put the truck in park, he could see the lights on upstairs and occasional movement behind the curtains. Geno couldn't tell if it was Agnes or Leonora, and he hoped the little girl wasn't home yet. If the wolf pack knew, the girl tribe would soon too. The story would never go further if Agnes didn't share it, but that was far enough. She deserved to know what had happened, and he was going to push Luke to come clean about not only tonight, but why he was really here.

And then Geno would know too, if only by Agnes's reaction.

"I don't think this is a good idea, man." Luke didn't move to release his seat belt, even as Geno unclipped his and opened the driver door.

"She deserves to know. Other people are now part of this. Do you think word won't get back to her? You think news travels fast in the North End? Wait until you experience warp speed here."

Luke still didn't move.

"Look, out of the truck, before I drag you out. Let's get this over with. Tell Agnes the truth about why you're here. She thinks you're on an open-ended vacation. She doesn't know about Walsh. How can she protect Leonora if she doesn't know what's possibly coming?"

Luke sat there, watching the lit windows. Finally, he said, "I'm trying to frame my argument. Give me a minute."

Geno got out of the truck and stood at the curb, leaning on the hood and looking up. Agnes must be home from her visit with the women, and her daughter might be back from her play date. His options were limited. He could leave Luke with Agnes to explain and he could take Leonora for ice cream. He knew she loved chocolate mint.

But then he wouldn't know for sure if Luke gave her the full story. Her brother might still harbor some misguided idea that Agnes in the dark was safer than Agnes alert and aware. He needed to stay and push if necessary, even if that meant putting Leonora in the bedroom with a movie and ear buds.

Luke finally opened the passenger door but hesitated once more. As if knowing patience wasn't something Geno had a lot of at the moment, he glanced over and shrugged, then slammed the door on his way out and dragged across the street, his shoulders hunched.

"When I try to come up with a rational explanation, I sound kind of stupid to myself. Was this such a bad idea?" He didn't look over to see how Geno took his admission.

"Your heart is in the right place. You're her brother and you worry about them. But you forget that Agnes is grown up. She's had to take care of everything on her own with little to no help from her family." Or her best friend.

"Man, that is harsh. True, but harsh. But out of sight, we tended to forget about how hard this must have been on her. And yet, she moved across the country, started a successful business, and raised an incredible little girl. I'd say she's done amazing things."

While he was glad Luke recognized this, Geno doubted this would make the coming revelation any easier. He wanted to get it over with. Most of all, though, he wanted some one-on-one time with Agnes. They needed to talk, now more than ever.

When they reached the front door, Luke paused without pressing the button. "Maybe you should tell her."

Geno raised his arm and punched a finger on the doorbell, considering if this was the time to let go of his peacemaker tendencies and deck Luke. Before he could make up his mind, Agnes came down the stairs and opened the door for them.

"And to what do I owe this honor? Checking up on me, Luke? You too, Geno?"

>>>>>

She might as well get it out of the way. They would hear about it soon enough. And Agnes wanted to be the one to explain it to them.

"Leonora will be home soon, so I only have a few minutes." She waved them into the living room and closed the door, checking her watch mid-motion.

She saw the pointed glance between the two men. Geno looked angry, an expression she'd seen a lot of in the past few days. Luke, on the other hand, looked guilty, and she knew from personal experience that he must have done something major to give it away.

"What's going on? Come on, you might as well spit it out." Because in a minute, she'd yell out what she exposed. No one would get a word in while they all argued about the wisdom of her admissions.

"What makes you think something's going on?" Luke's indignation would be laughable, except for the fear in his eyes.

"I know you, Luke Amendola. Now cough it up."

The smile came and left Geno's face so fast, she swore she imagined it. He stared at Luke and crossed his arms, and probably would have tapped his big sexy foot, if that was in his make-up. Since it wasn't, Agnes did the tapping for both of them.

"I have something to tell you. Maybe you should sit down. I don't want you to take this the wrong way. I was only trying to do what's best for you."

Geno threw his hands up in the air. She might have appreciated the show of frustration with more humor if she didn't have a sense this was going to be bad news.

"You must be one hell of an attorney if that's the best argument you can come up with," Geno growled.

Luke shrugged again, then stared at the wall while he rattled off his indiscretion.

"And?" She sensed there was more to come.

Luke glanced at Geno, who looked even fiercer than he had moments ago.

"Tell her," he said in a voice that bordered on violent. It was so unlike him, she stared for a moment. His protective stance and narrowed eyes clearly scared Luke into continuing.

"Do you follow what Conrad Walsh is doing now?" His tentative question hung in the room for seconds before she realized her brother expected her to answer.

She met Luke's gaze with a direct stare of her own. "Of course I do. He's Leonora's father, so I keep track of him. Besides, one day he's going to come to his senses and want to develop a relationship with his daughter. When he's ready, I'll be waiting."

A sound like a wounded animal came from across the room, and she turned to find Geno with his hands spanning the window frame, his eyes closed and his forehead against the glass. His face held no expression that she could see. The stark shift made her uneasy. Did he think she was merely using him last weekend? He should know her better.

But then, they'd been strangers for so long. She couldn't help but compare the stories about Conrad's antics with Geno's solid, earthy reality. Confusion swamped her. How could she expect him to understand when she didn't herself?

Crossing the room to stand behind Geno, she put a hand on his back. His flinch at her touch made her gasp.

"What's wrong?" She heard a threatening wobble in her voice and willed it to even out.

"Nothing, Agnes. Am I understanding this right? You want Walsh?" The monotone of his voice pushed distance between them. She stepped back in response, shrinking from the coldness emanating from him.

"Well of course I do. Leonora should know him, don't you think? I'm sure he'll mature, and once he does, he'll realize he has responsibilities."

Geno spun from the window, taking a step toward her even as she stepped back once again. He didn't look angry. More like disappointed. And hurt. And immeasurably sad.

"Did you ever consider you might not be his only responsibilities, as you put it? Where there's smoke, Agnes, and in this case, that smoke is probably a string of women left with children he's fathered. He's not a good man. You deserve better."

And before she could answer him, he stalked to the door, opened it with almost unnatural care, and disappeared down the stairs as he yanked it closed behind him. Luke sat as if frozen to the sofa, and Agnes stared at the door as it bounced open and swayed to a stop.

"Hi Geno. Where are you going?" Leonora's voice sounded from the outside door. Geno's answer sounded patient and calm, almost tender, Agnes thought. She heard the outside door close and Leonora's footsteps sounded on the steps. Agnes couldn't help pushing the curtain aside to watch Geno stalk to his truck. Right before he swung in, she thought he looked up at her and shook his head in apparent disbelief.

"Hi Uncle Luke, hi Mommy. Geno said he had an emergency and had to go. What's wrong?"

Agnes always tried to tell her daughter the truth, but in this case, it was impossible. She herself had no idea what the truth was, and she wasn't sure that even if she knew, she'd like the answer enough to want to give it a voice.

Chapter 27

Geno stared at the colorful mass of plastic and wires, wondering if this was a good idea any longer. He thought it would benefit Leonora, but Agnes might not agree. He had to face facts. While he believed she was his destiny, the woman had another idea. That idea was named Conrad Walsh.

Though how she could believe Walsh would be good for them was beyond his understanding. Geno had spent days trying to puzzle it out. The man was scum, even if only a fraction of the stories in the press were true. He hadn't been speaking anything other than the truth that night when he asked Agnes if she honestly believed she and Leonora were Walsh's only casualties. Paternity tests were pending on at least three other children.

He tried to shake off his depression over Agnes's words. That didn't change what he wanted to do, to give Leonora a birthday present she would truly appreciate. Seeing that little girl smile and have a chance to realize her dreams would be reward enough.

Damn, he was confused. He loved Agnes, but was it really love if it wasn't reciprocated? He loved Leonora like the daughter he never had, but he had no right to be in her life without a relationship with Agnes. He'd given up his opportunity a long time ago. Agnes's words last weekend seemed to confirm Luke's assertion. She still loved Walsh, despite his lack of support for the child he fathered.

A car horn beeped from the end of the driveway. He heard Lucky bound across the yard and bark in greeting. He wasn't good company no matter who was there. When Lucky continued barking, he got up reluctantly and peered out the workshop door to see who he needed to send on their way.

The small grey sedan parked outside the gate, and he didn't need to see past the windshield to know who was inside. It was Agnes's car. Lucky leaped up on the chain link fence, making the gate shake on its posts, delighted to see a friend as she got out of the car. Agnes put her hand through to give him a couple of scratches. She looked up at Geno before he had a chance to draw back inside. If her wave was tentative, he figured there should be a good reason for that.

He couldn't ignore her without being obviously rude. Ducking inside to hide the completed present, he returned to the doorway and leaned against the frame of the workshop. Agnes used the small gate next to the driveway to let herself in, laden with a covered tray in her hands and a tote bag over her shoulder.

Her hair hung down, loose and tossed in the slight April breeze. Jeans and a thick sweater emphasized her curves, and he felt a pang of regret that they'd only had that one night. He would enjoy getting to know her better in the biblical sense, but he was afraid that like a drug, each time would only pull him into a tighter snare of addiction.

She talked to Lucky as they walked up the drive. Whatever she had in the tray held the dog's soulful attention. When the dog lifted on his back paws and tried to get his nose under the foil covering, her laugh made Geno's gut clench in pain. As she came closer, her steps slowed and the laughter faded away. She seemed nervous as she met his stare.

"Hello Geno. We haven't heard from you for a few days, Leonora and I, I mean. I wanted to make sure there were no hard feelings about last weekend. You know, about Luke's big mouth. Mine too, for that matter. I shouldn't have told the women about asking you to marry me, not without asking your permission first. I'm sorry about that. I wanted to get it off my chest, and if it makes you feel any better, while they didn't chastise me, they understood your side more than mine. Hell, even I understand why you said no." She shifted from foot to foot in apparent ill ease as she continued to balance her packages and occasionally hip-check the dog.

Geno hid his surprise. He'd kicked himself about turning her down perhaps a thousand times. As much as he regretted his response that day, it sounded like Agnes was also sorry she put him in that difficult position.

But he couldn't bring himself to forget about it. He didn't say anything, because he didn't know what to say.

Agnes shifted her load again, the nip of teeth on her lower lip showing her agitation. When she took a deep breath, he watched her breasts rise and fall under her red sweater. Lucky sat at her side, drooling his approval at whatever she carried. Geno thought he could drool too, but in his case, it would be over the woman.

"You don't say anything when you get angry, do you?" A hint of indignation in her voice echoed the spark of anger in her eyes.

"You don't stop talking when you're nervous, do you?" Even as he was mad, he heard the humor in his tone. It was impossible for him to stay mad at Agnes for long. She meant too much to him.

"He speaks. Lucky, did you hear that? The great man speaks."

The dog barked in response, making another lunge for the foil.

"No, this is for him, not you." She extended her hands, balancing the tray at arm's length. "A peace offering, Geno. Can we please call a rewind? I don't want to lose your friendship again."

He sniffed, detecting the scents of sugar and cream. Unlike Lucky, who would forgive and forget if given any kind of food, Geno didn't cave that easily. Sniffing again, aromas from the pastry hiding in the tray warred with the warm, enticing scents of Agnes. If he didn't control himself, he'd knock the food to the ground and sweep Agnes off her feet. Lucky would probably be in favor of that.

"It's your favorite, *Genovese*, homemade cannoli. I stuffed them just before I came over, so the shells should be nice and crisp. Three are pistachio and three are chocolate. I remember how you love both flavors." She lifted a corner of the foil, giving him a peek-a-boo look inside, and as he sniffed again, the smell of chocolate added to his confusion. The cannoli looked great, but Agnes would taste even better.

He couldn't bring himself to say anything, fearing that he'd declare his feelings for her like a fool. She didn't need to ask for forgiveness. Even though he didn't understand her love for a man who wanted nothing to do with her, he'd willingly jump a tall building in a single bound to have the privilege of staying at her side.

"Please, say something. I can say it again. I'm sorry, Geno. I didn't mean to hurt your feelings."

He let himself exhale, not realizing he'd been holding his breath for so long. He didn't move, not trusting himself to get closer without wrapping his arms around her and laying his lips on hers.

"What's in the bag?"

She gave a relieved smile at his question. "Lasagna, garlic bread, and wine. I brought a picnic for us. Please, Geno, can we break bread and make up?"

He'd rather kiss and make up, but this would suffice – for now.

"Where's Leonora?"

"Luke's staying with her at the apartment. He said he'd be happy to stay for as long as I need to make this right with you." The pleading expression let him know she would stay until he said he forgave her – or sent her away.

Reaching for the tray and tote, he said, "Let's pull your car inside the gate and get this food in the house. I have something I want to show you."

She'd insisted they eat immediately. As she warmed the lasagna and bread and he set the table, he wondered if forgiving and forgetting without a discussion wouldn't be wisest move. What did he want more, Agnes as a friend, or as a lover? In the best future he could envision, she'd be both. He had to remind himself that, peace offering aside, she loved another man, one who wasn't worthy of her in any way.

Dinner came with a truce of sorts. He didn't bait her to explain why she would even consider Walsh good father material. She didn't ask him why he stormed out last weekend. She probably figured that out. Agnes talked about her surprise for Leonora's birthday, two weeks at art camp.

"Maybe it will be good for her. I talked to Noah about it, and he suggested I let her try new things and find her comfortable level of ability."

Geno tried not to feel hurt that she'd go to Noah with a question like that, reminding himself the man was a doctor as well as raising daughters on his own. It was logical for Agnes to turn to him, as the father of her child's best friend if nothing else. He never thought of himself as the jealous type, but he wasn't feeling too kindly toward Noah at the moment.

Would Agnes be angry about the robohand? He hadn't built it without her permission for any reason other than making it a wonderful surprise for Leonora. Agnes didn't like advice unless she asked for it. This gift could fall in that category.

"What did you want to show me?" She bit into a cannoli after asking the question, leaving a trail of chocolate shavings on her cheek.

"You got something on your face," he said, feeling the pulse of his blood pick up as her tongue darted out and tried to wipe off the chocolate.

"Did I get it?" She lifted her chin as if welcoming his inspection, shifting close enough to brush her shoulder against his arm.

"Ah, no. Allow me." And he leaned forward, intending to lift a napkin and wipe the food away. But this was Agnes, his Agnes. Her lips parted. Feeling lightheaded and crazed, he put fingers under her chin, tilted her head, and dropped his lips on hers.

She tasted like the cannoli, and something much richer. Every pass of his tongue over hers brought an affirmation that this was where he was supposed to be. Altimari and Amendola. They belonged together. Walsh hadn't earned any right to be in the picture. Except Agnes wanted him. That reminder made Geno back off quickly.

Agnes blinked up at him as if trying to focus her eyes. She breathed out a fast gasp and shook her head slightly.

"Did you get it?" Her question came in a hoarse voice that aroused him beyond sanity. His jeans had become more snug as the evening wore on, and now, the constriction was to the point of painful.

"No, I didn't. Let me see if I can remedy that."

He leaned closer, and this time, she kept her eyes open and locked on his. He noted the hazy desire in those darkened depths, as her lids sagged and long lashes swooped in to hide whatever she was thinking.

He didn't want her thinking. He didn't want her comparing him to any other man or imagining this was anyone other than him, Geno, kissing her. The need to have her focus that desire on him made him move faster and slide fingers into her hair to hold her mouth in place.

That might be his downfall, he realized, not that he didn't jump off this bridge willingly. One more night of Agnes was better than nothing. If he handled it well, he could drive all thoughts of Walsh out of her head, at least for a few precious hours.

He released her lips, trailing his mouth across her cheek until he licked off the pastry cream. She moaned, a small sound that made him consider where else they could drop some so he could lap it up. If she let him, he'd buy bags of cream and spend days finding inventive ways for them to enjoy it. He knew how they could burn the calories off.

"Geno? Do you forgive me?" An airy breathlessness as he tugged on the shell of her ear with his teeth made her tone a whisper.

He couldn't lie. "I'm working on it." He bit down a little harder, enjoying the tremble moving through her body and into his.

"Work faster," she said, as she grabbed his face and brought his mouth back over hers.

Her kiss tasted wild and reckless, sweet like the pastry and spicy like her. He wanted to lose himself in that amazing mouth, his reasons why he shouldn't getting lost in the flames rapidly eating him up from the inside out. Agnes made him this way, and he didn't want to question why it wasn't a good idea.

Her fingers dipped to his throat, gliding up and down under his beard until he felt the skin twitch even when she stopped. The scrape of chair legs brought her closer, almost sitting in his lap. If he had a notion they should move to the sofa, she waylaid it when her fingers traced down his chest and climbed back up under his t-shirt.

"We're wearing too many clothes." She nipped at his neck under his ear as she finished speaking, and the sensation went straight to his groin.

He slid his hands under her sweater as he said, "I couldn't agree more."

Completely in sync, they drew apart far enough to lift each other's tops off. Under the red, she wore more red, a lacy bra filled to overflowing with creamy skin. His fingers itched to trace the edge of intricate weaving and dip inside to tease her nipple. But Agnes seemed to have other ideas.

Out of the corner of his eye, he dimly registered her hand reaching for another cannoli. Then he got lost in her mouth, dipping deep inside and tracing her teeth with the tip of his tongue as she moaned. The sudden cold shock of something trailing down his chest made him draw back abruptly.

She held the cannoli against his skin, allowing the pastry cream to follow a path from his sternum down. Agnes seemed to be fascinated by its progress, and when his muscles jumped at her light feathering touch, she smiled.

"*Agnese*, you're stealing all the dessert." He heard the strain in his voice, and he was powerless to change it.

"I'll make you more," she said, still teasing his belly. Each time she did, muscles shivered, and his erection twitched and grew harder.

"That's not what I mean." He wrapped an arm around Agnes and let his fingers trail across the soft skin of her back, until he reached the clasp of her bra. He flicked it open and pushed the fabric aside, cupping a hand under one breast as he reached for another cannoli.

He waited until her dazed eyes rose to his, watched as her pupils dilated further and her lips parted on slight pants. Then he drifted the cannoli in circles around her breast until he reached the hardened nipple. "This is what I mean," he rumbled against her skin, right before he licked.

The taste of her, rich and heated with that hint of spice, overwhelmed the cheesy cream. He licked the goose bumps raised on her skin, biting gently on the tight nipple and tugging. Her fingers curled into the back of his head, pulling him closer, and she moaned louder.

"You taste amazing." He couldn't get enough of her.

"It's my grandmother's recipe," she said.

He paused, lifting his head in his confusion. Filling his mind, a sudden vision of Agnes's grandmother, a severe old woman always dressed in black, who berated anyone and everyone in old country Italian with a significant number of curse words thrown in, was a definite mood killer. He loosened his grip, intending to release Agnes and find a gentle way to extricate them both out of this haze of lust. Sex wouldn't solve anything.

"What's wrong?" Her hands remained locked behind his head, making it impossible to pull back completely.

"Your grandmother?" He almost laughed.

Her dazed look cleared quickly, replaced by narrowed eyes and an intense stare. "For the filling, you idiot. God, I cannot believe you. One minute you have me tied up in knots, and the next you're marching away like a righteous bastard. Here's what you can do with these damned cannoli."

There were three left in the box, and her nimble fingers grabbed one and slapped it on his chest with enough force to smash the shell to crumbs and splatter ricotta filling everywhere. The pistachios raked down his chest as she made a point to rub it on as much skin as possible. Her eyes snapped at him in time with the movements of her hands, kneaded the sweet filling into his skin as if intent on giving him a massage.

It was the sexiest thing he'd ever felt. His erection throbbed with sudden anticipation and he forced himself to move slowly. He wanted to grab her, lift her up, and settle her over his lap so that her heat met his. The cheese filling would combust.

"Agnes, stop." He wrapped his hands around her wrists to hold her in place. Her breasts bounced as he pulled her closer, needing more force since she was intent on destroying him with yet another cannoli. Putting both of her wrists in one hand, he replaced the cannoli in the box and pulled her in close, not caring that the filling now turned into gooey cement fastening their bodies together.

His gut didn't protest now. In fact, he felt lightheaded, like he was floating. Agnes still fussed in his arms, and he couldn't be happier. One more night was more than he thought he'd get. And this time, he'd show her how she should be treasured.

Agnes wasn't sure why she continued to struggle. Maybe it was on principle, because what she wanted more than anything was to nestle against Geno's lean chest and let nature take over. She didn't want to think, didn't want to analyze, and most of all, didn't want to fight.

He released her wrists and his hands moved to her back, rubbing up and down in a soothing motion as gentle as floating bubbles. His breathing slowed with exaggerated deep inhales, as if he was trying to hold himself back. She drew small circles in the ricotta still clinging to his chest. From somewhere close by, she heard the vague sound of slurping.

Beneath her fingers, she felt Geno's chuckle before she heard it.

"What's so funny?" If he said he was remembering something else from their childhood, she'd take the remaining cannolis, box and all, and dump them on his head.

"Are pistachios okay for dogs? Because Lucky's scored in a major way. We've made a mess."

She looked down to find the dog lapping up ricotta and pastry flakes from the floor, as eagerly as she'd been licking at Geno earlier. In her case, it had nothing to do with the dessert.

Returning to trace her fingers randomly through the cream on his chest, she looked up into Geno's eyes. They twinkled down at her, twin emerald lights. His mouth formed a soft tender smile. He lowered his head, putting his lips on hers with the slightest pressure as he teased the seam of her mouth with the tip of his tongue. When she opened, expecting an assault on her senses, she got instead a soothing caress. She felt buoyant, like they could remain locked together like this for days without touching down.

Too soon, Geno disengaged and leaned back, smiling down as her, the brilliance of his eyes looking a little misty. "We really have made a big mess. We should get out of the rest of these clothes before we get food all over them too."

That sounded like a damned fine idea to her, and without answering, she scrambled off his lap and reached for the button on her jeans.

"Wait, what's your rush? Allow me." He reached forward, covering her fingers with his and tugging her closer. He pulled her in, taking a moment to lick up her belly to her breasts. Oh god, what he could do with that mouth. The tickle of his beard sent heat throughout her body until she was sure the remaining pastry cream would vaporize.

"*Genovese*," she said, not sure what she wanted. But he seemed to know. When his fingers slid inside to unbutton her jeans, they sent a quiver of need through her. The zipper sounded unusually loud, as if it should be able to be heard on Main Street miles away. When he pressed her back into the chair she stumbled out of earlier, she felt incredibly disappointed.

But he wasn't done with her. She should have known better, because Geno never did anything without a reason. He knelt at her feet and put his hand at the heel of her boot, pulling with a tug. When the boots were gone, his hands moved again to her jeans, and she lifted her hips to help him. Each movement was slow, measured, and so erotic, she thought she might explode in a firebomb of need.

Soon her socks were history, and she sat there in only her panties. She should feel strange, naked like this in front of her childhood friend, but instead, all she could feel was the heat. When Geno stood, she was eye level with the huge bulge in his pants, and her hands reached out to cup him and trace the length without thinking.

But he grabbed her hands, holding her off. "Not now, Agnes, please. I'm trying to take things slow, but you're making it difficult. You're so sexy, so incredibly alluring, and I want you so much. I've wanted you for years."

That startled her. "Years? But when? How? You turned me down."

He nodded, his face pained for a moment. "Yes, and I've regretted that day many times. But I also believed it wasn't the right time. This, though, this feels like the right time."

He pulled her up into his arms and turned her away from him, pushing her hair to one side and resting his lips against the side of her neck. The trail of kisses made the heat surge in her body, until it was an almost unbearable ache. Then he bit down gently on her ear lobe, and she gasped at the surge of pleasure. She might come from this foreplay alone.

"You have some smooth moves, Geno Altimari."

She felt his smile against her skin before he lifted his head. His chest rested against her back, the fine hairs creating an itch only he could scratch. She heard the slow slide of his zipper and the rustle of clothes being dropped to the floor. His fingers hooked on the sides of her panties, trailing them down her legs at an unhurried pace until she could step out of the lace.

"We need a shower. And a condom." He gave her a little shove toward the bathroom door.

She tossed her hair, glancing at him over her shoulder. The heat in his expression, as if he couldn't wait to jump her, made her so happy that she laughed out loud. Dancing away from his hands when he would have grabbed her, she said, "Yes to the shower, no to the condom. We're safe, Geno, and I'd like to give you a first time too."

When he grabbed this time, she let him catch her, and she spun and wrapped her arms around his head, pulling him down to her. This was exactly where she always wanted to be.

She'd taken his hand, pulling him into the shower once the water warmed and soaping him up like she planned to slide all over him. Her mouth under his made him forget all reason. No matter how much he tried to slow things down, breathing deeply and willing his libido to stop racing, it was impossible when Agnes was in his arms.

As if they'd done this a thousand times, he lifted her at the same time she jumped and her legs wrapped tightly around his waist. Sliding inside her was like heaven's gates opening with angels singing. She was tight, so tight that he almost came on the first thrust. Again he tried to slow their pace, but she had other ideas. She rode him hard, her head thrown back and water streaming down her hair. She looked like a goddess of pleasure, and all he could do is hang on and hope he satisfied her.

When she came on a cry that ended in a moan, he cushioned her as he sank to the floor, finally finding his own release when she surged over him one more time. He couldn't hear, couldn't see. All he could do was feel. He'd never been this complete, this sated, this at peace. He never wanted to let her go.

The reality of daylight came too quickly. Responsibilities. Their lives. His promise. Watching Agnes drive away was wrenching, even though he knew they'd built something new last night. Her insistence on going bareback was an amazing gift to him. As his first time, he'd never forget it.

At his feet, Lucky shoved for attention. Geno shook his head, his mind filled with the magic that was *Agnese* in pleasure. With company gone, the dog should have sprinted away, but instead, he stayed where he was, sitting by Geno's feet and looking down the driveway as he continued to give a squeaky whine.

"Yeah, I know, boy. I feel that way too. I hope she's coming back."

Because after the shower, after two more rounds in his big bed, and after a playful but casual breakfast of leftover cannoli and coffee and fruit, he wasn't sure she was. She set a distance between them and hadn't said anything about seeing him later or soon or at all. He was afraid he'd given her what she wanted, a night of passion, and that was all she'd ever want from him. If that was the case, he needed to protect his heart, because it cracked open a little more each time he was near her.

Chapter 28

"Mommy, I'm so happy I can have a big party. Everyone said yes, even Geno. He said he's bringing me a special present. Do you know what it is, Mommy?"

Leonora danced around the spa, dodging furniture and knocking into counters in her glee. She'd been like this for the last two days, ever since she learned her birthday party would to be held at Tess's home at the end of Main Street. At first, Agnes had politely declined, afraid that a band of rowdy children was the last thing Tess needed in what was sure to be an elegant home.

"You think the place hasn't withstood the test of time? You haven't met our friend Gabby's boys, have you? Or the assorted pets? They can't break anything that matters, Agnes. Please, it's our gift to Leonora."

And before she could protest again, Serena had added her encouragement, and Roxy offered to provide the food, including a cake in the shape of a fairy princess. Agnes felt the tears come to her eyes even now as she thought about their generosity.

"Nonsense, Agnes. This is what the girl tribe does for each other."

And as easy as that, it was settled. She felt like she'd been picked for the 'in' crowd in high school. These women and their men were nothing but gracious and welcoming. No wonder Geno loved them.

She didn't want to think about what Geno might be giving Leonora, either. Ever since that night she went to his house, she'd been riddled with confusion. She assumed what he wanted to show her was something other than the sexy, overwhelming passion that made her heart beat faster whenever she thought about it. And she thought about it a lot.

Since then, he'd been smiling and easy with her, not pushing, not questioning. When she caught him watching her with a shadow in his eyes, he hid it quickly, fading back into the gently teasing friend she'd known years ago. She couldn't accuse him of putting distance between them, not when she herself was trying to do it.

Her brother was another story. He'd been hanging around with troubling persistence, some days sitting in the waiting room chair at the spa with faked nonchalance. She stared at him now, reading a gossip magazine of all things, as diligently as if it was a legal brief.

"Don't you have to study for the bar or something? Or look for office space? Or maybe an apartment?"

He glanced up from the magazine and put a halting palm in the air.

"Done, done, and done. You'll be happy to know that I'm going into business here in Flynn's Crossing. I'm buying into the Armstrong practice, you know, the office in the new space on Main that Powers built? Just as soon as I have my bar results. I've studied my ass off, and if I don't know what's different in California from Massachusetts by now, I shouldn't practice anyway." He checked off the items on an imaginary list in the air and lowered his head to the magazine.

She poked at him again, because part of her couldn't believe he was actually going to make this kind of commitment. "And where do you plan to be living?"

He waved at her as if shooing off a pesky fly. "I have a place lined up, don't worry. Besides, I like that B&B. The women who run it are a great pair, and around them, I don't need to worry about being chased for my good looks."

She smiled at that, since she knew the couple he was talking about. Still, something was up with him. His overprotective presence was one thing, but Luke trying to hide from the interest of a bevy of women? Unheard of.

"Look, Mommy, there's Geno and Lucky. They're going next door. Can I go see them, please Mommy? Please?"

Leonora jumped up and down, a bundle of energy today. If Agnes didn't know better, she'd suspect Luke had fed her daughter sweets instead of a sandwich for lunch. She cast a quick glance at her brother, but his frowning gaze stayed fixed on the magazine. Whatever was in there must be riveting.

"I'll take her over," Luke said from behind the pages.

"Yay, okay, Uncle Luke. Let's go." Leonora yanked at his arm in sudden encouragement.

"Hold on. What's the rush? They'll be working there for a while. When I talked to him – " Luke bit off whatever he planned to say next with a quick glance at Agnes.

She gave him the stink eye, the one she learned from her grandmother along with the cannoli secrets, and he shrugged.

"You and Geno are very buddy-buddy, Luke. Care to share with me why that is?"

He shrugged again, standing and letting Leonora drag him to the door. When they reached it, he paused and sent Agnes a serious look.

"You'll be okay here, right? We're only a scream away if you need us, you know. Both Geno and I."

"And me," added Leonora.

"I'll be fine, brother dearest. You are acting very strange. Is there anything you need to confess to me?"

Luke looked away quickly, then back again. His serious gaze made her a little nervous. He opened his mouth, then slammed it closed and followed Leonora out the door without another word. Something in the worry on his face made her shiver in a sudden chill.

>>>>>

The men stood at the front of the shop, splitting their attention between the activity on the street and the little girl and big dog playing in the rear of the unit.

"She's on to it, no doubt about it. It will only be a matter of time until either she learns about it or Walsh shows his face." Luke shifted on the balls of his feet with nervous twitches.

Geno asked, "Who is she going to learn about it from? It's not like he's taken a full page ad in the local paper, letting Agnes know he's looking for her."

Luke shifted again, everything in his stance screaming guilt. "I might end up telling her, if she pressures me enough. She almost made me cave last weekend."

Geno felt his own nerves rattle. Would Agnes confide in Luke first, even after she slept in Geno's arms? Though there had been very little sleeping involved.

Luke continued, "She asked me to babysit Leonora, and when I declined, she demanded it. She said she'd withhold any and all of the cannoli she was making. Did you enjoy them?"

Geno almost choked on the mouthful of hot tea, using it as an excuse not to answer immediately. Hell yeah, he enjoyed them, but not necessarily in the way Luke meant.

"They were excellent. I'm not sure which kind I liked better." He barely kept a grin of carnal delight off his face. It was easier to do when he remembered that Agnes was now acting like it never happened.

Luke didn't notice his sudden sobering. "I know what you mean. *Nonna Opa* was a mean old bitch, but the woman could cook. For some reason, when Agnes had Leonora, she took it upon herself to make sure my sister learned as many of the old country recipes as possible. Ma snubbed her granddaughter, but great-grandma stepped in instead. I even saw her crack a smile once, playing with the baby."

The men turned at a particularly loud girly giggle. Leonora had Lucky on his back, all legs up in the air, and he peddled like he was riding an upside-down bicycle. The girl laughed harder, and he peddled faster.

She should have a dog, Geno thought. Or a cat, if that was what she wanted. And whatever else her little heart desired, within reason. If only he could be the one to give it to her.

Turning back to Luke, he asked, "Is there anything new?"

Luke shook his head, his worried gaze returning to examine the traffic on the street. "Nothing. In fact, it's gotten almost too quiet. My sources say Walsh has reached some kind of agreement with the team owners and as long as he executes whatever he has planned and it's successful, he'll be in their good graces again. Otherwise, he will be forced out of his contract for immoral behavior. And yes, before you ask, his contract has a morality clause in it. How his agent got him to sign it in the first place is a mystery to me."

The whole situation made Geno exceedingly nervous. His ulcer twinged, reminding him that any time he wasn't on solid ground with Agnes, it hurt. He needed to figure out why she didn't acknowledge what they're shared, at least in private. But that would be something he'd settle only with her. He wasn't someone who aired his laundry in public.

Turning back to Luke, he asked, "Do you have any idea what he's planning?"

Luke shook his head, turning restlessly until he watched his niece again. "No, but I have my suspicions. Let's say that if I were his attorney, I'd say the redemption needs to be a major act. What makes a bigger statement than reconciling with your disabled daughter and the mother of your child in public?"

Geno put a hand to his gut as his ulcer suddenly burned like an open flame.

Chapter 29

Geno fingered the pink bow on the large box, straightening it once more. It was the umpteenth time he'd done that, his motions choppy and restless. Cleansing breaths weren't working today, nor were internal assurances that what was destined to be would be, and he could only partially influence the outcome. He'd never been a control freak, but now he understood why Agnes felt that way.

Tess and Powers had gone out of their way to make their main floor into a little girl's wonderland. Carrying the fairy theme throughout the party, the place was decorated in pink and white and yellow material so thin that you could read a book through it. Magic wands and crowns and costumes with full princess-like skirts made each of the girls look like she too could wave a wand and make everyone's wishes come true.

"Quite the party. I don't know how Bliss does it. She is amazing."

Geno glanced at Noah, similarly encumbered with a flat box with a yellow bow on it. He wasn't sure he liked him, even though, according to Leonora, Agnes had turned down every one of Noah's offers of dinner. The thought that he had a spy in the ranks and could keep an eye on things lessened the animosity he had for the good doctor.

Noah eyed him, taking in the big box. "Who's father are you?"

Geno raised an eyebrow at the query. He should probably have expected it. Would a grown man come to a fairy party like this unless his child was invited? Did wishing Leonora was his count?

Beside him, Lucky suddenly woofed, his body shivering in delight. He recognized his friend Leonora, and he adored her. Geno understood the emotion. He adored the child too, and he loved her mother.

He'd thrown in the proverbial towel on trying to convince himself otherwise. He loved Agnes Amendola, and if he could wean her away from her crush on Conrad Walsh, maybe he could have a chance at a relationship with her. Not the best friends from childhood kind of thing, but a full adult one, complete with kisses and intimacy and eventually, marriage. More babies wouldn't be bad, either.

Noah answered the call of a girl dressed in a blue princess skirt, leaving Geno standing in the doorway by himself again. Even Lucky had abandoned him, answering Leonora's command to come, sit, and shake. Her friends were suitably impressed as Lucky made the rounds, then dropped to the floor and rolled over. At least six little hands rubbed his tummy, and the dog's eyes rolled up into his head in apparent ecstasy.

"See anything yet?" Luke whispered the words as if they were playing a spy game. This was no game. They needed to keep Agnes and Leonora safe.

"Are you sure this is where your source said Walsh is going to make his move? At a child's birthday party? It's not his style."

Luke nodded in the affirmative. "What better way to break from the past than to do everything differently? I believe he's going to make his move here. Are the rest of the guys in position?"

Geno turned to look at Luke, shaking his head. "This isn't a game, Luke. Powers knows. Dane knows. Mac's working on those angles to track down Walsh's other children. Evidently a couple of the mothers are Hollywood players who like to latch on to celebrities and then sue for child support. I feel sorry for those poor kids."

Luke nodded in agreement, as both of them watched Leonora settle herself in a wingback chair with her pink princess skirt fluffing around her, Lucky seated at her side. Her friends giggled and settled around her on sofas and stools in a big circle. Presents were gathered and presented, and on the periphery around the room, adults chatted in small clutches.

Agnes stood by herself under an arch, looking to Geno like the most gorgeous mother of the group. She'd pulled her hair up into some kind of complicated looking knot on the back of her head, and she'd exchanged her usual slacks or jeans for a dress the color of lemons. To him, she looked stunning, or that's what he assumed his sudden loss of brainpower and air supply meant.

He didn't realize he'd walked over to her until he was standing beside her, looking down at the way her hair fell softly over one ear. Fighting the urge to drop the box and wrap her in his arms, he said, "Excuse me, Your Highness, but is this bit of floor taken?"

She looked up at him in surprise, the quick giggle of delight at his words bursting out of her as a blush washed up her cheeks. Agnes rarely blushed, so the sight of it threw him off whatever he was going to say next.

She batted her eyelashes at him, saying, "Why Sir Knight, it is not. Please, pray you, settle yourself here."

They both laughed, and Geno felt his tension ease. It was always this way. If he was worried, she could take his mind off his problems without even trying. When he was tense, she'd know what to say to make him feel better. In scary times, they supported each other and got through it together. Except, this time, she was the root cause of his fear.

Her laughter dissipated, her expression falling into solemn, wide-eyed examination of his features. He felt the flick of her gaze on each inch of skin. When she stared into his eyes once more, she licked her lips, and he nearly tossed the box at Leonora and grabbed her mother instead.

Agnes sighed, her eyes still on his. "Geno, I'm sorry. I've been thinking, and – "

"Geno, is that for me?" Leonora's voice broke into whatever Agnes planned to say, and he tore his eyes away from her with difficulty. Around the little girl, boxes and bags lay strewn haphazardly and presents were being passed around for examination by the children. Leonora held out her good hand as if commanding the box to rise and fly across the space and land at her feet.

Geno threw Agnes an apologetic look, one she seemed to understand and echo. He walked between children and bent on one knee, flourishing the present in front of Leonora.

"Fair princess, this is but a humble token of my esteem and admiration for you. I hope it is something that brings you hours, nay, days and weeks of joy and happiness."

He stayed on one knee, enjoying the look of unrestrained delight on Leonora's face. She tried to act haughty as she thought a princess should in these circumstances, but her giggles gave her away. Next to her, her friend Charlotte urged her to open the box. Even Lucky sniffed the package with eager pants.

Geno could count on one hand the times in his life he'd been as nervous as this. All of the others involved Agnes, and now, like mother, like daughter. He wished he'd made a bigger effort to get her mother's input on it, because if Leonora didn't like it, he didn't think his heart would stand it.

Everything seemed to slow down, each movement of Leonora's good hand as she ripped off the bow, tore into the paper, and started to reveal the carved wooden box.

"Oh, it's a treasure chest. Look, it has my initials in the top of it. Geno, you made this for me. It's the best present ever!"

He wasn't prepared for Leonora's sudden leap off the chair to land on top of him, and he tumbled backwards with the girl screaming in laughter. He looked up to see Agnes standing next to them and laughing too, though he could also see the sheen of tears in her eyes.

He righted Leonora, turning her back toward the box. "There's a treasure inside the chest, fair princess, so you need to open it up."

She skipped back to it happily, lifting the key where it dangled on the side and settling it in its slot. As she opened the lid, her eyebrows pulled together in that way her mother's did, puzzlement clouding her face when she didn't recognize the contents immediately. As he stood, he noticed the room had become unnaturally still, as if no one else was talking or moving. When he looked up, though, Agnes's mouth formed a perfect O of surprise that morphed into a big smile. For a minute, Geno thought she'd launch herself on him too. He kind of hoped she would.

"What is it, Leonora?" Charlotte peered over her friend's shoulder. "Oh, he made you a hand. Look, the fingers are pink. Cool."

He turned to watch Leonora's face mirror her mother's as she took the robohand out of the box and held it up. When her eyes came back to Geno's, her grin filled her face large enough to make his cheeks ache in response.

"You made me a hand, Geno. It's perfect! How does it work?"

>>>>>

"Okay, I have to admit you might have managed to come in on the very top of the cool gifts chart. What made you think of this? It's amazing, by the way. I can see she's going to be a natural with it."

Geno nodded to Noah's praise, feeling numb with happiness after first Leonora, then Agnes kissed him. The girl's was a peck on his cheek. The woman's, a hard press of lip on lip showing barely constrained passion. He showed Leonora how to put it on and gave her instructions on how to bend her wrist to close and open the fingers. The fit would need to be adjusted, but he expected that.

What he hadn't expected was the flood of warmth from every other adult in the room. Some of the women cried openly, and the wolf pack members slapped him on the back with ferocious expressions on their faces, along with a few shiny eyes.

Leonora didn't seem to tire of her water bottle demonstration, as she closed her robohand on the bottle and lifted it, then set it down with a few bumps and released it. Agnes broke away and walked toward him, a seductive sway to her hips and a smile wide enough to match her daughter's.

"Damn it, Geno, you make it impossible for me to do anything but love you, you know that?" She threw her arms around his neck and hid her face in his shoulder as she leaned into him. He thought he felt a tremble of emotion moving through her, and his body couldn't help but follow.

And his heart, his stupid heart, sped up in anticipation of undying love and devotion. That wasn't the kind of love Agnes meant. She loved him like a brother, or at best, an exceptional friend with occasional benefits.

He loved her like the only woman he ever wanted to spend his life with.

A commotion sounded from the area around the front door, and a tall man broke through the line of chattering parents and stood on the edge of the princess circle. His eyes scanned the room coolly, as if he expected to be noticed. He felt Agnes's arms loosen as she prepared to turn. Before she could, he took his chance.

Burying his face in her hair, Geno whispered in her ear, "*Agnese*, I love you."

She pulled back to look at him, opening her mouth to speak as a booming voice said, "Agnes, there you are. I hope I'm not too late for our daughter's birthday."

She thought she must be hearing things, because first, she thought Geno said he loved her. She didn't think he meant the best friend kind, either, based on the fear and desire she saw in his eyes.

Then she thought she heard another voice she never expected calling her name. When that voice mentioned their daughter, elation changed quickly to anger. She didn't want Leonora to meet her father this way. Not in public. Not in front of all these people. What the hell was Conrad thinking, coming in here without consulting her first?

"Mommy? Is that him? Is that my daddy?"

Leonora's frightened voice put her feet in motion, and she crossed the room and knelt by her little girl, wrapping a protective arm around her.

"Why don't we go outside for a little while, sweetie." She gave a little tug with the words, but Leonora's eyes were glued to the man who now stood alone. People faded away around him, and whispers grew to open chatter around the room.

"Mommy, tell me." Her mutinous face never turned away from the man, and Agnes gave up hope of moving this big reveal someplace private.

"Yes, sweetie, that is your father. He's never met you before. He's not that scary, I promise." She hoped. Conrad didn't look like the same man she'd crushed on years ago.

In fact, he looked like he'd slid by on his looks and his throwing arm for a little too long. What used to be a warm smile looked creepy now. His eyes were cold, without any human expression. His picture perfect features held droops and rough edges as if he partied hard and too often. He dressed like he was hanging out in some exclusive nightclub instead of a child's birthday party. Behind him, other similarly dressed men and women pushed to get a view into the room.

Powers loomed next to Conrad, his hand on the man's arm. "This is a private party. You'll need to leave."

Conrad shook off the restraining hand, laughing. It wasn't a happy sound. In fact, he sounded evil.

"I've come to see my daughter, to help her celebrate her birthday. Her mother has kept me away from her for long enough."

Agnes heard gasps from around the room, but for once, she didn't care what others thought. Leonora looked like she was about to cry, overwhelmed and uncertain about this strange man who didn't look happy to be there, despite his showy words. She stood and marched across the room, powered by anger and motherly protection.

Behind Conrad, she noticed one of his retinue had her cell phone raised, following his progress across the room as if she was shooting a video. She opened her mouth to yell at the woman, but Luke beat her to it.

"You cannot post a video of a child on the internet without the parent's approval," he said, putting his hand up to block her shot.

"Con's her daddy, and he said take the pictures so he can post 'em. So I got all the approval I need, sweet cheeks." The woman popped her gum in emphasis, though the vigorous nod of her head did nothing to move her over-sprayed hair.

Agnes spared a glance for Luke, noting his red face and obvious fury. She glimpsed Powers and his brother Dane moving as one in Conrad's wake. She didn't want to cause them trouble, so maybe if she got Leonora away from here, Conrad would follow. They could settle this someplace where they wouldn't be a spectacle in front of people she'd like to continue to call her friends.

Keeping Leonora behind her, she stood in Conrad's path and widened her stance. If he wanted to bother Leonora, he'd have to get through her first. She didn't dare look over her shoulder to see how her daughter fared in all this excitement.

"Conrad, what are you doing here? Why didn't you call first to see if this was a good time?" She pulled herself up straighter. Over the years, she'd forgotten how much taller he was, and unlike standing in front of Geno, Conrad made her feel like she should cower.

Behind her, she heard Roxy's voice and small shuffling feet. The kitchen door closed. Then she felt something in the small of her back. A hand. Looking down, she found Leonora standing next to her, holding on to her dress in the back with her good hand, her new robohand held in front of her.

"Are you my daddy?" Her young voice sounded unusually loud in the room, or maybe that was because everyone else had fallen silent, except for the popping gum from the bimbo.

Conrad barely glanced down at Leonora, instead flashing an ugly smile at Agnes as he looked her up and down. His eyes lingered where she expected them to, on parts of her he'd enjoyed ten years ago.

"Hello Agnes. You're looking good, almost as good as you did that summer, from what I can remember. We should get reacquainted."

The way he paused on the last word for emphasis left her with no doubts about what kind of acquainting he wanted to do. The disgusting smile made her skin crawl like a thousand ants tracking over her body, and she couldn't help the shiver of revulsion.

"Are you my daddy?" Leonora delivered the question again in a louder voice, and the women with Conrad giggled and pointed at her.

He glanced down with obvious boredom, then looked back again. His eyes narrowed with a predatory gleam, and Agnes wanted to pick up her little girl and run as fast and far as she could.

Conrad crouched down, but he didn't look at Leonora directly. Instead, his eyes locked on to the colorful robohand she held against the front of her body like a shield. He tapped it a couple of times as if testing to see how strong it was.

"You must be Leonora." His voice dropped from overly loud to a whisper. "You turned out pretty enough, though it's a shame about your hand. What is that, a toy to replace it? You don't need to wear that. In fact, it's better if you don't. Let everyone see your disability. It has much more tear-jerk appeal for the idiot masses. Yup, you two are going to be my ticket back to the golden boy spotlight. People will look at you and say what a saint I am for taking you in. Poor little disabled girl and her struggling single mother."

Agnes couldn't think for the anger rushing through her. How dare he belittle their daughter like this? He'd never been there when they needed him, and to waltz in now with some rotten scheme was insane. Hell, he was certifiably nuts, probably hit in the head once too often when he was sacked on the field, and the faster she got Leonora out of there, the better. She might deck him anyway. She still remembered how to throw a punch that could knock out her brothers.

She felt a hand on her arm, though whether it was in support or restraint, she wasn't sure. She didn't care. Her fists were clenched so tightly, she felt her nails biting into her palms. Powers and Dane were on either side of Conrad, and Luke shifted into her line of sight, watching her carefully as he squeezed the hand on her arm. Across the room, Conrad's buddies shifted from foot to foot, as if suddenly realizing they weren't welcomed here.

"Come on, *amatissimo.* I think you've worn that hand for as long as you should for its first test drive. Let's put it away and get you some punch, what do you think?"

Geno, caring Geno, lifted Leonora away from Conrad and moved back a step, and Agnes risked a glance at him. His focus was completely on Leonora, subtly turning her and blocking the scene with his body. Right before they disappeared behind the kitchen door, Leonora peeked over his shoulder and Agnes saw her daughter's tears. Leonora recognized evil and her father's dismissive attitude. That broke Agnes's heart, right before it made her blood boil over.

Stepping closer to where he still crouched down, she said, "Conrad Walsh, you are a bastard. Worse than that, you're an unfeeling asshole. How dare you say things like that to my daughter? How dare you say it to your own flesh and blood?"

Conrad stood and brushed his hands on his jeans, as if touching Leonora was a dirty proposition. He straightened his jacket and ran a hand through his hair, looking down at Agnes as if she was an annoying insect he intended to squash. He gave a disbelieving snort before continuing in a normal voice once more.

"Ah, Agnes. You always were a feisty one. But don't worry, I'll pay you well for this little lark. Just a few months. I don't need you around for long. The public's span of interest is wonderfully short. By the time we're into next season, the game will be all that's important to the fans and management won't care because we'll be winning. Come here, Agnes. Let's get a kiss on camera to fool my idiot fans. I know you love me, baby. You always wanted more of me. No, you can have a piece of Conrad again, at least for a little while."

He put out an arm for her to slide under. The hand on her arm magically disappeared. Luke no longer held her back. She would thank him for it later.

"You videoing this again?" Conrad called the question over his shoulder at his minions, and a couple of the women dutifully answered that they were.

"Yes, this will make for interesting viewing."

Agnes paused, her brain stuck on the voice. Tess. Then Serena said, "Yes, it will, I agree. Particularly the part where he belittled his fans. Does he think people are stupid or what?"

Conrad looked over at the women with a surprised expression, and Agnes followed his gaze. They both had their phones lifted in front of them on extended arms. When Serena caught her eye, she smiled and winked. Agnes felt a sudden rumble of relieved laughter bubble through her.

"Hey, I'm a public figure. You can't post something about me without my permission."

"We're not posting anything about you, Mr. Walsh. We're filming Agnes. You're just standing in her shadow." Tess gave a smug smile when she finished speaking, and Powers moved to stand next to her, as if anticipating a rush on Conrad's part. Dane did the same, putting an arm around his wife's shoulders. He leaned closer to see the phone's viewer.

"You framed that shot well, my love. I bet my contacts in the media would love to see this. I mean, Agnes is photogenic and gorgeous. And the audio volume is perfect, despite his whispering. People will hear every word anyone said."

The smug expression on Conrad's face melted away. The rough, nasty look that replaced it made Agnes wonder what she ever saw in the man. It would be a blessing if he didn't want anything to do with his daughter. Leonora would only be harmed by any contact.

"You never were that bright, and this just proves it. You could have had a nice little paycheck for a few months, Agnes. All you have to do was show up, bring the brat, and keep your mouth shut. Easy money. But no, you have to be difficult, like back then."

He flicked his hand as if brushing off a bad memory, and turned to make the same motion to his crew. His women tittered and made exaggerated faces of dismay, and the men laughed outright. As a pack, they swished out the door, their derisive words echoing back to the room.

Agnes felt her face burn with shame, but at the same time, she was proud she'd stood up to Conrad. An arm came around her shoulder, and she looked up into Geno's face. Pride filled his easy smile, and he dropped a quick kiss to her forehead.

"You planned to deck him, didn't you?" His face held tender amusement with the question. She nodded in response.

He kissed her forehead, then the end of her nose. "Good girl," he whispered.

"Mommy? Mommy, that man is not nice, and he's not my daddy."

A determined shove brought Leonora between them, clinging to both of them like she never planned to let go. Her face wore a determined expression and she directed an evil eye that would do *Nonna Opa* proud toward the group huddled at the door.

When Ages looked back, Conrad had stopped before the door and turned back to her. He looked her up and down dismissively.

"You'll be sorry about this day for the rest of your life. Enjoy your sad little existence, Agnes. And oh by the way, you were a lousy lay."

Geno couldn't help the jolt of anger. He was sure Agnes felt it too, as if he'd been struck by lightning. Walsh had no business saying any of this, not to Agnes, and never in front of their child. He released Agnes's shoulders, only to spin her and Leonora further away from Walsh and look into her eyes.

"May I?" While he asked the question, he planned to do what he wanted no matter what she said. Anger, frustration and vengeance made it impossible to step away.

"Be my guest." She pulled his face down and gave him a hot kiss, one that seared him to the core. When he turned back to the door, Walsh had a sneer on his face as he watched their exchange.

Geno ambled across the room, his measured pace a sure sign to those who knew him that he was pissed as all hell. Agnes would probably read it in the tension of his neck. He flexed his fingers in anticipation. Walsh kept the sneer but retreated a step, only to find Luke blocking his exit and the posse nowhere in sight. As his eyes flicked up to Luke's, Geno read the encouraging smile.

When he stopped a few feet away, Geno adopted a relaxed stance, like he was about to shoot the shit with the guy. He hoped Agnes had hustled Leonora back to the kitchen. He didn't want the child to see him start a fight, but it was one he was going to finish.

Geno said, "Walsh, this has been educational. It's always interesting to see what kinds of adults people become. And oh by the way, you're an asshole."

And he swung up his right, catching Walsh on the chin. When the quarterback's head snapped back, he looked stunned. Geno followed with a left that slammed into his nose, and blood immediately spurted out.

"What the hell are you doing? I'll sue you. You're all witnesses." Walsh tried to blot at his dripping nose, his face a picture of red rage.

Luke accommodatingly put a stack of fairy motif napkins in his hand, as he said, "Gee, I'm really sorry you ran into that doorframe, Walsh. Next time, you should be more careful when you're rushing out. Right, everyone?"

Around the room, loud agreement sounded from all of the adults. Geno shook out his hands, feeling strangely satisfied that he'd drawn blood and sorry Walsh didn't come back at him for more. He had years of anger to fuel a fight on Agnes's behalf. He could go a few rounds, and he was guaranteed to come up the victor.

Behind him, he heard sudden commotion. He thought he heard Agnes gasp out, "No, Leonora." He didn't have time to turn before rapid footsteps raced across the room and something landed against his back.

He was ready to turn and scoop up what he felt certainly must be Leonora, but he never had the opportunity. When the child stepped around him and crossed her arms in front of Walsh, she looked almost as fierce as Agnes had.

"You're mean and nasty and you say bad things, Mr. Walsh. I don't care if you are my daddy. I don't like you. It's my birthday party and you should go now."

No one bothered to hold back their laughter as a bloodied Walsh, the picture of outrage, spun on his heel and banged out the front door. The laughter continued as Geno scooped up Leonora and gave her a big hug. His peace grew as Agnes flashed a brilliant smile across the room. He felt his heart swell to the point of bursting when Leonora gave him a sloppy kiss on the cheek and patted the top of his bald head.

Behind them, a flurry of feet and chirping young voices announced the return of the other little girls from the kitchen. A flustered looking Roxy appeared, glancing around the room in apparent annoyance. "Did I miss the action? I was trying to keep seven little angels and the dog from attacking the birthday cake. Someone fill me in."

Agnes's smile widened as Tess and Serena raised their phones in unison and started narrating the videos. Geno walked toward her slowly, savoring the joy in her expression. Carrying Leonora felt as natural as if he'd been doing it her whole life. When they reached her mother, he lowered his head and gave Agnes his sweetest kiss, one full of promise and love.

"I think we have time to make up for, *Agnese*. I love you. I've loved you since the first grade, and there's no other woman in the world for me." He pulled her tight against his body and hugged Leonora in. He didn't want to let go, didn't want this sweet moment to end. He hoped that with time, Agnes would come to love him as more than a friend. Regardless, he'd take care of her and Leonora as long as they'd let him.

When they broke apart, Agnes's eye leaked big tears, and he felt wetness on his own face too. She reached up and brushed at his cheeks, laughing.

"Don't cry, *Genovese*. Altimari and Amendola. We're meant to be together. I love you too, Geno. It just took me a long time to grow up and figure it out."

When she pulled him down for another heart-stopping kiss, he let Leonora slide down to stand next to them. She didn't say anything. When he next looked down, the girl watched them with that big smile covering her face.

"I love you, Geno. Will you be my daddy? I want you to be my daddy."

Agnes burst out with a wet laugh, and he chuckled in response, agreeing that he'd love to be this precious child's father. Around them, he heard vague cheers and snuffles as their friends shared their perfect moment. He lifted Leonora to nestle her between them and the child gave him a big kiss on the mouth and patted his cheeks.

Geno looked into Agnes's eyes, the soul mate he'd known for as many years as he could remember. This was the only place he wanted to be.

"Ask me again, Agnes."

She looked confused for a moment, then her face cleared and her saucy grin spread from ear to ear. "Are you sure, Geno?"

"I am positive the answer will be different this time." He grinned back and lowered his head.

When his lips were a breath away from hers, Agnes said, "*Genovese Altimari*, will you marry me?"

"Yes, *Agnese Amendola*, absolutely yes." And he couldn't wait to prove it.

"I have a question," Leonora said.

"What's that, baby?" Agnes stroked the child's hair behind her ears as she gave Geno a tender glance.

"Mommy, what's a lay?"

Agnes gasped and sputtered as her cheeks turned bright pink. Geno thought it was one of the prettiest things he'd ever seen. As guffaws sounded around them, he kissed Agnes hard and fast and flicked a finger on Leonora's nose.

"Why, Leonora, it's one of the many things your mother does perfectly."

Epilogue – Three Months Later

The bustle of customers and prospects, business acquaintances and close friends, hadn't stopped all day. Hearty congratulations about her expanded business were only rivaled by best wishes on her engagement to Geno Altimari, and Agnes Amendola wouldn't have it any other way. The grand opening of the new and improved Bliss Day Spa was everything she could hope for, and the expanding love in her personal life was even better.

"Are you completely yakked out by now?"

"Have you been on your feet all day?"

"Where's Geno?"

She waved off the spate of questions from Serena, Tess and Roxy. One or more of them had been around most of the day, helping out with whatever she needed. She'd come to know some of the other girl tribe better as well over the past couple of months. With them, she felt like she was enfolded into a warm, loving family of sisters.

"Almost, yes, and I don't know," she answered, flopping into a chair for a brief moment of rest. Leonora whirled up, sweeping to a stop with her newest version of her robohand, holding in it a plastic cup she extended to her mother.

"I love the colors in your hand, Leonora. It's like a rainbow. I bet you're having fun with Geno when you make them." Tess reached out to turn that hand over and examine the palm closely.

"Yes, it's a lot of fun. We've already made improvements, and we shared those on the internet. There's a boy in Indiana who's going to try the last change we made. It's so cool to have friends all over the world who're all like me."

Agnes smiled and pushed a stray curl behind her daughter's ear.

"Besides, it smells good when we print things. Like pancakes." Leonora skipped away as she completed the comment.

The women burst into shared laughter.

Agnes added, "No, seriously, it's because of the material. It smells like breakfast cooking. I'll be in the house, and I can smell it all the way from the workshop."

Roxy asked, "And how is living together working out? Is there enough room for all of you?"

Agnes's smile widened. "Leonora has her own room. I'm still sharing one, but I don't mind sharing it with Geno, if you know what I mean. Besides, we're creating plans to build a great new master suite in the attic. Dormers overlooking the yard, a soaking tub for two, and even an office for me. We'll be rattling around in that place yet, just you wait and see."

Serena rubbed her protruding belly, the baby clearly planning to be big upon arrival. "And who knows when you'll be adding to that family, eh?"

They all laughed, but Agnes didn't mind. A big family of her own would be nice. She'd found one in these friends, even if they didn't share blood. Leonora would grow up with pseudo aunts and uncles and kids as close as cousins. Sometimes, your family of choice was bigger and closer than blood.

Looking around the room, Tess asked, "Seriously, where is Geno? I haven't seen him for quite a while now."

Agnes waved a hand, catching sight of the simple but perfect diamond Geno had put on it two weeks after he asked her to propose to him again. He said he'd bought the stone years ago because it reminded him of her, even at a time when they weren't speaking. When she finally stopped crying from the sentiment, she'd kissed him soundly and dragged him to the bedroom.

"Geno and Luke headed out on some mysterious mission a couple of hours ago. They were all hush-hush about it, whispering like a couple of Italian grandmothers. Honestly, I thought my brother was secretive, but Geno can be just as bad. He never did tell me where he went a month ago, some trip he said he had to make but wouldn't tell me about. I've never been able to get it out of him."

A bustle of activity came from the front door, and Agnes rose to greet the latest visitors. The grand opening had been terrific for generating new business, and she was more than delighted to welcome each and every one of her existing and new customers. She was proud of what she and Geno had made of this beautiful space. There wasn't another airy salon and spa like it in the region.

Sunshine from the street made it hard to see the faces of the people coming in, but it appeared to be a big group. She shielded her eyes and caught sight of Geno at the back of the pack, the shorter form of Luke beside him. Both men waved wildly, grinning like idiots, and she wondered again at what they had been up to.

A hand tucked into her fingers and she looked down to find Leonora smiling up at her. She knew she should be suspicious of that grin.

"You're going to be surprised, Mommy. And it's good surprise," her daughter assured her with a positive shake of her head.

"Well that's good, sweetie, but right now I need to greet these people. Time for business, okay?"

But Leonora didn't release her hand and step back, only turning to the group and smiling.

>>>>>

When Agnes looked up, Geno could read her face easily. Confusion and disbelief came first, then she blinked rapidly. A hint of tentative joy came next, and in the next instant, he was at her side. When he wrapped a supportive arm around her waist, he felt her tremble. When he pulled her forward, she looked up at him in amazement.

"Surprise, darling. I wanted to give you something very special as a present for your grand opening. This was the biggest thing I could think of."

Agnes stared up at him, her mouth opening and closing as if she didn't know what to say. That uncharacteristic situation made him laugh out loud. He pulled her forward again, and this time, she allowed him to urge her along.

A short, stout woman stepped forward from the group, and all talking ceased. She took another step forward, lifting hands that quivered toward Agnes. When fingers touched her face, he felt Agnes quake harder.

"*Agnese*? *Mie belle Agnese*."

And Geno felt that moment of perfect destiny when Agnes fell into her mother's open arms.

Pandemonium promptly erupted. Agnes was kissed, pinched, hugged, examined, and kissed again. Passed from mother to father to brothers, she had tears streaming down that did nothing to hide the joy on her face. When her eyes met his, she blew him a kiss and mouthed a 'thank you'.

"Geno, is it time yet?" Leonora waited patiently at his side, looking only slightly put off by the noisy group of relatives she'd never met before.

"Yes, sweetheart, go ahead," and he gave her a supportive push.

Leonora walked up to the imposing figure of Sophia Amendola with barely a limp. Again, the room fell silent, and it was as if everyone held their collective breath. This was the only part that worried Geno. Sophia had been silent on the subject of her grandchild. She might turn away, but Geno was hoping he'd convinced her to give it a chance.

In almost flawless Italian, Leonora welcomed her grandmother to California and told her she was happy to meet her. Then she extended a drawing she'd made at art camp, one of soaring mountains and a stream and a deer. Geno thought it was pretty darned good for a ten-year-old.

Over the child's head, he caught Agnes's worried gaze and gave her a reassuring smile. It would work out the way it was supposed to. Karma. Destiny, just like Altimari and Amendola.

Sophia reached out a shaking hand and took the picture, and then she took Leonora's right hand and stared at the missing fingers. The examination lasted for so long, he was afraid the girl would panic. Instead, she smiled at her grandmother with more confidence, and said, "Don't worry, *nonna*, it doesn't hurt."

Tears fell as the old woman took stock of Leonora's features. Then she pushed hair behind the child's ears and pulled her in for a tight hug, declaring, "This child is perfect. *Assolutamente perfetto. Agnese*, you've done good."

People started clapping and cheering, and someone yelled for wine and a toast. Geno felt his eyes misting up, and he closed them to enjoy the perfect moment. When he opened them, Agnes stared up in wonder.

"I don't know how you did it, *Genovese*, but you worked a miracle. Mama and Papa, and all the boys, and their families. I love you, Geno, I really do love you."

He pulled her in close and lowered his head. Each kiss they shared was perfect, special, and even better than the last. When he lifted his head, he felt the heat between them burn as hot as if they were in the room alone.

"Ah, *Agnese*, remember, it's destiny. Altimari and Amendola. We're meant to be together, and that's together forever."

THE END

About This Book

The inspiration for Measure Twice, Love Once came from two chance sources. The first was an article in Parade magazine in the Sunday paper. It featured a girl with Amniotic Band Syndrome (ABS) and her robohand, the Cyborg Beast. The facts about the support network helping to change lives for the better and the 3D printing of these simple prosthetics are real. To learn more about ABS, visit http://amnioticbandsyndrome.com/. To see the amazing things people are doing with robohands, visit http://enablingthefuture.org/.

My second inspiration came from the home of a dear Master Gardener friend in California. Her home is the model for Geno's little hovel, down to the fig tree! I've taken some artistic license with the carpentry features Geno would use, but like my friend's home, it reminds me of a cozy tree house, the perfect place to curl up with – yes – a good book and read away a rainy afternoon.

I hope you enjoyed reading this as much as I did writing it! Please leave an honest review on the site of your choice. Tell your reading friends. And help someone else discover the pleasure you've enjoyed!

Upcoming Excerpt

I hope you enjoyed this story about Geno and Agnes, reunited lovers destined to be together. Here's an excerpt from **Love's Fiery Prescription** (working title) due out in late 2015. Noah and Laurie have much to contend with!

He strummed his fingers along with the song. That riff, the one right there, was always the best part. Of course, it sounded best when the guitar player yelled the words and rocked it loud enough to deafen people in the next county. He and Gideon tried to imitate it, lyrics delivered in a wild screech, guitars yowling, and the drums' percussion deep enough to make the rake and shovel bang against the rack in the garage.

Gideon. One of the reasons they were here. The accidents he claimed were nothing more than that. Lives lost, lives Noah couldn't save. The drinking. The destructive behaviors.

"Come on, Char. Father is getting fidgety."

Noah swallowed the anger and hurt, realizing he wasn't living up to his promise to himself. Be in the moment. He used to be Daddy, or at least Dad. Elena decided those names were too gauche. She wanted to call him Noah, but he had to draw the line. He was grateful his younger child didn't yet look at him like he was an alien from another century.

Elena tapped her foot out of time with the music and watched her sister with marked exasperation. Charlotte was having a hard time selecting a binder for school. In the last few months, his outgoing ray of sunshine had developed numerous decision-making issues, from what to wear each day to which books she wanted to read. She'd become quiet as well, too quiet.

The psychologist assured him it was a method of coping with upheaval from the messy divorce. Noah understood the why, but he didn't know how to fix it.

"Would you like me to help you, sweetie?" He knelt next to Charlotte and examined the binders in their selection of styles and colors. Char leaned into his shoulder and he felt her nod. Up the aisle, Elena gave another frustrated sigh and popped her gum. The popping accelerated as her eyes focused on her cell phone, her thumbs typing faster than her jaw could chew.

His daughters brought him immense joy. He wouldn't give up time with them for the world, and he was eternally grateful this job came along. It gave him an opportunity to move the girls away from the less savory aspects of life in Los Angeles. He wasn't sure his kids felt the same way, but they'd come around. Or so he hoped. He hoped Gideon would come around too.

"Father," Elena popped to emphasize the elongated two syllables, "why can't we study online at home? Lots of kids do it. Amelia goes to school online and then she can travel all over the world with her mother. If I'm going to be stuck in this effing hick town in the middle of effing nowhere, I should be able to go to school online so that I can meet people who are more my type."

"Elena, language." He sighed, knowing this was a futile reproof. It didn't matter how many times he asked her to watch her tendency to curse. He'd even taken away her cell phone charger for a week.

"Father, it isn't like it's even a swear word. I mean, you say worse. I've heard you."

Yes, unfortunately, she had, on the phone with his ex-wife. Trying to be a good example, he'd set up a swear jar, and whoever said a bad word had to put a quarter in the jar. He hadn't yet figured out what would happen to the money. It was beginning to accumulate.

"Char, honey, how about this binder? Will this work for you?" He tapped a white one at the beginning of the rainbow of choices, and his daughter nodded solemnly.

He grabbed two for good measure and stood, putting them in the shopping cart.

"Father, I cannot believe you picked white. Only morons get white. I mean, really." Elena stalked over to the cart and picked out the binders with two-fingered distain. "Charlotte needs appropriate colors, or she won't fit in."

Her irritation sent the message loud and clear. His eldest thought he was a clueless dork and therefore unfit to do something as straightforward as picking out the correct binders for school. Elena took over the job of helping Char, debating the merits and reasons why each color might or might not work, and Noah realized they'd be there for a while.

The piped-in music changed to a heavy metal classic delivered in show tune fashion more appropriate to a doctor or dentist's office, but despite the presentation, he bopped his head along with the rhythm. He hadn't always been clueless. In almost everything else in life, he was the bomb. Wait, did anyone say that anymore? Maybe he should stick to gang slang.

But he couldn't help nodding along. If that made him un-cool, so be it. He was a clueless embarrassment to his girls, who were sure they knew more than him. God help him, when it came to raising children, they might be right.

Swaying with an occasional snap of his fingers, he let his eyes roam the stacks of paper and dividers further down the aisle. This early on a rainy Thursday morning, they had the place to themselves. He gave his shoulders a little shimmy when it came to the chorus. He grabbed a package of highlighters from the shelf and pulled off a passable dip and dive with the fake microphone, mouthing the words to the music. As absorbed as they were, neither of the kids would notice. And there was no one else to see his rock and roll tribute.

Except for her.

He stopped bopping, his eyes snagged on the person at the end of the aisle. She wore a grin that said she'd seen the whole exchange. The song moved on to the next verse, and as if she was part of the band, she bobbed her head back and forth in a parody of him. The movement made her braid of dark red hair toss on her back. Her lips parted when it came to the chorus, and he found himself grinning and playing along. Together, they lip-synced the words until they were cut-off by an announcement paging any available associate to help a customer by the printers.

The woman shrugged at their interruption, and he smiled in return. From here, the expression on her face was full of fun and mischief. What color were her eyes? Even hidden by a tan jacket with a logo on the front, he could tell her body was fit. And she was tall, but then, he wasn't. She might have to lean down to kiss him.

Where the hell did that come from?

Did he need to put a quarter in the jar if he only thought the words?

It didn't matter. He hadn't kissed a woman in so long, he couldn't remember how long it had been. He kissed his daughters, and he kissed his mother on those rare occasions when she breezed in and out of their lives. He occasionally did a cheek buss with colleagues who were good friends. But kiss a woman, lip on lip action?

"You aren't listening, Father. We're done. God, will you stop acting like such an embarrassment?"

"Quarter in the jar when we get home," he said in response. At least it showed he was listening.

"Charlotte is getting blue binders, because blue is cool. I, on the other hand, will have red, since red is a power color." Elena sashayed down the aisle as she delivered the information, already typing something into her cell phone as she passed around the corner out of sight. Charlotte followed listlessly, dragging her feet and leaving dark heel scuffs on the tile floor.

Noah knew how she felt. He wanted to stay here too and play rock and roll star with the intriguing woman at the other end of the aisle. Elena would never notice, and he'd be spared her derisive comments in front of the first woman to catch his eye in ages.

Still, he had no time for dating. His life now revolved around his girls, and Gideon.

The woman stood where she'd been lip-syncing, that sunny smile still on her face. When his eyes met hers, she raised her hand and gave him a big thumbs-up to go with the smile. Then she disappeared toward the back of the store as he stood frozen in place.

He felt a small hand on his and he turned his palm over automatically and closed his fingers, giving Charlotte a squeeze of recognition. When he looked down into her face, her serious eyes filled her expression. It hurt his heart to see her so silent and somber. She squeezed his hand in return and glanced back down the aisle.

Then she looked up at him, and she smiled. It lit up his world. She leaned in and he leaned down, because whatever she said would always be important to him.

"Daddy," she whispered, "that lady looked like fun."

About the Author

I love to hear from readers, so feel free to contact me through my website, www.yvonnekohano.com, or directly on Facebook as Yvonne Kohano, on Twitter @yvonnekohano, and at yvonne@yvonnekohano.com. Please leave an honest review of this novel at Amazon, Goodreads, or your favorite book discovery site of choice.

A HOLT Medallion Award of Merit recipient in Romantic Suspense, Yvonne enjoys channeling her characters' voices and passions as they overcome real world problems and discover love. Her Flynn's Crossing contemporary romantic suspense series is set in a fictional northern California foothills town not unlike the one where she used to live. Of course, the beauty and wonders of the Sierra Nevada Mountains and the surrounding counties play costarring roles in her work.

The first six books in the Flynn's Crossing series follow the developing love interests of the girl tribe, a group of successful women who work through real world conflicts and challenges to find acceptance and love - with some suspenseful happenings thrown in! In the next six books, single guys in the wolf pack find their true loves, but not without their own issues to conquer. Periodically, Yvonne will be adding seasonal novellas to the series, featuring the first person voice of a character from one of her previous books experiencing an event that we can all relate to.

Made in the USA
Middletown, DE
13 July 2015